THE FOOL'S JOURNEY

KRISTINA JACKSON

THE FOOL'S JOURNEY

THE FOOL'S JOURNEY

First published by Little Acorns Publishing Ltd 2012
www.littleacornspublishing.com

The right of Kristina Jackson as the Author of this work has been asserted in accordance with Copyrights, Designs and Patents Act 1988.

This book is a work of fiction and, except in the case of historical fact, any resemblance to actual persons, living or dead, is purely coincidental.

All rights reserved. No part of this book may be re-printed or reproduced or utilised in any form or by any electronic, mechanical or other means, now known or hereafter invented, including photocopying and recording, or in any information storage or retrieval system, without the permission in writing of the Publishers.

Cover design© Oephebia

Copyright © 2011 Kristina Jackson
All rights reserved.
ISBN:
ISBN-13: 978-1-909202-07-8

THE FOOL'S JOURNEY

DEDICATION

To Rik, for his ability to polish my work into a diamond.

To everyone who has believed in me; when all seemed dark and I would never get through, and to those who lifted me up on the power of their beliefs.

THE FOOL'S JOURNEY

CHAPTER ONE - AND SO IT BEGINS

The sky was flooded by the brilliant red light of the setting sun. As the fiery ball dipped towards the horizon, the sea became steely blue, tinged pink by the dying light. The last rays shone on Moira's hair, turning it flame red; its curls framing the pale skin of her face. Tears fell and coursed their way down her face and dripped off her chin. She sat there, idly tossing abandoned mussel shells into the water, musing on what her life had become.

Moira's job had long hours and gave her very little satisfaction. It had cost her a long-term relationship, her sense of morality and her pride. There was nothing she would not stoop to, just to succeed. Today had been one of those days. She had worked late. On her way out, her boss had called her into his office. He had demanded she satisfy his needs if she wanted to win the promotion she had applied for. He had taken her on the office desk, her skirt around her ears, whilst he grunted away like a rooting pig. Once his urges were satisfied, he dumped the used condom in the bin, discarding her with as little emotion in the same instant. She could hear him talking into the phone as she left the office.

One of the directors, Rupert, caught up with her at the door of the building. She had been asked to follow him here, to this deserted cove, where he too satisfied his urges, ripping at her clothes to get them off, discarding her broken panties into the sand. He had kept taking her until there was no charge left in his chamber. He had then handed her the letter confirming her appointment to the new role. As he left, he told her that he expected to be satisfied in any fashion, that she did whatever he demanded, any time he demanded it, otherwise she would be back down in the secretary pool where she had started.

Moira waited until it was almost completely dark. When she started to shiver she went back to her car. She wasn't prepared for some late night dog walker stumbling across her in this state: half ripped clothes, sand where sand should not be, mascara-stained face. She felt now, at twenty-six, she was plummeting to the utter depths of depravity.

Moira slowly drove back to her house, feeling her way on unfamiliar roads, eventually pulling her car up into its allotted parking space a little before eleven pm. She let herself into her townhouse, choosing not to go into the kitchen; despite not having eaten since lunchtime, Moira headed upstairs instead. Past the lounge and bedroom of the second floor, she reached her bedroom on the third floor, and immediately turned on the water in the shower.

Moira threw her ruined clothing into the bin and stepped into the warm, soothing water. She continued to scrub herself long after the sand had gone down the drain; trying to wash away the feeling that she was soiled and was no more than a cheap tart. Drying herself and wrapping up in her favourite pyjamas, she collapsed onto the bed and fell asleep.

Entering the office the next day, Moira was greeted by cheers and pats on the back. News of her promotion had quickly filtered through the ranks. Smiling and waving, she lapped up the attention, which almost washed away the unpleasant feelings from the night before. Not quite; something had woken inside her, which wasn't going to be laid back to rest that easily. Later that day, she moved into her new office, one of her own. This was what she had striven to get. She met her team and then started work as head of Advertising Campaigns.

Moira kept telling herself life was good; weeks turned into months and all the time, she was in the same sort of semi-denial. At times, she felt there was a part of her screaming. Rupert kept his word and would demand at least weekly sessions. It was nothing she couldn't handle, although the frequency was getting more alarming; but still she worked on. Starting here was the best thing for her. Realising that her body, which she had been teased about at school, was alluring to more mature men, she soon found that by using her brain and body, she could do well for herself. Now with her first advertising campaign heralded as a success, her confidence grew. Still, somewhere lurking in her soul was something; something making her feel uneasy, this was going too well, something had to give.

One day, when she was looking out of the window, wondering how to make the company's most uninteresting products appealing to the consumer, she saw Rupert. His sandy-coloured hair stood out against the greyness of the tall buildings surrounding the car park and the dull heaviness of the day, making everything look very bleak. He was talking to a heavily pregnant woman. Moira recognised her as one of the secretaries she had known when she had started. Her name escaped her. This woman had got fast-tracked and then left suddenly several months back. The woman stood there with her hands clasped, pleading him about something and then Rupert reached out to put his hand on her swollen stomach. Rupert withdrew his hand as if something had bitten him. From where Moira stood, she could not see Rupert's expression, but what happened next had her fleeing the office and going down the back way to the car park to avoid him.

Moira watched as Rupert struck the pregnant woman; not once, but picked her up and did this four or five times. The last blow sent her flying. She fell against the back of a parked car and collapsed in a crumpled heap, hitting her head on the ground as she did so. She didn't move.

Moira reached the car park in time to see Rupert sauntering back into the building as if nothing had happened. Kneeling by the woman, she felt for a pulse. Reaching for her mobile, Moira rang for an ambulance, merely saying that a pregnant woman had collapsed. Moira started to get up, to go back into work before she was missed. The woman was struggling to remain conscious and kept opening and shutting her eyes. The woman feebly reached out toward Moira.

"It's his. Rupert knows it's his. He told me to quit my job, as interwork relationships don't look good. He said he would look after me. It quickly became apparent what he meant by 'look after me'; a fat cheque in the post. Don't let it happen to you." With that, she shut her eyes again. Moira heard the wail of the sirens and fled the scene.

THE FOOL'S JOURNEY

Back at her office window, she watched as the ambulance crew tended to the woman and lifted her onto a trolley, then into the back of the ambulance. She fought down a wave of nausea and repulsion; but repulsion to what? So caught up in the scene and her thoughts, she was momentarily unaware she could hear Rupert talking to her secretary. The buzzer went on her desk, bringing Moira back to reality with a jolt.

"Rupert to see you,"

Before she could answer the door was opened and he walked in.

"Moira, your success has been noted by the CEO. There might be an opportunity arising soon on the board of directors. I'll need a few things from you to convince them you're the ideal candidate."

Moira's head spun. Director! She was barely aware of her internal voice clamoring for attention. She was in the giddy heights of the boardroom, company cars, executive lunches and all the trimmings that went with that seat: bonuses and large salaries. Dimly aware Rupert was speaking; she focused on the current situation.

"I'll need you to do one more successful campaign like the last, and if you can increase sales by more than thirty percent, that would be fantastic."

Moira nodded, already clear in her mind's eye what she needed to do to improve on her last success.

"You will be expected to demonstrate good team leadership and bonding skills. So the happiness and general agreement of your current team is critical."

Again Moira nodded, already aware she was well liked and ensured it remained so by being flexible and rewarding when things were done well. The Friday cake run was an all-out winner; which reminded her - she must get todays done soon.

"I will also need a special something from you personally. Just to ensure we understand each other."

"That is?"

"I am arranging a special weekend. It will show you can work well in a team situation; there will be another woman there and maybe a few more men. You will have to do things that will mean leaving your inhibitions at the door. If you manage to do that and satisfy us, the directorship is yours."

Moira stood in the middle of her office. She could not believe her own ears. For now, it was all about that BMW adorning her parking space, the larger salary, which in turn would mean a larger house. Moira felt like she was floating on air, in some sort of trance, aware of nothing more than the sugarcoated dream. She buzzed through to her secretary.

"Claire, I'm going to do the cake run, have you got the orders?" To her own ears, her voice sounded distant and far off.

"Yes, Moira. Jane is on a diet again."

"So that will be one cream éclair in a bag, handed over without anyone seeing then."

Claire chuckled "You understand us so well."

Cakes were bought and consumed and Friday ended like any other. With cheerful greetings for good weekends, everyone headed off out to various places or homes for a cosy evening with loved ones. As ever, Moira left the office last, turning out the lights. On her way out she spotted a note on top of her message book, which was on her secretary's desk. A momentary wave of uncharacteristic irritation swept over her, but it receded when she read the message.

'A Sister Watts from the hospital rang. She asked you to call her about someone called Sarah. I thought she had the wrong person, so did not bother you.'

Sarah. That was the name that had eluded her. She stepped back into the darkened office and rang the hospital from there, so that she was not seen, eventually getting to talk to the Sister named on the piece of paper.

"Hello," a slightly starched voice answered

"Hello, my name's Moira McNally. You left a message for me earlier about Sarah." Moira's brain frantically scrambled around in case they asked for a surname.

"Could you come in please? Sarah is very poorly, and during fits of consciousness has been asking for you."

THE FOOL'S JOURNEY

"Of course, I'll be there in about fifteen minutes."

Dimly aware she could hear footsteps coming down the hall and of whose they must be, Moira hid under the desk in her dark office. She fervently hoped he would not come in. He didn't; he just looked in, and when he didn't see her, he moved on. She breathed a sigh of relief. The tide of realisation swept over her and brought to the fore of her mind, what he had meant by 'working in a team' the mere thought of it made her want to scream. She was not certain she wanted to go that far. Now with the news that Sarah was laying in a hospital bed clinging to life sent her thoughts into a tailspin.

On the way to the car her mobile phone rang.

"You were not in your office." The tone sounded accusing.

"Must have been in the ladies." Moira answered lightly, walking faster to get to her car and get out of there before Rupert could come down.

"I was looking forward to a bit of Friday night satisfaction, before I went away for the weekend."

"Going anywhere nice?" plainly avoiding the suggestion behind the words.

"I am away until Wednesday morning; a mixture of business and pleasure." Again, there was the heavily weighted suggestion behind the word 'pleasure'. Much to Moira's relief, he finished the conversation off with, "I've got to get a taxi to the airport soon. I will catch up with you on Wednesday; be sure to be ready."

"Sure," Moira replied, trying to sound casual. With that, he disconnected and she ran the last few metres to her car. Driving out as fast as she could, heading towards the hospital.

Moira went to the main reception desk at the hospital and was told to go to Intensive Care. Sister Watts met her looking very grave.

"Her parents are still an hour away. They were on holiday in Cornwall and are making their way back up. Would you sit with her a while? She's been anxious to talk with you, I think."

THE FOOL'S JOURNEY

Nodding, Moira agreed and scrubbed her hands in the alcoholic gel. She went and sat by the side of Sarah's bed. Sarah's face was swollen and barely recognisable. She half-opened an eye.

"Moira, tell them who did this if I die."

Moira just stared, looking down at the monitors; one was strapped to Sarah's belly registering the baby's heart rate, the other to Sarah herself. Moira couldn't say anything. She didn't know what to say.

"Tell my parents not to tell the baby his father was a murderer. Tell them the baby's name is Joseph, that will please my dad."

"I will," croaked Moira.

Sarah clung onto her hand and lapsed back into unconsciousness. After a short while alarms started bleeping and going off. Moira stepped back whilst nurses adjusted drips and worked efficiently. Eventually, she was stabilised. Sitting back down, Moira kept up her vigil until Sarah's parents arrived.

Moira was dozing when a hand placed on her shoulder made her jump. Looking up into a she saw a familiar face, Lisa, her hairdresser. It took her a few seconds to realise she was Sarah's mother.

"Moira, I'm so glad it was you who found her! She regained consciousness once they brought her in. We spoke on the phone, she told me everything and that it was you that found her. We had just packed the car when the hospital rang and told us Sarah had taken a turn for the worse and we're rushing her down for emergency scans."

Feeling utterly helpless, Moira didn't know what to say. She felt weak, sick and scared.

Um," a gasp came from the bed, sounding more like a death rattle than the spoken word. "Where's Dad?"

"Here, love."

"Dad, he's Joseph junior, save him."

Moira left as the big man leant over the bed to his daughter, sobbing. His body shook uncontrollably as emotions poured out of him. Sarah's mother was in a no better state. One parent sat either side of Sarah, clinging to her hands, as if willing their lives into hers. Moira went home.

Moira's head spun and her heart ached. It was like she had been caught up in a tornado. It had picked up her and dumped her into someone else's life. Not knowing what to do next. Moira had thrown up the hospital sandwich she had bought on the way out as soon as she got home. She felt alone, scared to tell anyone what had happened. Who was there to turn to? With no answers to her questions, Moira cried herself to sleep.

Moira was woken by the phone.

"'Ello"

"Moira, she's dead." A double shot of espresso would have had the same effect as those three words.

"Lisa, what about–?" She was unable to ask the question.

"It was considered best he was delivered by emergency section. It might have given Sarah..." the sob came down the phone, " a better chance of survival. It didn't. She touched the baby when she came around. Died less than an hour after."

"I don't know what to say."

"Can Joseph and I talk to you later? We need to get a few things straight for our own peace of mind."

Swallowing hard, Moira answered in a slightly strangled whisper, "Yes. When would suit?"

"Can we say an hour from now, so about ten o clock? We will meet you in the town park."

Putting down the phone, Moira lay in bed for a while staring at the ceiling, uncertain what to say or what to do.

The meeting was hard on Moira. Sarah's parents asked about the events leading up to Sarah's hospital admission, wanting to know everything she knew. She passed on the wishes Sarah had uttered to her. They both nodded and decided no fathers name would be entered on the birth certificate and they would deny any knowledge they knew whom the father was. They would work out a story by the time he was old enough to ask any questions. As Moira took her leave, Joseph reached out and touched her arm.

"Moira, please do not let what happened to Sarah happen to you. Lisa is going to sell the businesses and we'll sell the house here. Soon as they've sold, we are going to move to our holiday cottage in Cornwall. Too many painful memories here."

Moira could understand that. Perhaps Joseph Junior would bear a resemblance to his father. In this town, tongues would wag.

"When the police asked, we said we were uncertain who the person was who found her. When they asked why she'd asked for you, we told them you were a friend…" His voice trailed off.

Gentle hot tears trickled down Moira's cheeks. Her heart broke, at his grief; this big man had considered her feelings and given her a chance to decide what to do. Understanding what she could not have voiced. He looked deep into her eyes, gave her a hug and left without another word, heading towards the hospital to pick up his namesake, their precious grandson: the one good thing to come out of this.

Moira drove out of town, staying on country roads with no particular idea of where she was going. Driving along, she kept trying to make sense of some of the thoughts racing around in her mind. The grumbling in her stomach reminded her she had not eaten properly for a couple of days. She spotted a sign showing a crown nestled amongst some thistles, with the large letters 'Rose and Thistle' underneath. She turned into the gravel car park of a quaint, thatched village pub.

Its steep sloping roof with newly laid thatch glistened in the afternoon sun. Its tall brick chimneys standing like oaks in a field of corn. The roof rested upon whitewashed walls that sparkled. The beer garden adjacent to the car park was decorated with tubs of flowering plants. Some had red geraniums standing proud amongst the marigolds. Some contained wide-leafed hostas surrounded by brightly coloured busy lizzy plants. There were wooden picnic tables on the lawn and table and individual chairs under a lean-to attached to the pub. From open windows, laughter was carried in the gentle breeze, along with the smell of good home cooking.

Moira stopped just inside the doorway, blinking to adjust her eyes from the bright light outside to the relative dimness of the low ceilings and dark-beamed interior. The mixed aroma of cooking and real ale filled her nostrils. Looking around, she looked for a table and spotted one nestled into a niche by a big fireplace, unlit in the heat of summer. Squeezing past a baby fast asleep in a modern looking, orange coloured pram. The woman gently rocking it looked slightly frazzled, suggesting she was the baby's mother and sleep had not been her companion at night. She smiled warmly at Moira and shifted the pram a little to allow her an easier passage.

"Thanks," Moira said, trying to prevent the lump in her throat from choking her voice.

The woman just nodded and went back to eating. Moira manoeuvred herself around a table where a large man sat. His stomach strained the buttons of his red shirt, and in front of him were a bowl of discarded mussel shells and a plate scattered with breadcrumbs. A girl of about seventeen or eighteen was clearing away the plates.

"Looks like you enjoyed that," she said, addressing the man at the table.

"Matt's cooking gets better. I am looking forward to trying the steak."

"He's just cooking it now, won't be long."

Sitting down, Moira tried not to gawp. The bowl of mussel shells had been big enough, and now he was talking about steak! He seemed familiar with the staff and the food here. Moira could not help wondering if he was a local or someone on holiday staying nearby. Shaking her head, she turned her attention to the menu on the table.

Moira's eyes were drawn to the lunch sized Lasagna but equally, the Chicken Caesar Salad sounded tempting. She was about to go to the bar and order, when the same waitress who was talking to the big man came up.

THE FOOL'S JOURNEY

"I'll take your order, Miss. It's just that busy in here today; someone will nab your table while you're at the bar."

"Great! Thanks." Moira beamed. "I'll have a pint of lager shandy and I think I'll go with the Lasagna off the lunch menu, please."

"Chips and side salad?" The tone of voice suggested 'no' would be a silly answer, so Moira agreed. Whilst her drink was poured and her food brought out, Moira sat back and surveyed the scene.

Moira watched whilst people came to the bar to order, then went back out carrying wooden spoons with numbers painted on them and sat in the sun. Two lads sat in an alcove by the window. They were both wearing designer sportswear, shorts and trainers and were discussing loudly the forthcoming football fixtures and whether Manchester United would triumph over Liverpool FC. A harassed woman in her mid-forties brought over Moira's drink and departed without a word, someone else at the bar demanding her attention. The girl brought out Moira's lunch asked about sauces, which Moira declined. The girl headed back to the kitchen for another plate of food.

The combination of the heat outside and so many bodies crammed into a small place was turning the air in the pub stuffy. With a satisfied sigh, Moira went to the bar to pay. She was looking through the various leaflets that were stacked by the till with interest, when one caught her eye; it announced 'Psychic Fair' in gothic script, listing various attractions and today's date. A harassed, red-faced woman in her forties came over and prepared Moira's bill.

"I am passing through here. Would you mind telling me where the village hall is?"

The woman looked down at the leaflet Moira held and grinned.

"Of course. Turn right out of the car park; it's about five hundred metres down on your right-hand side. Leave the car here; you'll not get parked down there today. Make sure you get a signed copy of Michael Stewart's book. He's a psychic medium and a real dish. I am going to go down later once my lunch shift has finished."

THE FOOL'S JOURNEY

Thanking her, Moira navigated her way through tightly clustered tables and out into the bright sunlight of the afternoon.

Wandering down the road in the direction indicated, Moira sauntered past chocolate-box cottages; some of them were painted white, some pink, and all had thatched roofs, overhanging like brooding eyebrows. The small windows that adorned the cottages were thrown open to the day. Bees buzzed in the pyramids of sweet peas that grew in some gardens. Other gardens had clusters of pink and white aquilegias and the tall purple spires of delphiniums.

The village hall was situated next to a particularly pretty cottage garden. Around the edge, tall heavily scented roses grew with lavender bushes at their base. The cream coloured gravel matched the cream of the cottage and in the centre of the gravel grew sweet peas. Double-flowered and with frilled edges, all of the most unusual hues. Moira stood admiring the scene, momentarily forgetting why she was there, until she heard two women come out from the hall giggling like school girls. They looked near the age of fifty, judging by the grey streaks in their hair.

"Oh, Michael Stewart is such a dish," exclaimed one of the women.

"I know," agreed the other. "Especially as he's such a famous person too! I just love his show."

Moira could hear them continuing to discuss this as they walked down the road. Now with a little more curiosity than that which had initially drawn her, she walked into the village hall. It was like she had stepped into another world.

CHAPTER TWO - THE FOOL
Beginning – Spontaneity – Apparent Folly – Faith

    The village hall was one of those rectangular constructions. Just inside the entrance was a lobby, where the toilets and coat hooks were. At the end of this lobby were the double doors that lead into the main hall. Just inside the main hall, on the right, there appeared to be a small kitchen area. A woman with long, dyed scarlet red hair, her arms covered in bangles and wearing a lively coloured maxi dress came out. She was carrying a mug and her expression showed she was feeling slightly frazzled. Moira took a step back to avoid colliding with the woman.
    "Oh, sorry deary!" She grinned, as she placed the mug on a table. "It's just been that manic this morning, I've not had a break for a cuppa yet."
    Moira, smiled warmly. "Don't tell me, everyone is flocking to see Michael Stewart?"
    "You're not?" she asked, looking at Moira with her head slightly on one side.
    "Ummm, actually it was just curiosity that brought me here" Moira's voice trailed off, hoping she did not sound too silly. Overtures of self-doubt started playing within her soul. For the first time since she had realised she had a toxic combination of brains and beauty that could be used to her best advantage she felt insecure. It must have shown.
    "Don't worry deary, you've come home now. You'll be fine. Now let's see who we can find to advise you." Picking up the mug in one hand and taking Moira's hand in the other, she led her into the main part of the hall.
    Moira let herself be led like a child. Her senses overloaded as she entered. At the back of the hall was a raised wooden stage, on which there was a picture, a pile of books and an empty chair where Michael Stewart had sat. Laughter could be heard, combined with the faint sound

THE FOOL'S JOURNEY

of whale music. The combination of incense, wax, wooden floor polish and the rose scented breeze wafting in through the open side doors took Moira straight back to her childhood.

"My name's Amber. I am psychic medium," she said, giving Moira a card. "You don't need me today. You might do later; keep it." When Moira had put it in the back of her purse, Amber carried on "Off you go, have a wander and see where you feel drawn."

Moira had spotted something already; the smell had brought it back. She turned to thank Amber, but she had already gone. She saw her heading towards the stage, her red hair making her easy to spot. She focused her attention to what she had seen and made her way over.

The table where Moira was headed was draped with a deep plum velvet cloth, its folds touching the ground. On the front of the cloth, embroidered in silver thread, was the sign of the Triple Goddess; the symbol of a waxing crescent moon, a full moon and a waning crescent moon, all touching on their rounded sides. The words 'Triple Moon Tarot Readers' were written below the symbol. Behind the table sat a woman, Moira guessed in her mid-thirties, wearing a pale pink summer dress, her dark hair tied up in a bun. About her neck hung a necklace of the same design as the front of the cloth. Moira approached with a little trepidation.

"I would like a tarot reading done please," Moira half whispered half croaked.

The woman behind the table smiled. "Please sit down. I am guessing this is your first reading?"

Gratefully, Moira sat in the chair indicated, simply nodding as she did so. The woman handed Moira a list of types of readings, saying, "I have to advise you, due to legal requirements, this reading is for entertainment purposes only. It does not replace medical or legal advice." Moira nodded, unable to speak. She read the list for a moment or two.

"What is a Celtic Cross Spread?" She asked, wondering frantically if she had enough money with her.

THE FOOL'S JOURNEY

"The Celtic Cross Spread is ideal for looking deeply into a question. It gives you depth and extra knowledge. It will look at the whole situation and the cards will be able to advise you what is on your path. Ultimately though, destiny is still firmly in your control. It is up to you whether you take the advice the cards offer."

Moira checked her purse and handed over the amount of money indicated on the list. "Can I have one of those please?" She sat there clasping and unclasping her hands in her lap.

"My name is Alison. Triple Moon Tarot is run by three of us. It is my turn today." Grinning, she added, "Well I did have to come and meet Michael Stewart after all." Alison slid three decks of cards over to Moira.

"Would you choose a deck that takes your fancy?"

Moira selected a deck with the picture of a sun on the front of the box. It announced itself as Universal Waite. After being handed the cards out of the box, she was asked to shuffle them whilst thinking about her question. She handed them back and asked, "Where do I go with my life now?" Alison smiled and spent a very short while just sitting quietly, then began to lay the cards out.

Whilst she did so, Moira looked on in interest. Apart from two cards, one placed on top of the other, the others were all turned so just their blue backs with a star was showing.

Alison spoke. "The Tarot Deck is made up of 78 cards. Within the deck we have 22 Majors. These signify the major events on our path. We will also encounter each archetype of the Majors within any one cycle of our lives."

Moira listened wide-eyed. She felt drawn into the pictures of the cards, almost willing them to reveal their secrets. The picture shown on one of the cards gave the distinct impression things were going to change.

"For the first cards, in the position of 'now', we have The Tower. Lightning has struck the Tower; it has blown the crown cap off. Within fire is beginning to rage. The two people who had dwelled there are

THE FOOL'S JOURNEY

being thrown out, falling towards the rocks below. This card shows the world, as you know it, and it is falling down around your ears. Events have happened which have shaken all you believed in."

Alison moved the second card back over the first.

"The Tower is crossed by the Eight of Swords. A woman stands loosely bound and blindfolded amongst eight swords. The suit of Swords is representative of our thoughts. This card suggests that you are confused and do not know what to do or where to turn. All the woman in the card needs to do is shake off her bonds, remove her blindfold and walk free. Whilst the Tower may seem like a hideous card, sometimes we need to destroy things in order to build afresh. Like a forest fire destroys and destructs, it also acts to aid germination of fallen seeds, so new life can spring forth. I instinctively get the feeling this Tower is something you've unconsciously brought down yourself. If you stop worrying what to do and release those bonds, a path will become clear."

Alison paused.

Moira felt like she needed to say something, not just sit there dumbstruck. What Alison had just said did make sense. She just couldn't find the words to admit it yet. Instead, she nodded, swallowed hard and waited for Alison to carry on.

Alison looked across at Moira. She was sitting there in well-tailored, tasteful clothes. Yet she almost looked afraid. Alison felt that whatever had happened had been very recent and still very raw. Deciding it was best for her to carry on and listen, she turned the next card over.

"This is what lies in the past. Whilst it lies in the past, it has a bearing on what is happening now. This card is The Devil. A horned and winged creature perches on a metal pole. Tied to this pole are a male and female, with a loose chain around their necks. This doesn't mean you've had dealings with the devil or with anything demonic. It means you've become a slave to a situation. This could be the pursuit of worldly goods over spirituality, or doing things some may consider 'evil' to achieve advancement. As this is in the past, it suggests you have removed the

THE FOOL'S JOURNEY

chain from your neck and walked away free. This situation has brought The Tower down."

"That's true more than you know." Moira felt her familiar world growing more distant, quite literally as if it was falling down around her ears.

There were no further comments from Moira so Alison carried on.

"What is known? The Ace of Swords. A hand holding a sword with a crown at its tip is coming out of a dark cloud. The sword appears to shine. We've already talked about swords being about thought, and aces are about new beginnings; this suggests you are already beginning to think differently about things, looking at things from a new vantage point. You are already beginning to come out of the debris of The Tower and into a brighter light."

Alison turned over the card below the two cards in a cross shape, the fifth card in the spread.

"What is unknown? A man tiptoes away from a battle camp, carrying off five swords, leaving only two behind. This card suggests you might feel that by making these decisions, you take more than you feel you deserve.

"I don't know about that yet," Moira ventured. "I have to be honest. I only found out this morning that someone I knew had died."

Alison looked at her with her head slightly on one side.

"Is this part of your indecision?"

Moira nodded.

"Let's see what is next."

Moira felt that she shouldn't be surprised. Something felt familiar, like she had seen the cards before. Not in her hand, but in someone else's. Right now she just couldn't figure out whose. So she kept her focus on what Alison was saying. Moira gasped as Alison turned over the sixth card.

"Near Future. Death. Another one of the tarot cards with preconceived ideas. This does not show you will die, merely the end of one phase and the beginning of another. Here, a skeleton clad in black

THE FOOL'S JOURNEY

armour is riding a white horse, and it stands over a dead King. At the horse's feet is a male child, showing that though one era dies another one dawns. The rising sun seen coming up between the two towers represents this. I see this card as a physical change, as much as an emotional one. Leading on from the previous cards, this suggests you might consider a physical change of location, ending what has begun emotionally with a physical change. Whilst all endings are not without a level of pain, things must end in order to begin again."

Moira felt a tear trickle down her cheek. She wiped it away with the back of her hand.

"It seems life and death are rolled into one at times."

Alison nodded, "The triple Goddess, our symbol, is about that. Those who follow the Wheel of the Year believe in the Maiden, The Mother and The Crone. As we come out of winter and into spring, the Maiden becomes the Mother and then as we head back again towards winter she becomes the Crone. As the seasons give life, they also take life."

Moira knew now where she had heard this before. It went with the memory of the smell that was around her. Her grandmother.

Alison felt a shift in Moira. Something was stirring that had been dormant for a long while, perhaps waiting for a chance to come out. She seemed less introspective and more assertive, bracing her shoulders for what was going to happen next. So she moved on, turning over the seventh card.

"You, as you. This card represents the way you see this situation. Eight of Cups. Eight golden cups stand on a sandy shore. Five golden cups on one row and three on the top row. There are spaces within the top row. On the other side of a small stream, a figure can be seen with its back turned to the golden cups heading up a rocky road. This card suggests you are leaving behind a lot of things you once considered needed; these are now not so and would hinder you on your journey. The fact there are gaps within the top row, suggest the figure has taken some of the cups with him. You are leaving one way of life behind, but starting out on a new chosen path. You take with you some of the things you

THE FOOL'S JOURNEY

hold dear. The path you use may be rocky, but it is chosen. This card may also suggest a more spiritual path. The Moon is eclipsing the sun. An auspicious sign for those choosing a different path."

Alison looked over at Moira, who was leaning forward. Alison got the feeling she was trying to see what she herself could see. She turned the eighth card over.

"Outside influence. Another Major; Justice this time. A woman wearing a red gown sits between two pillars. She holds aloft a sword in one hand and scales hang from the other. This suggests legal matters may influence you. This may have a bearing on what you choose to do."

Moira sat upright. Yes, legal matters. She knew what to do about the situation with Sarah's death now. Things had become a lot clearer. She needed a little thinking time to work things through, but the fog was certainly clearing. She watched as Alison turned over the ninth card.

"Hope and Fears. Another Major. This card is Temperance. A winged angel stands with one foot in the water and one foot on the shore. Her eyes are closed. Water appears to be flowing from one cup to the other. This card suggests you are hoping for balance. An equilibrium where life is not about all or nothing. There are also spiritual connotations about this card. Learning to balance thought with action, perhaps by undertaking meditation. Ultimately it is about learning to live life in balance."

"That would be nice," Moira whispered.

She gazed into the distance, her mind racing with what it was she had to do. Alison turned over the last card, the tenth.

"Outcome. The Fool. Another Major. A gaily-dressed figure holds his head up, looking at the sky. He is about to step off a cliff. How high is that cliff? A white dog is at his side, preparing to take that leap, suggesting the cliff is not high and a leap of faith is required. This card suggests you might consider a leap of faith, by starting something new. Listen to your gut reaction, your subconscious, as suggested by the white dog in the card. This is also the beginning of the Majors; he is the fool whose journey we follow through each Major Archetype. This card

THE FOOL'S JOURNEY

indicates a new beginning is awaiting you. You just need to take a leap of faith."

Alison couldn't understand. This client was clearly interested and taking in the information, yet there was a lack of questions and a lack of response. Had she made things clear enough? Time to summarise.

"The amount of Major's within your reading suggests these events are of considerable importance. Not something to be taken lightly and serious thought should be given before taking any action. There seem to be a lot of endings and beginnings. The journey may have its rocky patches, but ultimately I believe the cards are suggesting you let your heart and head guide you."

Moira sat there for a moment looking back at Alison. Then she started to speak.

"I saw someone killed; well, she did not die then, but it was an assault that caused the death. It was by someone I know. If I report it, I bring my world around my ears, for sure. Yes the indecision was whether I should do so or not. It looks as if, subconsciously, I've made that decision. I cannot thank you enough. What you've said feels right." With this, Moira got up, shook Alison's hand and left, never even noticing Michael Stewart, accompanied by his wife, who happened to be Amber, return to the stage or even what this might mean to her in future. For now, Alison watched her go, with a feeling of slight puzzlement. It was quickly replaced by one of understanding. Moira seemed to have a good strong instinct about the cards and their messages, even if she was not aware of it. She then turned her attention to the next client waiting at the table.

Moira spent the rest of that weekend planning what she must do, researching and making lists. Walking around her sparsely decorated home, she thought about her course of action. She had kept on top of the mortgage and bills, but it left her little money for anything else. The promotion she had gained had started to improve things; she had some savings, but were they enough to see her through? It was the only thing to do. People would no doubt question her judgment and think her a fool. She just had to trust this was what was right and hope things would work

THE FOOL'S JOURNEY

out as she had planned. Moira walked into her lounge and over to her laptop. She clicked on the print icon on the screen and the printer churned out a letter that would change her life forever. She was resigning from a well-paid job and moving on from this life, as she knew it. Would it be though for the best?

THE FOOL'S JOURNEY

CHAPTER THREE – THE MAGICIAN
Action – Conscious Awareness – Concentration – Power

Moira headed towards the Severn Bridge, the echoes of her mother's disgust and her father's laughter ringing in her ears. He told her she had spirit, her mother told her she was insane; she had left with her parents arguing with each other.

These last weeks had gone by in a blur. First there was the meeting with CEO, who admitted he had seen the whole business with Sarah and had chosen to go to the police. Moira then gave them her version. As CEO, his word would be used in court. She was pleased to be free of that. The CEO had discarded her resignation letter, offering her voluntary redundancy instead. Moira reflected on how this left her feeling - that she had taken more than she had perhaps been entitled too. How strange that the tarot cards saw that with the Seven of Swords. The sale of her house was only a few days away from completion. The first person to view it snapped it up. She would soon be homeless. Now she was heading into Wales and to Pembrokeshire, where all her happiest childhood memories were. Here, she was to view a house that over the last few hours of the drive had her questioning her own sanity.

Moira pulled up outside a lime-washed building built in the eighteenth century. In places, the lime wash was missing, exposing the stone beneath. The slate roof looked new and complete. The driveway to the house was overgrown with brambles and long waving tufts of bleached grass. The front gate hung loosely on its hinges, and the front path to the door was newly laid with flakes of slate. The grassy areas either side of the path were overgrown. The cottage had a brooding look, as if it was watching onlookers. It stuck out like a sore thumb amongst the neighbours' trimmed lawns and groomed hedges. It was no wonder they grew the hedges so high. Perhaps now was the time to walk away from this house. Yet she couldn't; something was drawing her towards it.

A sleek black BMW pulled up behind Moira's car. She gulped hard, trying to swallow the feeling of what she had lost and concentrated instead on what was ahead. A women in her mid-forties tottered on high heels towards her. Her plump body strained the clothes too young and small for her, creating the impression she had just been poured from a jelly mould. Her bleached blonde hair looked brittle in the late summer sun. Her face was heavily made up. Moira heard in her head the voice of the CEO as she left his office, 'Your body is cute. Your brain is better. Figures go but your brain stays forever.' This woman's figure had certainly gone and looked like she had failed in the bid to hold back the oncoming tide.

"I'm Mary, you must be Moira. Oh, this place is so..."

Moira switched off the prattle, letting the estate agent's spiel flow over her.

Mary let them in through a new stable-style front door. The house had a musty odour, suggesting no one had lived in it for a while. There were abandoned dustsheets and discarded paint tins in the hall, as if they had just been dropped there. Mary led them into the kitchen. On one wall, nestled in an alcove, was a solid fuel range cooker. Underfoot was an uneven quarry tiled floor. Here and there plants tried to grow in the crevices. The kitchen led into what must have been the old scullery. There was evidence of plumbing for a washing machine. The scullery window had a broken pane, and beneath it the floor was mossy. The backdoor was nailed shut with a board. Yet strangely, Moira was filled with a sense of roses and laughter. Blinking, she was back in the dim light of this partially rundown house, ignoring the ceaseless prattling of Mary, trying to sell the quaint charm of the house. Moira instead just relied on her own instincts. Oddly, she was now curious about the house.

Entering the lounge, she found it was not as big as she had expected. The large bay window gave the room a pleasant airy feel, despite the low ceilings. On the main outside wall, away from the door, was a newly installed wood-burning stove. The walls had been painted white, adding to the brightness of this room. There were recently installed pine skirting boards, which still needed painting. The moth-eaten velvet of the bay window's seat needed changing. It started to puzzle Moira why the cottage had been started, but not finished. Along the opposite wall from the fire stood a newly attached radiator. Moira could not remember seeing a boiler. Going back out into the hall and past the stairs into the back room, Moira thought she heard the creak of the stairs; like someone trying to stand very still, but not quite managing it.

The back room had plaster missing, exposing the bare stonework beneath. Lines had been chiseled, Moira presumed, for the up-to-date electrics the house details had boasted of. It had rotten timber-framed French doors leading onto what looked like, through the grime, an overgrown garden. Mary had ceased her chattering and was trailing Moira around like a jet skier in the wake of a speedboat.

Moira and Mary explored upstairs. The three bedrooms were in a reasonable state of repair, having recently been re-plastered and the bathroom suite still had its shop wrapping on. Thoroughly perplexed, Moira asked the question that had been brewing in the back of her mind.

"Why is the cottage being sold unfinished?"

The question, by the looks of contortion on the features of Mary's face, was one she was not looking forward to answering.

"They ran out of funds," came the answer in a rush, as if holding onto the blatant lie would burn her lips.

Moira did not push it further. She was certain she could just hear someone say, 'Yeah, right!' Feeling she knew the reason, she questioned whether she was ready to take on a project like this, despite it being under budget. Standing back outside amongst the tall grasses and bramble entangled borders, Moira knew what the right decision was.

That was ten weeks ago. It was now rapidly approaching Christmas. The legal process and survey went surprisingly smoothly. What had not gone smoothly was finding people to install an air source heat pump and glazing to make the house habitable. Local people, for some reason, would not go near the house. In the end, Moira enlisted the help of her uncle, a retired builder, to provide contacts and help oversee it. Moira began to understand why people might be avoiding the place. The plumber swore he had left his tools in the kitchen, only to find them in the bathroom upstairs. The glazier had dropped a pane of glass, much to his company's annoyance. He swore someone was pulling at his clothes. In the meantime, Moira worked for her board and lodgings at the local pub, finding this a good way of meeting the locals and integrating with the community. Finally, she was able to move in.

Sitting on her sofa in the lounge with the fire lit in the wood-burner, Moira listened to the wind blowing rain against the windowpane and whistling around the chimneys. With a notepad resting on her knee, she started detailing what else needed doing to the house. As she was making a list of what she thought she needed to do with the kitchen, she became aware of the sound of saucepans moving. Taking a deep breath, she got up to investigate.

Moira approached the kitchen like a cat stalking a mouse. She stood in the doorway and watched. A saucepan was being lifted from the cupboard where she had put it and was trying to hang itself on one of the hooks by the range cooker, only to fall flat on the floor with a clang. It then repeated the process, finding itself falling towards the floor again.

"They don't have holes in the handles to hang them by," Moira said to the room at large. The saucepan then was slammed to the floor with enough force to dent it.

"OK, when I can afford it, I will buy some with holes in the handle and hang them. Happy?"

For an answer, the dented saucepan put itself back in the cupboard. Moira went back to the lounge with a giggle in her throat, half manic and half amused. She vowed a phone call would be made.

The next morning dawned bright and clear. During the night, the wind direction had shifted from the west and turned northerly, heralding a change in the weather to a colder snap. Moira woke shivering. Today, amongst unpacking the remaining boxes, she would have to try and cut some logs up and get the range cooker fired up to help with the heat pump. The sound of logs clattering on the kitchen floor had her out of bed and downstairs in an instant.

As Moira approached the kitchen, she could see logs floating around in mid-air, and then dropping to the floor with a clatter, missing the log basket that stood by the side of the range. Moira ran to the front door. She unlocked it and ran outside, closing it behind her, leant against the door breathing hard. She was suddenly aware of someone walking down the road with a dog. Here she was, standing outside in pink pajamas and fluffy bunny slippers. She waved a cheery good morning and raced back into the cottage, blushing scarlet. At least the logs had stopped floating around and were just messily strewn across the floor. Cleaning them up Moira said, "OK, I get the hint. I'll light the range."

In response, a box of matches flew across the room and struck Moira. After a little fumbling and blowing, Moira managed to light the range.

A while later, wrapped up in a warm coat against the biting wind, Moira went to work at the pub. Whilst she was there, she put a phone call through to someone who might be able to help her with her matchbox thrower, before it did some expensive damage.

Christmas came and went. Her mother refused to talk to her. It was a lonely Christmas. But it wasn't a quiet one. The unseen presence in the cottage would make itself known if it was unhappy about something. If the range went out or she was back from work late, logs would be thrown across the floor or the coalscuttle would be turned over. It was a welcome relief when the New Year was past and her awaited guest was due to arrive.

The morning her guest was due to arrive dawned with a heavy sky. There were a few flakes of snow being blown in a keen wind. Moira stalked about the cottage, peering out at the darkening sky. She twitched folds of the bed linen and swept the still uneven floor for the umpteenth time. Even the unseen presence seemed to pick up on her mood and hid. The allotted hour came and went. Moira started to worry. The skies looked so heavy; it looked like the snowfall would be significant. She forced herself to sit down, making herself jot the ideas down of the plans she had started to make. Being a barmaid was fun but it wasn't enough. Nearly an hour later, a battered looking Land Rover pulled up on Moira's still weedy, if less overgrown, driveway. Out got the scarlet red hair she had been expecting.

"Amber! I am glad you've got here."

"Blinking M4 was snarled because of a few poxy flakes of snow. Barely a centimeter and people reacting like it's a huge amount."

Amber looked up at the sky.

"Looks like there's more than a centimeter in that. Come; let's get inside out of this wind."

Sure enough Amber was right. As they drank coffee and Moira explained about her unseen presence, the snow started to fall. The wind dropped and the snow fell silently and softly. As the day turned towards night, the unseen presence in Moira's cottage began to make itself known.

Upstairs, Amber and Moira could hear things being moved in the room Amber was staying in. They went upstairs to explore. Amber had put her overnight bag on the bed. It was now on the floor by the chest of drawers. Amber picked it up and put it back on the bed. They both watched as it floated across the room and landed forcefully back where it had previously been.

"It does not like things on beds," Moira conceded.

"Perhaps now is the time to see if this presence wants to explain itself."

Amber walked over to her case and took out a black velvet bag. Together she and Moira headed downstairs.

In the lounge, they cleared the furniture back to make a space in the centre of the floor.

"We may as well be warm. Spirits are not always very keen to communicate."

THE FOOL'S JOURNEY

With that, Amber took out a container of sea salt from her bag as well as four candles and some crystals.

"Sit in the middle of the floor," Amber suggested to Moira.

Moira did as she was asked; around them, Amber drew an outline of a circle in the sea salt. Once this was completed, she placed a candle in a holder at the compass points of the circle. In between the unlit candles, she placed four different types of crystal: amber, amethyst, jade and obsidian. Amber lit the candle at the north point and said, "Watch keepers of the north protect us."

She then repeated the process. Calling on each watch keeper in turn. Returning to the centre of the circle, she held her arms aloft.

"I call upon the higher power to watch over and protect us, as we aim to communicate with the spirit that dwells here."

Sitting down next to Moira, Amber went quiet for a few minutes.

"OK, let's begin."

To Moira, Amber's voice sounded different, as though it was coming from a distance, not from right next to her.

For what felt like an age, Amber said no more. Then she called out, "Come closer, Jimmy, I won't hurt you."

Moira was aware of the fire in the stove dip and then roar. The candles on the edge of the circle flickered.

"I am not scared of you. I just don't know what else lies out there. You like Moira? I am just keeping her safe."

In reply, the logs by the wood-burning stove moved back to the basket. The monologue carried on for a while longer. The candles on the edge of the circle had burnt down a little way, and the snow outside was now several centimetres deep and still falling. Moira sensed a change in Amber as she stood and raised her arms again.

"Thank you for your protection."

Amber dropped her arms. Moira thought she could sense a change in the atmosphere; it became less electric and back to the normal feeling of the room. Turning to Moira, Amber said, "Go get that bottle of malt whisky you promised, and I'll tell you what I found."

THE FOOL'S JOURNEY

Moira left the circle being careful not to break it.

When Moira returned to the lounge with two glasses, Amber had extinguished the candles and swept up the salt. They moved the furniture back to where it was. Moira poured a large slug of whisky into each of the two tumblers.

"Thanks. Nice glasses. Who is Maud?"

"My grandma's name was Maud. She bought me these when I bought my first house. She died soon after…." Moira's voice trailed off.

"She's watching over you. You'll do well. Now, let me tell you what I've learnt."

Amber took a sip of the smooth liquid, rolling it around her tongue before swallowing.

"You've picked up your grandma's taste for whisky too. This is good malt! Now, onto Jimmy. He's not certain how old he is. He was never very good at his counting. He does not like men. Some men are better than others. A lot of men scare him. I think he's probably late teens early twenties. There is a childlike quality. These days, they'd say he was autistic. He said men use to throw stones at him. One day, he got angry and threw the man. The man was hurt. I think he was probably a big built lad. After that, his mum would not let him go out on his own. He didn't mind. The men were not mean to him and did not make him angry. If he did not get angry, he did not hurt people."

A saying of her grandmother's came back to Moira: 'talk for those who have no voice and protect those who are vulnerable'.

"What happened to him?"

"One day his mum got sick. He promised her that he would not leave the house without her and no one would come near. He stood by the gate and shouted that his mum was sick. Then he got sick too. His mum died in the kitchen. He died a little while later with his head on her lap. He didn't leave her. He promised her he would never leave her. Before she died, unaware he was sick; she made him promise that he would look after the chest that was in the attic. There it still is, to this day. He is troubled that the chest will come to harm. He promised his mum he would never leave the cottage. I am not certain exactly when this was. He said it was during Queen Victoria's reign."

Moira saw a tear trickle down Amber's face. Feeling she might also shed a tear, there was a moment of solemnity. They both stared into the fire.

After a while Moira got up and looked out the window. The snow had stopped falling and moonlight was reflected upon its crystals. Feeling like a child, Moira ran to the hall and pulled on her wellington boots and coat. She ran out into the snow. Amber had risen to see what she was doing, and then joined her. They ran around like children, treading in virgin snow and lying on their backs making snow angels. They laughed. They laughed like there was no other care in the world. Soon the more adult part of their brains kicked in. Shivering and wet, but still giggling they went back into the house to get dry. Draping their coats over chairs by the range, Moira suggested, "Let's go find the chest."

Moira felt her clothes being tugged. Something was trying to pull her.

"I have to stay here. I am not allowed. He says you are."

Moira let herself be led; up the stairs and then the tugging stopped below the loft hatch. She stood there wondering how she was going to get up there. A pole came floating through the air, one with a hook on the end. Moira had to stifle a scream as it hung there in mid-air. Gingerly, she took it and hooked it onto the mechanism on the hatch. Giving it a tug, the hatch came down with a ladder attached. Moira's heart was in her mouth, and the palms of her hands felt sweaty. Aware of the thudding in her chest, she climbed the ladder.

It was cold in the attic. Her breath hung in the air. The solitary light bulb cast only a dim light; it rocked slightly by some unseen and unfelt force. The shadows danced. Moira took a deep breath. The laughter of earlier seemed far off. Up here, it felt eerie. The air had a metallic tang. Moira felt the tug at her clothes again and stepped forward carefully. Stooping slightly, treading only on the wooden beams, she moved carefully, questioning what she was doing. A voice, no more than a breath said, "That's it."

THE FOOL'S JOURNEY

Then she saw it in front of her, despite the gloom. It glowed faintly. As she reached out and touched it, it moved. She screamed. What was in the chest?

THE FOOL'S JOURNEY

CHAPTER FOUR - THE HIGH PRIESTESS

Non Action – Unconscious Awareness – Potential – Mystery

Moira could hear Amber calling her from below. She couldn't answer. She took a few steps towards the chest. It seemed to be drawing her to it magnetically. Moira couldn't help but think the chest was scared. Reaching out again, she stroked it gently, cooing softly to it. It seemed to stop quivering.

"I think we need to bring it down," Moira called to Amber.

"I can't come up. Something does not want me up there. This feels like something you have to do yourself. This is something you've been chosen to do."

She shook her head, as if trying to shuffle her thoughts to make sense. Nothing seemed to fit right now.

"In the morning, then. I am tired. I am coming down now."

Later, when Moira was talking to Amber, she said she could have sworn that she felt that she had passed some sort of test. Amber said nothing, but just gave her a package that she had left in the car and announced she would leave in the morning, because of the forecasted snow.

The morning dawned, although no sunrise could be seen. The skies were grey and heavy. All sounds seemed to be muffled; even the fire would not draw well. The world gave a feeling of expectancy, as if holding its breath. Amber had left at first light, the sky hastening her journey even before she had originally intended. Sitting in the still battered window seat, Moira swung her legs idly. A growing sense of unease forced her off her perch. First she went in search of more logs. Secondly, she went to visit her elderly neighbour. By the time she had returned, the first few flakes of snow had begun to fall, slowly and lazily

THE FOOL'S JOURNEY

falling down to earth. They were settling, unwilling to move. She closed the door on the snow and the world let out a breath.

The sky began to empty itself; the first few lazy flakes were soon followed by more of its companions, the snow angels and footprints were rapidly filled in. Soon, there were a good couple of centimeters on top of the last fall. Moira turned her attention instead to the package Amber had left her. It was pyramid in shape, wrapped in peacock-blue shiny paper. It was quite heavy, so Moira sat on the floor in front of the fire and opened it.

Inside the package were four individually wrapped packages. Moira unwrapped the first one; it was small enough to fit in the palm of her hand, wrapped in red tissue paper. It was a little box. Inside the box was a necklace. It was a pentagram hanging from a silver chain, with a note that read: 'For protection.'

Somewhere in the misty depths of Moira's memory, she saw something similar hanging around her grandmother's neck. Didn't she have it somewhere?

The next package was about the size of a deck of cards. This was wrapped in pale blue. It was a deck of tarot cards, much like the ones Moira had had her reading done with, back in the summer.

'Alison told me you had a feel for these. Contact an organization called TABI (Tarot Association of the British Isles) - they run online courses. Highly recommend them for professionalism.'

Trembling, Moira opened the box and flicked through the cards, seeing images vaguely familiar, yet at the same time almost alien. Looking down at the pile of tissue-wrapped packages, she reached out for the one wrapped in the same coloured paper as the deck of cards. It was a book entitled *Learning the Tarot* by Joan Bunning. The book had slightly curled pages with creases down the spine.

'I used this to learn tarot many moons ago. Goes with the TABI course.'

THE FOOL'S JOURNEY

Thumbing through the book, Moira saw images similar to those within the deck of cards she had just opened. It was a comprehensive book with key words and explanations.

She opened the next package; it was a bit smaller than the last one, yet it had the feel of another book. This time this one was entitled *The Real Witches Handbook* by Kate West. The cover showed a pentagram made up of sticks and tied at each point by coloured ribbon. The note for this package read, 'Food for thought. Only you can know where your path lies. Just felt this might be of interest to you.'

Moira put the contents of the packages on the sofa behind her and walked over to the window. She stared with unseeing eyes at the ever-increasing depth of snow; unaware that depth now was impeding exit from the front door. The daylight was leaving, being replaced by the full darkness of the night.

Moira was brought out of her reverie, when the box of matches that where on the mantle came flying across the room and smacked her on the side of the head.

"Ouch! What was that for?"

Then she saw that the snow had piled high, cussed quietly under her breath and left the room. Hastening to the backdoor she found it was covered by nearly a foot of snow. Feeling like a child on an adventure, Moira ran around the house then put a big torch by her bed. She shut the other room's doors, putting tall white candles in the silver spiral candlestick holders that adorned her mantelpiece. They were a lucky find in a local charity shop. She had just settled herself on her favourite perch, the battered cushion window seat, to watch the snow continue to fall when she jumped. The hand of realization scraped its fingernails along the blackboard of ignorance. She was blocked into her house. Starting from her perch, just like a bird that realised it has been caged, she ran to try and force the back door open, sinking to the floor when her efforts were in vain.

Moira had not made her way up the ladder in her previous life by body alone. She picked herself up, pulled on her wellington boots, which were warming by the range, wrapped herself in a coat, hat and gloves and returned to the backdoor. Opening the top of the stable-style backdoor, Moira hoisted herself over it. She found herself momentarily stuck, with one leg on the outside, one caught on the door. She suppressed a giggle. She felt herself being pushed back and landed in the snow with a soft thud. The giggle was now audible. Stifling the obscenity that floated on her lips, Moira instead went about the task that had brought her out here in the first place.

She made her way with dogged progress to the small shed that was on the left facing down her garden. Its door was protected from the worst of the snow by large overhanging branches of a pine tree. She soon had it open and retrieved the shovel that she had stowed there. Closing the door again, she progressed slowly to the backdoor, shoveling away enough of the pile of snow from it so that it would open. Just as she was about to go inside, the gentle buzzing from her back pocket signaled someone needed her attention. Pulling her glove off and retrieving the handset, she looked at the caller ID. With shaking hands she answered.

"Hello," she said, trying to keep the quiver out of her voice.

"This is emergency response. Blodwen Jones has activated her emergency alert alarm. She's fallen and needs assistance can you respond?"

"Y-es," stammered Moira.

"I'll let her know you're on your way." With that, the phone was disconnected.

Closing both sections of the backdoor, Moira made her way to her elderly next-door neighbour.

After picking herself up from falling in the snow, with damp clothes clinging to her, she made it to the front. Here she found that she had to dig the snow away from the door to find the key lock with the key hidden inside. Letting herself in, Moira found herself in Blodwen's photo adorned hall. Pictures hung in frames from every available space. Black and white ones from when she was a child to family portraits on white

THE FOOL'S JOURNEY

backgrounds and ones of her great, great grandchildren playing with brightly coloured balls.

"Blod?"

"In the kitchen, Bach"

Moira was aware of the booming loudspeaker voice.

"Miss McNally, the ambulance is on its way."

"It won't get here; the roads are under a foot of snow at least."

"Jolly good show. Time to call in the big red bird then," came the cheerful, if unprofessional, loudspeaker voice.

Moira found Blodwen on the floor in a crumpled heap at the bottom of a small stepladder.

"I was just getting the torch down, in case the power went out. I heard a noise from outside and turned and fell. I think I hit my head. It's sore. I think I've broken my hip. I did the other one several years ago; it feels the same as it did then. You said the road was blocked with snow. There wasn't that much last time I looked."

"It seems to have fallen heavily in the last hour. It's just fallen on icy cold ground and what was there before."

"This reminds me when I was child..."

Moira let Blodwen talk. Talking seemed to distract her from the pain she was in. She liked to hear tales of her childhood, when she would sleep top to tail with her two other sisters in a bed, in a cottage much like Moira lived in now. There had been sixteen of them. She was the youngest and although her mother died when she was only a few years old, she never felt like she had missed out. Her eldest sister was then married with young ones of her own, but she would pop by and help her father out. One of the other girls who had been sent to 'do service' as an undermaid in a house down in Cardiff, returned and thankfully took over the role of caring. She talked of her father fondly. A big, kindly man, who never drank much and played cards on a Friday night. She talked of how three of her brothers were killed in the Second World War. Periodically, the boom of the loudspeaker emergency response person would inform them on progress. After one update she scoffed, "Get the bleeding tractor out! This is nothing compared to the time when the whole village was under over three feet of snow…"

Eventually, the now very cheery loudspeaker voice announced that the Welsh Ambulance Helicopter was now only a few minutes away.

Moira let herself back into her own home. It was completely dark and despite a brief respite of an hour, the snow was now several centimeters higher than when she'd left. The back door, however, was still mercifully snow free. Kicking off her boots and dumping her wet coat on the floor, Moira poured herself a whisky and headed straight up for a long soak in a hot bath. Well, that at least was the plan.

Steam rose and bubbles bubbled as the water rushed into the bath. Easing her cold and aching frame into the welcoming waters, Moira pondered on the last few hours; the arrival of angels in flying suits, the kindness and tenderness they had shown to Blod. The clearing of the path to enable a safe and smooth progress out to the makeshift ambulance in the shape of a tractor and trailer. The slow but gradual progress to the field where the helicopter had landed; everyone walking alongside, making sure the stretcher that bore Blodwen was secure. Before Moira had returned home, she had secured Blodwen's house, rang her family and fed the cat. She sank deeper into welcoming waters, closing her eyes and breathing deeply. Thud! She sat bolt upright. She listened hard but heard nothing more than silence. Relaxing again, she heard it one more time: the same pattern as before. After the third time, Moira called out, "Jimmy if this is you; I've had a hard few hours. I am cold and tired and need to warm through and relax."

The reply was the trinkets on the dresser in the bedroom being moved around. This was a sign he was upset about something, but then this was drowned out by another thud. A sense of eeriness crept over her; the water around her no longer felt welcoming. She dried herself and put on her pyjamas to the accompaniment of thumps. They seemed to be coming from the attic. It sounded like something was moving heavy objects, dropping them as they became too much. Grabbing her torch, swallowing a mouthful of liquid courage, she went to the loft hatch in the hall and opened it. Mounting the ladder, she poked her head up into the space of the loft and screamed.

The chest that had been in furthermost corner was now only a short way from the hatch. It seemed to be trying to get out. It seemed to back away from her. Hoisting herself onto the edge of the hatch, Moira just sat there. The chest edged its way forward, falling back with the thump she had heard in the bath. When it was within touching distance, she reached out slowly. She touched the aged wood. It was a simple chest made by a skilled carpenter. There was no lock, just a small iron-sliding bolt, held together by rust. It was not as big as it seemed last night. It was probably forty centimetres long and twenty centimetres high and wide. Moira clasped the chest with both hands. It moved beneath her grasp. It felt uncertain. Just resting her hands on it, the chest seemed to settle. No longer was Moira afraid. It had the feeling of a frightened child. Moira tenderly picked it up and nestled it under her arm. She carefully made her way back down the ladder. She placed the chest in the room she intended to use as an office. Shutting the door on it with probably more haste than was needed, she made her way back downstairs and ate a late supper.

The next morning someone knocking on the door awakened Moira. Bleary-eyed, she stumbled downstairs and opened the door. Why had she not thought of the front door opening inwards yesterday instead of her gymnastics and digging?

"Err, umm, err. Are you, umm, Moira?" asked a red-faced, tall, solidly built man, probably only a few years older than Moira.

"Yes."

Moira realized she was standing there in her pyjamas with hair still ruffled from sleep. She in turn blushed like the setting sun, recognizing his face as one that adorned the walls of Blodwen's hall.

"I am Leo, great-nephew to Auntie Blod."

Moira smiled: the much talked about great-nephew. She was not certain whether 'favourite' could be applied, since Blodwen seemed as much to scowl over his antics as praise them.

THE FOOL'S JOURNEY

"I've come to thank you. Dad rang me last night, when Uncle Bryn rang him. I was nearest with the only suitable vehicle."

Moira looked beyond him into empty space.

"It's down the hill. I forgot to fill it with fuel." If it were possible, his existing blush deepened. "I'll be around until Auntie Blod gets out of hospital and on her feet. Oh, I forgot; I didn't tell you, her hip was broken. She'll do fine. So just to let you know." With that he darted back up the path as quick as he could.

Shaking her head and putting him out of it in the same instant, Moira shut the door. She went to the kitchen and put the coffee on to brew.

When Amber had rung Moira the previous evening to announce her safe arrival, she advised her to draw a tarot card a day and to write that day's card down in a notepad; then at the end of the day, to write down her thoughts about the day. When she had done that, to check the keywords within the text. This would help her learn about the cards' meaning and how it translated into everyday life. Whilst the coffee brewed, she shuffled the cards and drew The High Priestess. She put it on the coffee table in the lounge to remind her to find a notepad and write it down later.

The snow still fell, with less intensity now, although the accumulation would takes days to melt, if not weeks. Moira rang into work and was told not to go in until the roads were open. Curling up with *The Real Witches* handbook, she started to read. Half way through the book, she put it down and searched the internet on a few points, then went back to reading it. Turning the last page left Moira feeling that it had answered some questions about what she felt, yet it had left others unanswered. Perhaps time would answer this one. At least now, she knew what it was she that she felt.

Moira made a stew and put it onto the range to slowly cook and went about working on the business plan she had started before Christmas. She wasn't certain yet where she was heading with it. Did this area offer her the potential to do something like this? It seemed the watchword for the day was 'time'; it all seemed to be unclear and wrapped in a cloak of

THE FOOL'S JOURNEY

confusion. More research was needed and with over a foot of snow blocking all roads, she was not going anywhere soon.

It was approaching her bedtime when Moira remembered she had not searched for her notepad and written the day's thoughts down. She went into the small boxroom, which she was intending to use as an office, in search of the necessary items. She had momentarily forgotten about the chest that she had stowed there last night. It seemed to have moved itself into the shadows of the far corner, not where she had put it. Reaching down to touch it, it felt just like any other wooden box, but the lid was stuck fast. It was like a solid wooden box with no lid. Leaving it where it was, Moira went back downstairs to note down her thoughts of the day.

She rested *Learning the Tarot* on her knee, open at the page of The High Priestess. Looking over the keywords and descriptions, she saw in so many ways how this card had reflected her day. Non-action. Well, she had been stuck in here all day and there was nothing she could do about it. Unconscious. The seeking of inner guidance and opening up to her inner voice. That felt slightly surreal considering she had spent a good part of the day researching and reading about being a Witch, understanding now this is how she felt. Potential. That had certainly been working on her business plan. Mystery. Chewing the end of her pen, Moira pondered this one. She read the description of it, but didn't quite feel this fitted in with her day. Deciding that not every attribute listed would be reflected, she took herself up to bed.

She had only been asleep for a little over an hour when Moira was woken from her sleep by what sounded like someone weeping. There seemed a distinct lack of a Jimmy presence and the ambience of the house felt different. Colder, older, as if the time was not now, but in the past. Gingerly stepping out of bed for a moment, Moira thought that there were hard floorboards beneath her feet instead of the soft carpet. The feel of the carpet then returned. Creeping towards the spot from where the sound originated, Moira's heart thudded wildly in her chest and she licked her dry lips. She stopped to listen. The sound seemed to

THE FOOL'S JOURNEY

come from the boxroom. A faint glow shone from under it. She opened the door and held her breath.

There in the middle of the floor was the chest. It was shaking; the sound was coming from it. Moira reached out and stroked the chest with her fingertips, gently as if settling a nervous cat. Beneath her fingers, she felt the chest try to snuggle itself against her. She bit hard on her lip, stifling the scream that was lodged in her throat, stroking it now with the full palm of her hand. The sobs stopped. An odd thrumming noise came from the chest, not unlike a cat's purr. Slowly she caressed the chest, as she held it on her lap. It continued to quiver and ripple. Suddenly the lid sprang open. The chest was empty, apart from a scrap of paper. Written upon the paper in a childlike hand, were the heart wrenching words "Where did my family go?"

CHAPTER FIVE – THE EMPRESS

Mothering – Nature – Abundance – Senses

Moira stared at the piece of paper in her hand. The chest seemed to have exhausted itself. It sat there quietly, not quite inert. Carefully lowering it back to the floor, Moira scrambled around in the packing boxes that occupied a portion of the room until she found her spare blanket. She wrapped the chest in it and placed it gently by the window and closed the door.

Winter seemed to trudge on forever. Although the roads opened quite quickly, the snow seemed to linger. It had become an unwelcome visitor. The night freezes often left the roads like ice rinks, where some of the snow had taken the hint and melted away during the day. It was early March when the first shoots of spring lazily poked up their heads, with very late snowdrops being the first to make an appearance. Blodwen had stayed in hospital for almost a month after an infection complicated things. By the time spring had arrived she had only been back home for a few weeks. Leo had returned to his home whilst she was in hospital. Moira had looked after the cat and generally ensured that Blodwen's house was kept clean. When Blodwen returned home she was much weakened and a lesser person in spirit as well as in stature. Leo returned, but Moira saw nothing more of him and had pretty much forgotten his existence in any other way other than as a character in Blodwen's tales. Moira had spent a good deal of the winter researching gardening and making plans for the planting. The chest had been quiet and Jimmy was just as mischievous as ever. In short, nothing to note. Moira had made plans for other things as well. In no time at all, the day arrived.

March 21st dawned bright and clear. Perhaps a little too bright and clear. Something about the weather suggested this would not last. As the days were still chilly, Moira got up early and completed the morning chores of stoking the range and feeding logs into the wood-burning stove. Work had been slow at the pub and she could not afford to run the heating much. While she waited for the back burner to heat the water, she made a few phone calls. She then swept the lounge and cleaned and dusted. This took longer than she had planned, but by the time she had finished, the moment she had spent the last month planning for had arrived.

Feeling like a child on the first day of school, Moira went upstairs and ran a bath. Instead of relaxing in the bath as usual, she went through a cleaning process. Wrapping herself in a towel, she walked downstairs to the lounge. Dropping the towel at the door, she entered the room she had prepared.

In the middle of the room she created a circle of little tea lights. In the centre of the circle she had laid the pentacle she had bought, one as close as she could get to her grandmother's. A polished wooden-hinged box no bigger than a paperback book was also there. A single white candle was secured on a saucer. Entering the circle, she used a lit taper to light the tea lights. She stood there, naked and unadorned. Her damp auburn hair curled down the white skin of her back and over her well-formed breasts. From the box she lifted a small container of salt. Sprinkling the salt in front of her she stepped onto it. She put down the salt container. She then lifted a bottle, half the size of her hand. The bottle contained a carefully blended selection of oils she had prepared earlier. She took the cap off and placed it at her feet. The fire and the candles gave the only light; the curtains remained drawn, blocking all outside light. Taking a deep breath, she lit the white candle and stood there for a moment, feeling the warmth on her face and the heat of the fire and tea lights caressing her. She thought about what she wanted from this spiritual path on which she was about to embark. Moira swallowed hard and spoke, "I am a child of the god and goddess, and I ask them to bless me."

She poured a little oil on her hand and anointed her forehead then said, "May my mind be blessed, so that I can accept the wisdom of the god and goddess."

THE FOOL'S JOURNEY

Closing her eyes she anointed her closed lids and carried on, "May my eyes be blessed, so I can see my way clearly upon this path."

Opening her eyes, she used a little oil and touched the end of her nose. "May my nose be blessed, so I can breathe in the essence of all that is divine."

Picking up the bottle again she anointed her lips. "May my lips be blessed, so I may always speak with honour and respect."

She stroked the oil over her chest and stroked it down over her breast. "May my heart be blessed, so I may love and be loved."

She anointed the tops of her hands. "May my hands be blessed, so that I may use them to heal and help others."

She stroked the oil over the top of her genital area and spoke the words, "May my womb be blessed, so that I may honour the creation of life."

She sat on the floor, with her feet resting on the salt. "May my feet be blessed, so that I may walk side by side with the divine."

In a much clearer voice than she had hitherto managed she uttered, "I pledge my dedication to the god and goddess. I will walk with them beside me and ask them to guide me on this journey. I pledge to honour them, and ask that they allow me to grow closer to them. So mote it be. With thanks and blessed be."

Moira hung the pentagram around her neck and sat there quietly for a little while, savoring the scent of orange, patchouli, sandalwood and camphor. She felt aroused, not so much as the desire for physical communication, rather a heightened sense of awareness.

Moira snuffed out the candle and generally tidied up a bit, enjoying the sense of freedom not wearing any clothes gave, although the impracticalities of this was made clear as she dribbled hot wax from one of the tea lights over her hand and onto her stomach. She heard Jimmy sniggle from outside the door. She put out all the candles and went back upstairs. Moira got dressed and turned to the other task of the day. Just as she had done every day since the discovery of the note from the chest, she put her head on it. It was quiet and slumbering. It had not moved from the blanket. The message played on her mind. She would like to know what it meant, but where was she to start? Sighing softly, she closed the door.

Moira armed herself with pegs, string and a shiny new spade and went out into the bright sunlight of a spring morning. She stood there for a moment, sniffing the air like a rabbit. The scent of rain, damp soil, composting vegetable matter and wood smoke filled her senses. The sun had a little warmth to it, but the keen breeze sent Moira back in for a warmer jacket. Choosing an area to the left of the back door but just a few paces away, Moira measured and pegged out an area for her first vegetable bed. Retrieving the strimmer she had borrowed, she started to strim first around the area and then inside. After the string threatened to get caught in the strimmer for the umpteenth time, Moira removed the pegs and finished clearing the whole area. Bits of grass and bramble were flying everywhere, in her hair and over the path. Moira reinstated the pegs and then began to dig.

The rich dark soil was damp and clung slightly to the spade. The smell filled Moira's nostrils. Despite the chill wind, she had discarded her coat and perspiration broke out on her brow. Wiping it away with a mud-covered hand, Moira continued in earnest with her task. Feeling the invigoration of physical work added to the arousal still left over from the morning's dedication. The act of preparing the ground to create life was sensual. She stretched her back after finishing the first border.

Silently, a male visitor made his way up the side path. He had heard the noise of the spade as it pierced the ground. He rounded the corner and just stood there, gawping. Despite being mud-stained and covered in obliterated vegetation, he felt for that moment she must be some divine goddess raised from the freshly dug earth. He had had women, women of sculptured beauty, women that would have men crawling through the dirt at the mere blink of curled eye lashes. This woman would have made them all look like trashy tarts. She had something that not only stirred his loins, but his soul. This time he was determined not to turn into a spluttering, stuttering schoolboy again. He cleared his throat and swallowed a few times.

"Errr," Nope, she had done it again. He tried again. "Umm, hello
What was she doing to him?

Moira turned and saw him. He was well over six feet tall and broad at the shoulder, tapered at the waist. He looked vaguely familiar. The thought, knocking to gain admittance, finally succeeded.

"Hi, Leo."

She watched as he coloured scarlet again, like he had the first time they met. This time with clear non-drowsy eyes, she viewed Blodwen's infamous great-nephew.

His hazel brown eyes gazed on. He tried to smooth the unruly black curls into a semblance of order, having spent over a month here, away from his usual barber. He wanted to touch her, wanted his lips to caress the swan-like neck. He wanted to run his fingers through her fiery red hair. OK - reality check momentarily kicked in - after she had a shower! Still, he needed her like he had never needed a woman before. He still had to speak coherently to her and right now she was probably thinking he was a bumbling idiot. He had a message to impart and then…

"Auntie Blod says can you come over for tea about 3 o'clock." His voice sounded weak and pathetic. Oh, just to touch that skin. Shaking himself, he pulled himself together a bit, at least he hoped he had.

Moira felt an uncharacteristic urge to hug him. He looked like a lost and frightened schoolboy, not this daredevil rogue Blodwen had made him out to be.

"That will be great! How is she today?"

"Still very weak. But seems full of spirit and mischief for some reason."

"It is good to hear she is recovering a little. I'll see you later?"

"Yes." Again he coloured up.

She watched his retreat for a little while, before starting to tidy up.

Moira approached Blodwen's front door with a degree of trepidation. For some obscure reason, it felt like she was going on a first date, instead of going over to her elderly neighbour's for afternoon tea. Her favourite steel blue dress felt too loose on her. Her lack of funds was encroaching on many areas of her life. She hoped with the herald of spring that people would come out more to the pub where she worked, and she would be able to go back to double shifts again. She had to keep her reserve funds to set herself up in business. She was so busy with these thoughts that it drove away her nervousness. Ringing the doorbell with restored serenity, Moira was not prepared for what answered it.

    Blodwen stood there leaning on her walking frame. Her skin had a yellow tinge; she looked like a waif, but her sunken eyes twinkled, giving her an appearance of a fairy tale pixie. Following Blodwen in, Moira noticed that a lot of the photos had been removed from the walls, leaving darker scars of where they had once hung. Blodwen led the way into the lounge where certain changes were also noticeable. Considerable numbers of ornaments had been removed and a few paintings that had hung on the walls were gone. Blodwen had caught her glance. Indicating she should sit on the sofa, she explained.

    "The infection has damaged my liver. I may have not long left in this world. I am ninety-two now. I've rehomed some of my beloved photos and mementoes to the family already. The others have instructions as to whose is whose. In case of any arguments, Leo has put stickers on them."

    Blodwen chuckled, but ended up coughing. She sank into the mass of cushions that adorned her armchair. Leo came in, carrying a tea tray. Blodwen looked at him with her head on one side as the china on the tray chinked, and his normally steady hands shook.

    Time passed pleasantly. Blodwen noticed how Leo seemed to turn into a schoolboy again. Awkward and bumbling. He looked on Moira like a lovesick puppy. That certainly had not been in the script, but a welcome addition nevertheless. Moira seemed to be equally interested in him. As time progressed, Leo dropped some of his nervousness and Moira and he were eagerly discussing vegetables to grow in the garden. Even if he did start to wax lyrical about the benefits of organic

THE FOOL'S JOURNEY

gardening, Moira seemed not to notice. There was definitely chemistry afoot there, if she was any judge. The tinkling chime on the carriage clock indicated it was now four o clock, time for Cathy to play her part in the script. As if on cue, the doorbell rang.

"Leo, go let Cathy in for me. There's a dear."

She watched as he reluctantly left the room.

Leo did as he was bade. How he did not want to leave her side. Her eyes, the same colour as her dress seemed like deep pools, ready to drown a man. He would drown in them. He would. Bringing himself back to the business in hand, he answered the door to his cousin. Auntie Blod's granddaughter. He had always found this weird, as she was now in her forties. His dad had been a menopausal accident. A happy one as his Grandma, Auntie Blod's sister, up to that point had only managed to conceive one child. Uncle Bryn was then twelve years old. Cathy stood there, tall and willowy. Her long dark glossy hair fell over her shoulders. It was only the streaks of grey that gave any indication of approaching middle age. Her eyes shone like those of the child that clung to her knees.

"'Nuncle Leo," the child said, throwing herself at him.

Grinning, Leo swept her up into his arms, beckoning Cathy to follow them in.

"How's my pretty little Princess Lottie?"

"Nuncle Leo, I am four now. But I will still be your princess if it helps."

Smiling, he carried her into the lounge, closely followed by Cathy, carrying a brown cardboard box.

Leo sat next to Moira with Lottie still in his arms. Cathy took the chair he had vacated, sitting with the brown box on her knee. Blodwen grinned. She had not felt so alive in years. She turned to face Moira.

"I have a special little gift for you. You went out of your way for the month I was in hospital, feeding Helix, making sure this place was kept on top of as well as visiting me, never taking a single penny, although I know your funds are tight."

THE FOOL'S JOURNEY

She drew breath and nodded to Cathy, who placed the box onto Moira's knee. Moira lifted the lid.

Inside, curled up fast asleep, was a little silvery grey tabby, just like Helix, Blodwen's cat. He opened one eye lazily, stretched and yawned. He fixed on Moira the most intelligent gaze she had seen on any animal, or on many humans for that matter. It stood on its legs and put its front paws onto the edge of the box. Moira tenderly stroked his fur. She looked across at Blodwen who was grinning from ear to ear.

"Thank you! But my words barely seem enough."

Blodwen grinned and turned to Leo.

"Now go and get the box from under the stairs."

Moira watched as he gently deposited Lottie onto the sofa and walked out whistling under his breath.

"This is Silver Fox Archibald," Cathy explained. "Great, great-nephew or something similar to that to Helix. I breed them."

"I think I'll call him Archie," Moira giggled. "Can you imagine shouting 'Archibald' at the top of your voice?" They both giggled.

Moira lifted Archie out of the box, and he seemed happy just sitting there gently chewing on her fingers. Lottie had moved closer and snuggled into Moira. Almost without thinking, Moira lifted her arm to accommodate the child. Above her bent head, Cathy and Blodwen exchanged a look. Lottie was a very shy child.

Leo entered the room, wearing a smug expression and carrying a larger box. He had felt a little guilty about abandoning his great aunt's house to go back south. He had taken the opportunity to start work on renovating his own house. He had gutted it and left it in the capable hands of his cousin, Uncle Bryn's eldest son and his team of builders. When Aunt Blod had suggested that she gets Moira a kitten, he had thought that it would be nice if he got her a few things to go with it, and they were the contents in the box he carried. If it helped win her favour, all the better. He could afford it. No one except his immediate family knew that he would never have to work again. A failing business he had bought when he left university had just been bought for a large six-figure

THE FOOL'S JOURNEY

sum. It had left an empty space. It was his baby; his first project, but no means his last. Now he would only be called a conductor. He now had people playing along to his tune. All he had to do was metaphorically point his baton and the appropriate instrument would be played. Now, something else had entered his life. Little Lottie by the looks of things had given her seal of approval. Now, he had to win his desired prize.

That night, Moira tucked up in bed, chuckled to herself as she looked at the card she had drawn that day. The Empress. Who said motherhood was just about humans? As if to emphasise the point, Archie started wailing from the kitchen.

Heavy-eyed and feeling out of sorts, Moira stared at the card of the day: Five of Pentacles. It did not bode well: a lame beggar boy walked past an intricate stained glass window. Ahead of him, his mother was wrapped in a tattered cloak: snow was falling and had settled on the ground. Last night Archie had wailed until she had given in and taken him up to her room. She had just drifted off to sleep when the chest started whimpering. It seemed to be reacting to a disturbed sleep. Shaking herself a little, she fed Archie, who seemed transfixed by something in the corner (which she had named Jimmy's corner) by the range. She could feel him there. She went outside under a heavy grey sky to dig the base for the greenhouse. The one that she found on Freecycle would be arriving today. She could not believe her luck: a brand new greenhouse still in its packaging. It had sat in the previous owner's garage over the winter, but when her company announced she would be moving, she advertised it on Freecycle. She was the winner as it was free. It had only cost her the petrol for Wally, the local odd job man to collect it and a few pints of beer to build it. She now could grow cucumbers and tomatoes.

At lunchtime, she popped back in to feed Archie again. He was curled fast asleep in his basket, now situated in Jimmy's corner. Her poltergeist guest had taken to the little kitten. Maybe she would get some sleep tonight. Forgetting again to feed herself, she went back out to finish the digging. Shifting the large gravel to the dug out base ready to take the greenhouse, she heard Wally's truck pull into the drive and went to meet him. Her head swam and she threw up before she reached him. She put on a brave face and went on. They were manhandling the parts of the greenhouse off the back of the truck quite successfully. Moira began to feel as weak as little Archie inside. She leant against the front wall of her house while Wally carried the bits down the side. It started to rain; it was almost as if someone had turned the tap on. She was just about to get up to go in, when she heard screeching of brakes. That was the last thing she was aware of.

CHAPTER SIX – THE EMPEROR

Fathering – Structure – Authority – Regulation

Moira awoke to bright lights and the sound of beeping. She was aware of a grey-haired man with startling sapphire blue eyes peering over her.

"She's awake!"

"Dad?" Moira croaked. "What happened?"

"Hush love. You'll be just fine. The doc will be around soon to explain all."

Moira's senses, that had taken the opportunity to have a quick coffee break, came back with a rush.

"Ow! Dad what have I hurt?"

She looked up into his usually smiling eyes; they were lacking their usual joviality, and she knew it couldn't be great. A feeling of panic washed over her, the beeping grew more intense and triggered alarms.

"Hush love, hush my poppet."

Moira lay there and wept silently. Hot tears trickled down the sides of her face and over her ears. She could feel a collar around her neck; her whole body felt on fire. All she was aware of was her dad gripping her hand like it was a life raft.

"Dad, I am not going anywhere. You can let go a little."

His face came into view again.

"You can feel me?"

"Yes?"

"Oh thank the saints and apostles!"

Before he could say any more, a tall doctor appeared; he had dark circles under hazel-brown eyes, his dark hair was flecked with grey. His stomach was beginning to show signs of flab. He spoke in a broad Irish accent.

"Thank sweet Jesus. You had us worried for a while there."

He performed various tests. All she was aware of throughout was her dad's eyes returning towards their normal level of joviality.

Over the next week, Moira gleaned bit by bit what had happened. A car had taken the bend at the top of the road too fast and spun on the wet road surface. He had managed to get the car straight, but by doing so had careered straight into Moira. She had fractured a couple of vertebrae in her spine, broken one leg that had required surgery and pinning. The driver of the car had decamped and was in the process of doing a bunk. Leo, hearing the commotion, cannoned out of his aunt's house and chased the man down. The same Air Ambulance crew that had taken Blodwen to hospital flew Moira. Leo had then undertaken the vigil, much as Moira had done all those months ago, until her dad had arrived. Her mum was still not having anything to do with her, declaring she was no daughter of hers and had taken leave of her senses. Her dad had commented that proved she was no daughter of hers, as Moira had sense! Moira had often wondered why he had stayed with her mother, although her hissy fits had tended not to last as long as this one. Leo was a frequent visitor, bringing her little treats every time he came. His understanding of what she liked was uncanny, above any information her Dad could have given him. The day before she was due to go home; having shown that she could manage the basics without help, her Dad came in looking worried.

"Poppet, I don't know how to tell you this." He stood there a little while and twiddled his handkerchief in his hands. He then blurted out, "Your house is haunted."

"Oh dear. What has Jimmy been up to?"

Her dad sat down with a thump.

"Is that what the pest is called? He hid my shoes in the warming oven of your range. I let the range go out, and he started throwing logs around the kitchen. I shouted at it, the logs then started flying at me. I had put some of your clothes on the bed to take with me today. He put them back away again. So, if I have forgotten anything blame him!"

Moira could not help but giggle. Her dad sat there looking red-faced and flustered, his worried look long since departed.

"Jimmy was a simpleton; he died sometime during the reign of Queen Victoria. He does not like men much as they used to shout at him. He is very particular. He does not like things on beds and does not like the range to go out. Best thing is to explain who you are and what you're doing there. How is Archie?"

Moira's dad's face split into a soppy grin. "Oh, he is such a sweet little soul. He's taken to sleeping on my bed at night, now he can make it up the stairs."

With the help of you, Moira thought but did not press it.

The day of her homecoming was unseasonably cold; the sky looked like it might throw something other than rain. Her dad had wheeled her out to the car, swaddled to the point suffocation in blankets and roasted her with the heater on the painful forty-five minute journey over winding mountain roads. Out of her window, Moira watched as they passed the blue-grey rocks protruding from rough grasses cropped by sheep. A few flakes of errant snow flew around in the wind. The journey seemed to take forever. Glumly, she thought about what it was she was doing here. It had seemed a good idea all those months ago; now, perhaps like the Fool in the Tarot card, she found some of the going was certainly rocky. Right now there was no way out. Her dad seemed to sense her mood. He reached over and gently squeezed her hand. Her mood intensified as they approached the winding roads of her village on the hill.

There was a light on in her cottage and Moira could have sworn she saw the curtains twitch. Her dad unloaded a wheelchair from the boot, helped her into it and wheeled her in. As she came through the door a dark-haired child with forget-me-not blue eyes came whizzing out of the lounge to greet her. It was Lottie.

"Welcome back! Wait and see what Nuncle Leo has done for you."

THE FOOL'S JOURNEY

On cue, Leo appeared at the doorway beaming. Her dad handed her the crutches, and she followed him down towards the backroom. On the left, where there had been a sealed up under-stairs cupboard, was now a toilet and hand basin. Hidden inside was her uncle.

Over a delightful tea spread, including sandwiches, cakes, bite-sized scones filled with cream and jam, all made by Cathy, they gathered together. Blodwen looked old and tired, as she sat in the corner of Moira's sofa. There was no laughter within her eyes and the years had fallen on her like autumn leaves. Lottie had proudly produced a misshapen jelly bunny. She reliably and frequently informed Moira that she had made it herself. Sitting in her favourite chair, Moira hugged the child close to her. Her uncle had called up to the cottage to see her dad, his brother. Leo just happened to be coming back from shopping when he turned up. They knew each other through a club they both belonged to. Between them, they cooked up the plan of putting in a downstairs toilet to help.

The week after she was out of hospital had been fun. Cathy and Lottie had stayed with Blodwen. Lottie had been in and out of the house every day, playing with Moira's dad and Archie or curling up in Moira's lap to have stories read. Leo helped her dad in the garden and sometimes, if Blodwen was feeling strong, they would all have tea outside. However, the third week after the accident proved tiresome. Lottie and Cathy had to go back home as Cathy's husband had to work away for a few days and the cats needed looking after. Leo disappeared back south for a few days to take care of some business of his own. Jimmy seemed to have gone away for a bit; he did not seem to like the fact that Moira's dad was in the house.

Moira was in the boxroom, hammering away on the keyboard of her laptop, whilst her dad whistled happily outside hammering some raised beds for her to plant veggies in. The happy sound only seemed to frustrate her further. She watched as Archie stalked bugs or unseen creatures in the grass. She turned and throwing back her head, she let out a primeval scream of rage. Slumping, she began to weep. Life was just

THE FOOL'S JOURNEY

not meant to be like this. Since she pledged herself to the god and goddess what had they done for her? They had made her life more trying. She took her pentacle off and threw it across the room. It bounced off the wall and landed on the blanket-wrapped chest that was nestling in the opposite corner to where Moira had left it.

Moira stared blankly at the wall. The hum of a childhood song could be heard, barely audibly. It went. Moira turned in her chair, feeling stupid that she had had such a paddy. Perhaps the god and goddess had protected her? After all, the MRI scan was not clear whether her spinal cord had been compromised. Wincing, she got herself off the chair and retrieved the fallen necklace. Hanging it back around her neck, Moira heard the sound again.

"Twinkle, twinkle, little star."

The brace she wore made it difficult to bend. She lowered herself to the floor. The chest wiggled a bit, causing the blanket to fall off and opened up. Inside were three old-fashioned clothes pegs, dressed in scraps of material to make dolls. The lid of the chest remained opened until these pegs were lifted out. There was nothing else in the box: nothing but bare wood. The lid closed and Moira once again wrapped it in the blanket. By shuffling a little way on her bottom, she was once again able to lever herself up and with the aid of crutches she sat herself back in her chair.

The next morning Moira drew a card for the day. Three of Cups. Three prettily dressed women held three golden cups aloft, as if making a toast. Around their feet, were fruits, berries and garlands, a scene of merrymaking. Moira meditated on this card, looking into its depths. She could feel the happiness and sense the laughter. The meaning of this card bode well for today.

Several hours later, with the sun shining warmly, Moira and her dad made the journey of two weeks ago. This time she was back, brace free and her leg had been put into a different sort of cast, which made moving around a lot easier. In the lower fields of the mountains, newly born lambs skipped and jumped, enjoying the mid-April sunshine. They

THE FOOL'S JOURNEY

stopped at the local nursery to pick up some vegetable plants and some fleece to cover them with, in case of a late frost. By the time they returned it was mid-afternoon. Parked in the driveway, was a bright yellow Volkswagen Beetle.

"Jenny!" Moira exclaimed.

Her best friend since childhood had arrived.

Later that evening, Moira's Dad made himself scarce and took himself off down to the pub. Over a bottle of wine, Moira told Jenny everything: about becoming a witch; about her plans to not only learn to read tarot cards for herself, but sell readings when she was experienced enough. She talked about her garden and her plans for that. Jenny listened with amused tolerance, although she questioned her friend's sanity when she was relying on pieces of cardboard to advise her on her life. Still, she seemed happy enough. The evening was drawing to a close and the heavy weight of sleep hung on Moira's eyelids. Jenny said, "Your mum thought you'd suffered a nervous breakdown. She's been on the phone every day since your accident."

Moira grimaced. Poor Jenny. She had always been a surrogate child to her parents. The second one they had dearly loved.

"Apart from questioning your sanity about reading Tarot cards, I have to say, despite everything, I've not seen you look so serene. I'll report back that you're in total command of your faculties."

They hugged and Moira went to bed. Dozing off, Moira heard her dad come back from the pub, singing in the tone of one marinated.

Moira slept late, only to be wakened by someone tugging at her bed covers. She opened one eye; there was no one there. Rolling over, she tried to get back to sleep. A short while later, she could hear logs being thrown across the kitchen. Jimmy has returned, she thought to herself. She lay there for a while in a half doze. She was brought to full wakefulness as Jenny's scream tore upstairs, ran around and then faded.

When Moira managed to get downstairs, she found Jenny, who had been sleeping on the sofa, shaking and looking pale.

"There were logs flying around the kitchen!"

THE FOOL'S JOURNEY

"Yes. That's Jimmy."

The matter of fact tone in Moira's voice seemed to still the trembling Jenny.

"I'll make a coffee and tell you all."

Whilst the coffee machine bubbled, Moira took out the pegs and the snippet of paper and showed them to Jenny.

Sipping coffee in the spring morning sun, Moira and Jenny discussed how to solve this puzzle. A few old clothes pegs made into dolls and the words on the paper were nothing to go on. Moira's dad came out into the sunlight, smiling indulgently as Jenny's blonde head and Moira's red head were bent together, their hair entangled. It was a scene from childhood again. The old yearning rose. The one he had never been able to fully put to bed, the emptiness left by the feeling of only being able to father one child. Swallowing hard at the lump in his throat, he spoke in a hoarse voice just above a whisper.

"What are you two so engrossed in?"

Moira then re-told the story and showed him the items. They ended the session by going upstairs to where the chest lay, still wrapped in the pink fleece.

The chest, now unwrapped, sat between them on the floor. Moira's dad stroked the lid of the chest; an indistinct sound came from it. Perhaps it was a giggle. So he did it again. This time a sound like a child giggling could be heard. Jenny sat there and shivered.

"It's possessed by a child!" she exclaimed.

"I think it's more complex than that. Although I think the chest probably belonged to the family."

Again the giggle. The giggle this time ended in a cough.

"Did you die from whooping cough?" Moira asked.

Jenny and her dad looked at her as if she taken leave of her senses. Pretending not to notice their glances, she persisted.

"Did that nasty cough cause you to die?"

A voice, as chilling as ice said, "I am alone."

The chest went quiet and became quite still.

THE FOOL'S JOURNEY

They all went out to lunch at the pub where Moira worked. None of them felt able to sit in the house for much longer; those last words had torn asunder the fabric of their hearts. Sunlight had left the house and even the return of Jimmy and his reorganising the saucepans did not lighten the mood. They discussed it in hushed voices as they ate ploughman's lunches whilst supping a pint of local ale.

"Where do you think her family could have gone?" Jenny asked

"What makes you think it was a girl?" asked Moira's Dad.

"Uncle Cliff, when did you think boys play with dolls? She's obviously sad and alone."

The weight of the last sentence weighed heavily on the fabric of reality. Eventually the fabric split. They were no longer talking about an inanimate wooden chest, but a soul. One that had lived, died and now felt all alone.

After Jenny left later that afternoon, Moira and her dad set about doing some research, trying to find a date. Without any specifics, not even when Jimmy had died, they got nowhere. Generically, the best they could manage was something in the reign of Queen Victoria. Feeling as if they had failed, they went to bed and to sleep.

The next few days passed relatively hassle-free. That was until Moira's dad had a blazing row with her mother on the phone one day. He had put down the phone and in an exasperated tone said, "She's a wicked bitch. Why do I stay married to her?"

"I've often wondered that," mused Moira.

"Why the hell didn't you ever say so?" he yelled, storming out the room.

Moira watched his retreating back with a degree of sadness. She had never seen her kindly giant of a dad so upset. She wondered what her mum had said. She, however, did not have long to ponder this.

The house was filled with a roar, a primeval roar, one that bypassed the brain and struck at the nervous system. Moira's dad came running into the room and held Moira. The house began to shake. Around their heads ornaments and chairs levitated. They huddled into the corner, too

THE FOOL'S JOURNEY

afraid to move. A voice shouted so loudly, Moira tried to stifle the noise by putting her hands over her ears. It was to no avail, the voice was heard inside her head and it bellowed.

'Hell shall fall on the man who turns against his daughter. He shall die.'

"No. He means me no harm," screamed Moira.

Her voice was drowned out by the sound of a huge swarm of bees. None could be seen. Items whirred ever closer; things were being directed at her father. The fire poker crashing into the wall by the side of them.

"Stop," she wailed.

Looking across at her dad she could see him mouth the words 'do something'. But what could she do?

Around her head, her items whirled. Archie had crept into the room; his silvery fur went up on end. Some unseen force levitated him up toward the ceiling, and he was caught up in the mass of rotating objects. His screeches overrode the buzzing of the bees. Then she knew what she had to do, what she was told not to try, unless in extreme circumstances. This was one. She just hoped the threat would be enough.

Getting to her feet, ducking as the vase flew over her head, Moira grabbed at the box she kept on the fireplace. She lifted out the salt and her pentagram.

She began sprinkling salt; her heart felt like a herd of wild horses was galloping away from a heath fire. Trembling, she traced an outline of a circle and beckoned for her dad to come nearer. Crawling on his hands and knees, he entered the circle, smudging the line of the salt. Moira repaired it and sat by the side of him. She squeezed his hand. In a voice that rang like a bell she called out, "All evil that has congregated here, I …"

It worked! Everything fell down in a clatter and clunking. She watched as her best vase broke into pieces at her feet. Archie fell onto the sofa and scrambling off, he raced across the room and straight up

THE FOOL'S JOURNEY

Moira. His needle claws scrabbled at her back, until he nestled against her neck.

Slowly, they cleared up the broken pieces, both of them feeling like they had been caught in a tornado. Poor little Archie followed them around like a lost sheep. Moira's dad decided he would go back the next day after discussing it with her mum. Moira lay awake for a while pondering things. Archie had taken residence on the bed by the side of her. There was no way he was going to be left alone, not that night.

Morning dawned bright and clear with the promise of being a fine day. Moira's dad packed up the car. Giving her a hug he said, "Poppet, we need to work this out. I've been too soft on her for too many years. If there is chance we can work it out, we will. Be my little poppet and sell up and move out. This house is not good."

Moira watched the retreating bumper of the car until it was out of sight. She turned back towards the house and thought about her dad's words. What should she do?

THE FOOL'S JOURNEY

CHAPTER SEVEN – THE HIEROPHANT

Education – Belief system – Conformity – Group Identification

Moira rattled around the cottage for the rest of that week. It felt empty, and not only because her dad had gone home. It felt as if it had lost something. Jimmy had pushed a barrier and now she had lost trust in him. Perhaps this had happened before? Two pieces of brightness broke up the greyness that seemed to have settled in her world. One was an email from TABI, saying she had a place on the next course starting soon and Leo returned back to his Aunt's house. It amazed her how much he had become part of her world in such a short space of time.

They were sitting in her back garden one evening, watching the bats swoop overhead. Archie sat on Leo's knee watching them with keen interest, trying to work out whether they were toys to be played with or meals on wings to be caught. Archie tensed his muscles and prepared to leap. Archie took a leap at the nearest bat, missing by a mile and ending up in vegetable border amongst the growing potatoes. He was not amused. Then a third category entered into Archie's feline brain. Things to be ignored. Moira retrieved the disgruntled Archie, who curled up around her neck and purred whilst she told Leo about her course and what it would entail. Archie was not bothered by such trivialities such as Tarot cards. He had his slave and she fed and loved him. What else could a cat wish for?

The day of the start of the course came. Moira felt ridiculously excited by being at a computer; communicating in the metaphorical sense to people she had never met, via her keyboard. They were given their first assignment and a week to complete it. She had the advantage of having drawn a daily card since receiving her deck in the New Year. It

THE FOOL'S JOURNEY

was quite an enlightenment as she delved into seeing what the picture told, not just what the book told. For this exercise, she chose the Ace of Pentacles. Her card for today. From storm clouds emerged a hand carrying a shining gold pentacle. Below the hand was a richly laid out garden. Within a hedge of roses was an arch. Through the arch one could see mountains. Chewing the end of a pen she was twirling in her hand, Moira pondered what this card was suggesting to her. Looking again closely, she thought it was saying that she had all the financial resources she needed now to go off and start something new. She felt too that she was being protected; everything was, to coin the phrase, in hand.

Moira found herself eagerly awaiting the next installment. However, she was also now working hard to get her business plan in order. As the cast had been removed, she could now drive. The only thing that had fallen foul was her job at the pub. Her back meant she could not spend as long on her feet as she used to. While Liz was very understanding and tried to make it work for her, Moira had felt it was not fair on Liz. Now, it was more imperative than ever to get something going and get an income coming in. The Ace of Pentacles suggested all would be well.

The next portion of the course concerned the Major Arcanas. The question had been asked. What did she feel about the Fool's Journey, the meeting of the archetypes of the Major Arcanas. Moira looked back over her last year. A year - surely it must be close to a year now when she looked on that fateful day. She shuddered involuntarily. She felt a pang of guilt that she hadn't made any attempt to find out what had happened to Sarah. She realized she had in fact surgically removed the whole episode from her life. But like surgery, scar tissue remained. Promising herself that she find out what had happen and track down Sarah's parents, she turned back to the task in hand and pondered the Fool's Journey.

Moira decided that one went through several journeys in a lifetime. These may be quick, or they may be long. They may not happen in the chronological order of the cards, but they would all happen. This phase of her life, she decided, was in chronological order. She had taken the blind leap of faith and quit her job. These were definite characteristics of

THE FOOL'S JOURNEY

the Fool. With the Power of the Magician she had bought her cottage, forcibly setting things into action. Next, had come the High Priestess: inaction caused by being snowed in, working life out, just thinking things through. Of course, there had been the mystery element. The discovery of the chest and that poignant note. With the Empress had come her pledge to the divine, the mothering of Archie and creation of a garden. Then the Emperor card had happened. She had had her accident and her dad had come to her rescue. It was not so much a structured authority, rather the fatherly aspect of the card. Here she was now at her next major juncture, the Hierophant. Now she was conforming to certain standards set by the course, being at work within a group structure. Learning - she was learning to read tarot cards, not just looking at the definition in her book. The Lovers was next. Although Leo and her were not officially an item, she had a strong suspicion this would be the next big phase. The way he was going, this might take some time in coming.

    Moira very nearly missed the next deadline. A phone call from Leo saying his aunt had taken a turn for the worse and was going into hospital. Blodwen had a special place in Moira's heart. It had upset her and she found she was unable to concentrate on anything. The day she had heard the news, she had drawn the five of pentacles again. She was learning to dread this card. Today, as she settled to the coursework in hand, Blodwen was coming out of hospital. She had difficulty settling down to it and found the task of learning the suit qualities hard. That was, right up to the last question. This stopped her and made her look at the qualities within herself. She was fiery, passionate and creative. She was impetuous and on occasions over confident. Today - today restless could be applied. She was quite clearly a Queen of Wands. Although, perhaps, in a previous existence she was more Swords. She typed a note to her tutors to ask whether one could change suit qualities. The question had been put to the group as a learning exercise. Moira found herself believing that fundamentally personalities are the main characteristics, but in certain situations people may take on qualities of other suits that mask their underlying characteristics. When Moira had discussed this

THE FOOL'S JOURNEY

with Jenny that evening, Jenny had thought she was really beginning to lose her marbles!

Moira's thoughts were on other matters. Midsummer's solstice was approaching and she wanted her first one to be done right. She wanted to feel she was conforming to the belief system, not feeling comfortable enough within her faith to choose her own way of celebrating it. She purchased a quartz crystal and decided to charge the crystal as she had read at morning light, whilst standing naked in the morning rays. Then she would have a barbecue. She busied herself putting things into action, and soon it was the eve before Midsummer. The barbecue was going to be a small one; no one except Leo and Blodwen seemed that interested. Liz was working in the pub and Jenny's car was in the garage for repair. This was fine; she had Archie and Leo was coming; that was enough. She stifled the doubt that this was enough and assured herself that with her new work she would make friends.

Moira's alarm went off and she rose stiff and bleary-eyed to meet the dawn. She showered, dried herself, and wrapping herself in a dressing gown, she went downstairs and out into the garden to greet the sun. She thought she could just hear Jimmy sniggle. He, nor anyone else would stop her in this. She sat for a while listening to the world waking up, the snufflings of creatures coming out of their sleep ready to go in search of breakfast, the birds beginning to flutter and stir. She stood as the first hint of brightness flooded the horizon to her left. Walking into the centre of the garden, past the block of Blodwen's house, she shook off her gown and stood with arms aloft, one hand carrying the crystal. As light flooded over her body, accentuating her curves and bathing her pale skin in its fiery light, she could feel it charging her with energy; her connection with the masculine and the feminine of the divine were in perfect balance now. Pulling her gown around her, holding off the slight morning chill, she sat and watched the sun flood the sky with its light and felt blessed to be there.

Little did she know from the next-door back window, Leo had woken early from a restless night's sleep. His thoughts were purely of Moira; his

THE FOOL'S JOURNEY

yearning to be near her in more than one way was becoming like a physical pain. His heart ached and his body reacted in its own way. When he drew the curtains of his room, which overlooked Moira's back garden, he got a surprise that didn't help either yearning. He watched the beauty of her, his heart breaking with his need to hold her close. Yet, he also knew that if he held her close like that, he would not be able to control the boiling pot that his urges had become. Drawing the curtains, he went for a long cold shower.

Settling down to her tarot homework, Moira tried to design a spread. There was so much she wanted to know. She wanted to look at the situation with her and Leo. He stirred in her a strange cocktail of emotions. There was the physical desire, to want to have his toned body next to hers; there was the urge to look after him, to protect him; then the unfamiliar desire that burnt like ice, the want of never being without him. Part of her was afraid too. Then she wanted to look at where she should go with her business. She flicked through a couple of the other books she had bought. Restless, she plumped for a spread that showed card one as where she was now. Card two as where she was going next and card three as outcome. The churning noise of the tractor and buzz of bees filtered in through the open window. Putting her pen, paper and cards down, Moira decided to go outside into the garden instead.

Soon it was time to light the barbecue and get things ready. Moira laid the flowery cloth over the old plastic table, the deep red mixed in with the greens and whites were echoed by the rose growing nearby the trellis work. Lavender from the planted edging of the patio thronged with bees and butterflies. A jug of Pimms stood ready and the glow of the fire burnt within the barbecue. Moira got up and sat on the edge of the raised borders, feeling the furry leafed sage under her fingers and then pouncing over to where the table was. After what felt like an age, Moira caught sound of Leo's cheerful whistle, but there was another sound too.

Wide-eyed, Moira looked on as Lottie ran around the corner flinging herself at Moira to be caught up in a whirl of hugs. As Moira looked over Lottie's head, she saw Blodwen being pushed in a wheelchair. Her skin was sunken and yellow. Her once dancing blue eyes seemed to be leaden grey, like great looming rain clouds. To stop the tear that pricked at her corner of her eye, she looked on at Lottie who was playing quite happily with Archie. As if sensing her glance, Lottie said, as though addressing the cat, "Great Granny is dying. But she is old and that is OK. She will go and see the other dead people who she loved soon. When I am old and die, I will see her again then."

Cathy caught this conversation and looked on, her mouth hanging open. Not knowing quite what to say, she busied herself with taking foil wrapped dishes into the kitchen. Moira followed her in, giving her a hug when her hands were empty.

"Leo said you were having a barbecue and I knew Granny was not well, so it sounded an ideal situation. I've marinated some chicken and there are some of your favourite cakes. Lottie has made jelly but that is still setting in the fridge next door. I'll get that later."

Cathy chattered on, uncovering more dishes than just chicken and cakes. Jimmy decided that he wanted in on the action and decided that trays would need to be in size order. Cathy almost screamed as one tray was lifted and replaced with another.

"Thanks Jimmy," Moira uttered haughtily.

Cathy, regaining her composure, mouthed an 'Oh'. Jimmy had been a much-discussed topic of conversation.

"Is Blod dying?" Moira asked Cathy. "I know she is dying, but I meant shortly?"

Cathy stood in the doorway looking out in the garden at Blodwen covered in a brightly coloured, granny-square blanket. Archie and Lottie were chasing bugs in the grass and Leo was pouring the Pimms into awaiting glasses.

"I didn't know. I mean I don't know," she said, standing there ringing her hands. "Last time Lottie said something like that, it proved true. Luckily, it was a happier situation and her best school friend's Mum found she was pregnant with twins." There was a look in Cathy's eye that she recognised in her own dad, one of longing and emptiness. A sudden shriek of laughter brought back the usual familiar warmness.

The barbecue on Midsummer's Day seemed the most appropriate way of spending time. Lottie crawled around with Archie, getting covered in grass and mud. Once the sausages, burgers, chicken and kebabs had been consumed, marshmallows were being toasted on the dying embers, Lottie and Cathy retrieved the wobbly bunny jelly from Blodwen's house. Proudly, Lottie served it up into bowls. Jimmy, deciding he wanted a bowl, lifted one up and it floated around the kitchen, much to Lottie's amusement.

"Ok, you can have that one then," she announced to the floating air.

Whilst Cathy and Leo cleared up, Moira's back and legs were aching. They told her to sit down, and gave a running commentary on how many times the bowl of jelly either flew about the room or wobbled. Jimmy was very much like a kid with a new toy.

Blodwen and Lottie's eyes began to droop and with the instinct of a mother, Cathy whisked them both off to bed, leaving Leo and Moira alone in the falling dusk.

"I know we've been in each other's company a lot and I feel like a school boy asking this, but…would you go on a date with me?" Leo asked after they had sat there for a while.

Smiling, Moira looked into his doleful eyes "That would be lovely. Does this mean I am now your girlfriend," she teased.

Leo gently kissed her lips for the first time. "Yes."

Grinning like a pair of teenagers, they sat with their hands entwined, whilst the birds and animals Moira had heard that morning went to their rest. Moira lay with her head against Leo's shoulder, wondering whether this would work out. For now, she should be satisfied, shouldn't she?

CHAPTER EIGHT – THE LOVERS
Relationship – Sexuality – Personal Beliefs – Values

Moira fell asleep quickly that night and not even the whimpering from the chest could disturb her. When she woke, the sun was already high in the sky and it held all the promise of a hot day. With a mug of coffee in one hand, she opened the door of the boxroom. Coffee spilled over the edge of the mug as she was brought up short by the chest in the middle of the floor; it was quivering and out of its blanket and had moved from its normal place. Lowering herself to the floor carefully, she stroked its lid and hummed a wordless tune under her breath. Soon it stopped quivering. She lifted it onto her lap and the lid came up. Moira's quick reflexes saved her from being struck in the face. Inside was a note.
'I want my Mummy.'
The lid shut and the chest went still. With hot tears streaming down her face, Moira put the note up on the shelf with the others and wrapped the chest in its blanket. All thoughts of work were driven clean out of her mind. Instead, she went back downstairs and sat in the window seat, sobbing, great heart wrenching sobs. The note may as well have been a dagger; it pierced her heart and burnt her soul.
Archie came to investigate why his human was making this funny noise as she sat in the window. He jumped up and batted her with a paw. She seemed not to notice him. This was not like her. He tried a meow. She just sat there with her head on her knees and her long red hair tumbling down around them. The noise stopped but still she sat there. He was hungry and needed his breakfast. Desperate times called for desperate measures. He jumped up on her back, sinking his claws in just a little to get her attention.
Moira reached around and gently pushed Archie off her back. He was right - it was no good sitting here crying. She needed to find out what

THE FOOL'S JOURNEY

this was about. First, she had to feed the poor starving feline, and then, with a smile that flashed across her face like the rising sun, she would talk to Blodwen. It would give her a chance not only to see Lottie and Cathy, but Leo too. She closed her eyes and remembered the sensation of his warm muscular flesh as she had lain her head on his shoulder the night before. She definitely wanted more than that. It had been too long.

Carefully packing the items into a soft bag, she called Archie and they both made their way across to Blodwen's. A delighted Lottie opened the door.

"Nuncle Leo said you are now his girlfriend. Does that mean you are going to marry him?"

Archie jumped out her arms and curled himself around Lottie's legs, stemming any further questions.

Behind her, Leo stood grinning. Moira was glad she had dressed herself in her light summer dress. She was still too thin for it, but it certainly showed her figure off to its best. With a slight pang, she thought about the scaring on her legs where they had had to be pinned. He didn't seem to care. The look he gave her certainly seemed to have a wolfish air to it.

Moira watched Lottie and Archie hunt for bugs in the garden. Shaking her head, she tried to decide whether he was part human or part dog! He certainly seemed to understand and wanted to play Lottie's game. Turning her back on the scene, she put the things out on the kitchen table in Blodwen's kitchen and explained everything that had happened right up to that morning. She included Jimmy's part in her account.

Blodwen turned a peg doll over and over in her hand.

"I use to play with something similar when I was a child. I had a whole family of them. Mummy, Daddy and several babies. There are only three here; this makes me think these belonged to a child who was perhaps the eldest in the family."

Moira looked across at Cathy, who held the note that said 'I want my Mummy' in trembling hands, staring blankly at Lottie in the garden. She shrieked with laughter when she discovered a bug floating in through the open back door. Without saying a word, Cathy left the room. Blodwen, too, had a faraway look. She turned to Leo and said, "Go fetch the floral papered shoe box from the top of my wardrobe. I think there is something in there that might help us shed light on this."

The air in the kitchen had taken on a somber mood. Not even the laughter and birdsong from outside or the light flooding in through the windows and doors could lift the gloom.

Leo came back into the room carrying the box, followed by Cathy who had red-rimmed eyes. Leo put the box on the table then went over and grabbed the coffee pot. He refilled the mugs that were on the table, like guardians protecting the exposed contents of the chest. Blodwen lifted a couple of books out of the box.

"I bought these a while back. These are history books of Cardigan. That's where my family lived. There might be something in them that might help you shed light on what has happened. In the early nineteenth century, after the Napoleonic wars and great famine, there was a mass exodus to America and Canada. There were boats that sailed from the riverside in Cardigan over to the Americas around this time. I am not saying this is what has happened, but it might be a starting point."

Wordlessly, Moira accepted them. She had a strange sensation that the puzzle now had gained a corner piece. As Moira was leaving, Cathy pressed something into her hand.

"Look when you get back. Give it to the chest," she said blushing.

Moira squeezed her hand and smiled into her eyes. Leo offered to walk her home, to which he got a chorus of sniggles and an overture of knowing looks. He walked beside Moira. Archie, who was riding curled around her neck as normal, thought this was great fun and contented himself with batting any part of Leo that came within paw's reach. Once they had ambled the short way to Moira's front door, Archie jumped down and sauntered off into the cottage.

"Are you free tomorrow night?" Leo asked.

"Yes."

THE FOOL'S JOURNEY

"That's great. Cathy and Lottie go home tomorrow morning and I would like to take you out to dinner. I'll make a few phone calls and book a table." Kissing her gently on the lips before she could reply, he sauntered off whistling, his hands in his pockets.

As Moira bathed in lavender bath salts, she breathed in their essence, trying to calm herself. It was still two hours before the taxi Leo had arranged would come to collect them and she felt like a cat on a hot tin roof. Jimmy, as though sensing something was afoot had made himself scarce. As she lay in the water, her mind churned over the package Cathy had given her. Inside it was a bear, no bigger than the palm of her hand. Cathy had written a note saying that she had bought it for Lottie, because she collected them, but could easily get another and I should give it to the spirit of the chest. Maybe it would help her a little. That evening Moira had unwrapped the chest and explained that someone who cared about her had given her this special bear. The lid had opened, revealing an empty inside. Moira placed the bear inside the chest and wrapped it back up again. The chest bothered her a little, but Amber had reassured her it was not evil and if anything, she had been chosen. Moira was not certain whether this had made her feel any better about it or not. Still, tonight she had more important things to attend to.

Agonising over what to wear, Moira stood in front of her wardrobe wrapped in a towel. Since having to quit her job because of her back, she had been surviving mainly on vegetables from the garden, meat from the local farmer whom she helped with his accounts and dipping into her savings occasionally. As a result, she had lost the weight she had gained whilst inactive, and her dad was cooking for her. She was more angular now than curvy, and some of her old dresses looked more like sacks on a scarecrow than showing her figure off at its best. Eventually she chose a peacock-blue dress; it tucked in under her breast and flared out over her hips. She relished the shimmer of the fabric. The way it changed hue slightly with the light was the reason she had bought it all those years ago. Now, to find the shoes.

THE FOOL'S JOURNEY

After turning her wardrobe out and putting everything back in, Moira went to search in the spare room. She looked across at the chest; it seemed happy. Moira could not work out why; perhaps it was the atmosphere in the room. After the third, still unpacked box, she found her little silvery kitten heels and wrap. Moira glanced up at the clock on the wall; she raced back into her bedroom. She quickly blew dry her hair and then used the hair dryer to dry her nail polish. She had just about enough time to put her make-up on and get dressed. She was spraying herself with her favourite musky-scented perfume when she heard a knock at the door. There was Leo, looking smart in well cut beige trousers, a light blue linen shirt and wearing a rakish grin.

Moira felt as if she had been transported into a different world. The 'taxi' transpired to be a chauffeur driven car. The restaurant was in an old Victorian manor house. The wisteria covered red brick walls carried a steeply pointed, gabled, red-tiled roof. The owner of the house greeted them and they were shown through to the lounge, where they sat in leather armchairs. Pre dinner drinks were ordered and they browsed the menus. Moira had great difficulty hiding a wince at the prices on the menu. Noticing her anxious look, Leo merely said, "I like the best, the best is sometimes free, sometimes expensive. This is a very decent restaurant with great service. Compared to what I pay back home, these are middle-ranged prices."

Moira smiled a shy smile. She knew that Leo was an 'entrepreneur' and reassured her on many occasions that he was comfortably off. It still came as a surprise to Moira who had watched every penny since she started work, that this level of lavishness was commonplace to him. The gin and tonic helped her relax. They ordered their food and talked about various topics, comfortable in each other's company.

They were shown into a high ceilinged dining room, from which chandeliers hung. They were escorted to a candlelit table surrounded by red velvet cushioned chairs. The chairs were comfortable and the soft piano music created a very romantic atmosphere. They sipped delicious champagne whilst they ate their starters. Moira enjoyed her tiger prawns immensely, having never tried them before with lime and ginger. The combination was exotic. The sea bass when it came was lightly grilled, the flesh beneath the crispy skin moist and succulent. They laughed and joked and found more often than not that they were picking up the other's train of thought, often without realising. They shared a desert call Eton Mess which consisted of meringue, cream, strawberry coulis and strawberries. After they had finished dinner, they were shown back into the lounge and served coffee. Leo ordered them each a large brandy. Now, they just sat on the sofa in comfortable silence, Moira resting her head against Leo's firm, muscular shoulder.

The car journey back seemed to pass much too quickly. Moira tried to work out what her next move should be. She did not want to rush things and be perceived as a wanton hussy, yet the closeness of his body aroused urges in her that had been suppressed for a long time. They held hands in the back of the car as they travelled back. They pulled up outside Moira's cottage and Leo jumped out and held the door for her. He took her hand and kissed it as he did so. He turned to the driver and said, "Thanks Chris. I'll see you back home in a few weeks."

"Been a pleasure, Mr. Leo, see you soon."

Moira stood there wide-eyed with her mouth open. Leo grinned, his white teeth glinting in the moonlight.

"Aunty Blod disapproves of me using Chris this way. But Chris has been with me for many years. He loves driving and has a niece in Cardiff. It suits us both."

Moira took a deep breath, gazed straight into Leo's eyes and asked the one thing that was on her mind.

"Would you stay the night?"

For an answer, he leant down and kissed her passionately.

They entered the cottage and Archie was there waiting for them. They both absently-minded patted and stroked him and watched as he sauntered back into the kitchen. He seemed to sense they had something else on their minds. Moira led Leo up the stairs by his hand. In the bedroom, she undid the buttons of his fine linen shirt, exposing his toned but not over muscly body. There was a noticeable firmness in his trousers.

    Leo kissed her, a little roughly perhaps, but his desires were at the boiling point. He zipped off her dress exposing bare breasts and skimpy panties. He lowered her down to the bed. Unzipping his trousers and slipping off his silk boxer shorts, he stood there with his manhood erect.

    Gasping, Moira wriggled out of her own underwear and beckoned for him to come and lie on the bed beside her. They kissed and gently touched each other for a while. Her feelings were unfamiliar; situations like this had never arisen before. The tenderness of the situation made her hungry in a way that food could not satisfy.

    Gazing at her, Leo stroked his hand down her breast and over the flat of her stomach, kissing at the fine white skin, drinking in the fragrance of her perfume. He wanted more yet needed to take it slowly. His body ached with the wanting. Gently, they touched each other. Taking deep breaths, he held in the feeling, not wishing to ruin this moment. This was the moment that he had often dreamt about.

    It was more than he had expected. He felt her quiver beneath his hand's touch. Looking at the fire burning in her eyes that mirrored his own, he whispered, "Shall I?" Her hand guided him down to where he wanted to be. She arched her back in ecstasy as he entered her velvety depths.

    Leo woke first and looked at Moira's naked sleeping form. The sunlight streamed in through the undrawn curtains turning her red hair to fire. A feeling overcame him; he wanted to protect her, he wanted to care for her and most of all he wanted her for himself. No man should ever have this woman. Last night had been gentle. They were getting to know each other and he sensed that she had hidden passions to equal his own. Lying back on the pillows, he grinned at the ceiling. He would talk to Aunty Blod later, but he knew what to do.

    Moira made coffee and cooked breakfast that morning without the usual help from Jimmy. She sensed he was off sulking somewhere. In

THE FOOL'S JOURNEY

truth, since their encounter in the lounge, he was less prevalent in the house. This morning she didn't mind; this morning she was enjoying a new sensation: cooking breakfast for a man. She found herself thinking about future mornings and knew then that she loved him. The feeling scared her but excited her in the same instant.

Leo returned later to his aunt's house and Moira found herself on edge, feeling as if she was waiting for something to happen, something momentous. She grabbed the cards from their place on the mantelpiece and thought about the whole situation. What she was experiencing. Unsurprisingly, it showed her The Lovers. A purple and red winged angel hovered over a naked woman and a naked man. Behind the naked woman was an apple tree with a serpent entwined in it and behind the man was a leafless tree on fire. The union appeared to be blessed. Still unable to settle, Moira did a little light housework, tidying her already tidy house. From the window she could see Leo walking up the path, with a devilish grin on his face. She opened the door before he could even knock. Moira just managed to stop from throwing herself into his arms.

A little time later, Leo and Moira walked along the beach, whilst children with buckets and spades made sandcastles and their parents ran around fussing over hats and sun cream. They did not talk much, but clung to each other, as if they had were magnetically attached. Sitting on a rocky outcrop, Leo turned to Moira, "I've got something to ask you. If you need time to think over things that's OK with me."

Moira looked at him, her brow slightly creased in puzzlement.

"Will you marry me?

THE FOOL'S JOURNEY

CHAPTER NINE – THE CHARIOT

Victory – Will – Self Assertion – Hard Control

    Moira stared at him for a few moments, looking for any sign on his face that it might be a joke. Seeing nothing there but plain honesty, she whispered, "Yes."
    He held her tight in his arms, not daring to let her go. It was only the approach of the incoming tide that made them get off their rock. They walked back up the beach grinning like children, then went and bought ice cream to celebrate.
    Blodwen received the news with great delight, Cathy and Lottie had whooped and screamed with glee, so much so that poor Leo had to hold the phone away from his ear. Leo's dad called him a dark horse and his mum started planning wedding hats. After the warm and welcoming reception of Leo's family, it was with some trepidation that Moira rang her parents. This was her life and she was going to live it. It mattered little what they said, but still she would have preferred their blessing. To her uttermost horror, her mum answered the phone. She had managed not to speak to her for over a year now. Normally, she spoke to the answering machine.
    "Mum."
    "Moira."
    Moira twiddled her hair. There was a pause. Moira would have found plucking toenails out more comfortable. Eventually, her mum broke the silence.
    "Are you recovered?" There was a genuine note of concern in her voice.
    "I am getting there. I'm a lot better than I was. How are you?"

THE FOOL'S JOURNEY

"Actually, I am good. I went to the doctor after your dad and I had a row. It transpires my thyroid was dicky and has been causing all sorts of odd mood swings. I've felt better than I've done for... well...ages."

Moira smiled at the phone and felt her heart lift. Her mum had always been a cantankerous Madam, but over the last year or so and certainly recently, it had become worse. She was glad there was a reason for it.

"Mum, I am going to get married."

"Cliff, Cliff. Come here, quickly." Moira heard her mum down the phone calling. "Tell your dad too."

"What's up, poppet?" Concern radiated in his voice.

"I am going to marry Leo, Dad."

The explosion of delight that came from the other end of the phone was almost as deafening as the one Leo had experienced.

"Your dad and I are coming up! We'll leave tomorrow morning. This is marvelous."

With a smile, Moira put down the phone and hugged Leo.

Leo had sneaked off that afternoon for a short while and returned with a red velvet box, containing a solitary diamond ring, the size of Moira's little finger nail. Moira gasped in delight; it was more than she had ever dreamed. It captured the dying rays of the evening sun, exploding brilliance back, reflecting their love for one another as they sat in the yard, sipping champagne. The air smelt of roses and night-scented plants, the sound of cows lowering and sheep baaing could be heard in the distance. That moment in time was peace, pure peace.

The next few days went by in a blur. Leo and Moira felt like they were rocks caught up in the ebbing and flowing tides. Moira's parents had greeted Leo warmly and treated them to a meal out. Cathy, Lottie and Cathy's husband, Lee, arrived. Cathy explained that Lee's sister was cat sitting. Leo's parents came and started planning a big get together. It seemed that Moira's parents had things in common with Leo's and got on like a house on fire. Eventually, there was peace in their lives and they could plan for the future.

THE FOOL'S JOURNEY

Moira and Leo, with Archie curled up between them, sat on the sofa one wet afternoon, as a storm raged outside. Claps of thunder punctuated their discussions, like an erratic comma fiend. There were questions about where they would live, what Moira was going to do about the business she had been planning. They seemed to be caught in a whirlpool, not able to break out. Until, that is, Moira had an idea.

"Let me get my cards."

Leo agreed. They were getting nowhere. They both wanted to be together, but there were other considerations.

Moira laid her emerald green reading cloth on the floor of her lounge and shuffled her cards. She lay three cards face down on the cloth. Turning the first card she said, "Card one, where am I now?"

The card was the seven of cups. Seven cups were resting on a cloud, each cup contained different things. The figure standing in front of the cups was silhouetted.

"Seems like I have too many options and don't know which one to choose."

"You're not wrong there," Leo mused wryly.

Ignoring him, Moira turned over the second card.

"Card two; what do I need to do about the situation?"

The Chariot. A man stood in a chariot, and in front of the chariot were two sphinxes, one black and one white. Moira considered this image for a while.

"I feel this is suggesting I need to take control of the situation. I need to make decisions and stick to them. But make these decisions in a controlled and balanced way."

Leo watched, his eyebrow raised in genuine respect and interest.

"Card three, how do I move on from here?"

Six of Swords. A man was punting a boat across the water to the land beyond. In the boat sat a woman and child. All three had their heads bent. In the front of the boats were six swords. On one side of the boat, the water was calm and smooth, on the other side was a small expanse of rough water.

THE FOOL'S JOURNEY

Moira rested back on her heels as she studied this card. She wasn't certain what it meant in relation to her question. There was an element of sadness; the bowed heads suggested this. The area of rough waters was smaller than the area of smooth waters, suggesting that this was a move on to a better life. Perhaps some element of sadness or going through a rough patch had galvanised this move. Instinctively, Moira felt what this sadness was; she knew in her heart Leo could never live here without Blodwen next door. At the same time, moving on from here with him would be an end to her rough waters. There would be an element of sadness for her, but she loved him. Feeling his questioning gaze on her, she looked up into Leo's expectant brown eyes.

"I need to think about this a bit more. I feel this suggests we will move away."

She reached for the book 'Learning the Tarot' and flicked through the pages until she found the six of swords and handed it to Leo without saying anything. He read it whilst she tidied up the cards. She was just about to put the Six of Swords back into the deck, when it was whisked out of her hands and it hung there in the air. She could hear the faint words, 'Move on now.' Moira made a mental note to ring Amber, and said it out loud.

"OK Jimmy, I'll seek advice on this one and see if we can send you to your rest."

The card fluttered to the floor and the atmosphere of the room changed.

Moira had thinking to do and decisions to make. She needed time to think and be still, to put into the place the necessary thought processes in order to work this out. Her consent to marry Leo had changed the dynamics of her business plan. The cards suggested they would move from here, which meant she needed to change tack. She looked at Leo, still forlornly staring at the words on the page. He looked up and asked in a hoarse whisper, "Do you think Aunty Blod's going to die soon?"

THE FOOL'S JOURNEY

The question was expected, yet it still hit her like a bag of wet cement. Her mind bubbled in turmoil. Moira took a few deep breaths, and centering herself, she listened to her instinct, "Yes."

Leo nodded. "Cathy told me that Lottie had picked up on it as well."

Moira took his hands in her's and held them tenderly. "We knew she was old and that she was going to die. It will be sad. Let her pass on quietly when the time comes and without pain. We have to forge our own lives, perhaps create the next generation. Life has to end sometime to give way to new life." She kissed him on the forehead. "Go and take her out for the day, spend some time with her. Do what it is you have to do to feel happy."

Leo looked up into the steel blue eyes. There was a look that suggested arguing would be a waste of time. Instead, he plumped for the tack, "Why don't you come with me?"

"No, I need time to work things out for me and you need time with your aunt alone. Now go. The day's still young and the weather looks like it is breaking."

Leo got up, dislodging Archie who glared at him as only a cat can do. Hugging Moira, he left without a word. Moira made herself a coffee and went upstairs to the boxroom to try and put some of her thoughts into place. When she entered the room, she found the chest had moved. However many times this happened, it still unnerved her. She took a deep breath and put her coffee on her desk and went to sit by the chest.

The chest nestled against Moira's legs, seeming to want nothing more than human company. Moira leant against the wall, reached up to grab her coffee and sat there talking to the chest. She talked about her situation and the fact she was going marry Leo. The fact she was going to have to work to pay the bills and she did not know what to do about it. Throughout, the chest quivered and nestled as if answering her. Moira asked the question that was uppermost in her mind.

"Can I move you?"

She felt the air around her swirl. The temperature of the room dropped. In front of her, the faintest outline of a girl appeared. She was about six years old, wearing a long white gown; her hair hung loose down her back. She was smiling; she nodded then faded away.

Warmth returned to the room and the chest became still. Moira carefully lifted it back to its normal position and wrapped it in the blanket again. Picking up her empty coffee cup, she left the room and went outside to think.

By the time Leo returned, Moira was curled up in the corner of the sofa and had a notepad full of jottings and the laptop on her knee. So engrossed in what she was doing, if it were not for Archie jumping off the sofa and running to the door, she probably would not have known of Leo's return,. One look at him showed her that he was more peaceful than he had been that morning.

"How did the day go?"

"I'll make a coffee and tell you all."

He walked into the lounge holding two mugs of coffee and put them on the table. He perched himself on the window seat, half staring at the gathering clouds and half looking at Moira.

"She says she's probably not got longer than a few weeks." Before Moira could say anything, he continued, "I've spent part of the day sorting out her affairs with her lawyer; she's made provision for everyone in the family, even you."

"Me?"

"She thinks it is important that she's seen, as she phrased it 'as matriarch': to be seen as accepting you into the clan." Leo grinned ruefully. "First time I've done anything she's approved of." Taking a sip of his coffee, he continued. "She has also suggested we buy a place together, not one I've created and not this one. I agree with her. I don't love the house I've created and will sell it now it's complete. We'll choose a home together and make it a family home." He took another sip of coffee before he carried on with a gush of returning charisma and humour. "She's also drummed it into me that I've got to let you have your head to a degree. She said if I stifle the fire, I'll stifle what I love."

THE FOOL'S JOURNEY

Moira felt herself blushing. His words had brought home what she feared and cleared up her underlying worry in one sentence. She went and sat by him and held his hand. With a twinkle in her eye, she asked, "What does my lord and master want for his dinner?"

"You!" He turned to grab her and kissed her fiercely. The ringing of his mobile interrupted where his hands were starting to go.

"Leo! Put Moira down, bring her over and order in a Chinese. There's a good boy," came the laughing tones of Blodwen down the phone.

Grinning, they both went over, holding hands and giggling like children.

The next few days passed in a fairly normal way. Moira worked hard on setting up a website, so she could sell business services. After all, she had been a secretary. She was more than qualified in computer accounting and had made her name, albeit for a short time, in advertising. It was not the advertising agency she had planned, but when she knew she would move with Leo to a different area at some point, this seemed flexible. The Internet made things so much easier. Leo seemed to spend most of the next few days on the phone, or over in his aunt's house where he had made his makeshift office. That was until one day at the beginning of August.

A humdinger of a storm woke Moira in the night. It sounded like a steam train was out of control. The trees on the branches swayed and the rain drummed down so hard it bounced back up again, before sloshing away down the road in a torrent. It sounded like some psychotic maniac applauding a would-be murder. Thunder clapped as lightning stabbed. Moira watched from the window as the flash of lightning struck and split a tree not more than thirty metres from where she stood. The energy of the force rent the tree and sent Moira backwards. Leo woke muzzily to find Moira sprawled on the bed. She got up gingerly, her back aching. More alarming was the fact the tree branch was swinging precariously close to Blodwen's roof, over where Blodwen slept. Leo looked over her shoulder and shouted above the din, "I'm going." Then clad in no more

THE FOOL'S JOURNEY

than the shorts he wore in bed, Leo tore downstairs, threw on the raincoat and raced next door.

Moira stood transfixed, watching the tree sway alarmingly. The phone beside her bed rang.

"I've got an ambulance coming. Get some clothes on. Bring some for me. She's dying," came Leo's tear-strangled. The phone line went dead. Without a word, Moira did as she had been bade.

Through the torrent of rain, the screaming siren of the ambulance could be heard. Moira and Leo sat either side of Blodwen, holding a hand each. She looked up at them and with a breath that rattled she spoke, "My time is nearly here, the reaper man waits. Look after Helix. Moira, I am glad you've tamed the lion, which is Leo. You have a gift of second sight. Use it well. I love you both, I love you all."

With that, she closed her eyes and her breathing ceased. They bowed their heads, their hearts weighing heavier than lead. The wailing of the siren was outside now and a hammering on the door alerted them to the paramedic's arrival. Moira stiffly went downstairs and left Leo sobbing over the body of his aunt. He cried like a boy, without shame, without guilt and without the burden of manhood.

As she let the paramedics in, a fear ran through her like a knife and sent her racing back upstairs.

"Leo, lift her, move!" she screamed. A banshee could not have wailed a more terrifying cry.

Without a word, he lifted his aunt from the bed and had stepped out of the room when the half split tree came down on the roof, breaking through and onto the bed where Blodwen had lain. It was too much for Moira; she sagged to her knees in relief.

The rest of the night and early hours of the morning passed in some sort of trance. The ambulance crew pronounced her dead on their arrival. She was laid to rest in the spare bedroom, until the funeral directors were open in the morning. The doctor was called to certify death and as it was known natural causes, a post mortem was not necessary. He left and returned wearily to his bed. The storm that raged outside eventually passed, but not before it had soaked through the hole the tree had left. Thankfully, nothing of value, sentimental or material was ruined. It seemed the sky cried tears of the passing of this soul.

Leo informed the family and they informed the outer family. There would be many swollen red eyes and it would be a while before they could give thanks that their beloved mother, grandmother, aunt, great aunt and great grandmother had a happy and long life. Moira was swept up into the turmoil and grief as a long-standing family member and not one only by engagement of a few weeks. Still, Blodwen had lived and they celebrated that.

Leo stood looking over the body of his great aunt. He felt as her soul passed on to where it would go, that part of him had passed on too. For that moment, it felt that it had left a void. A strong, sensible levelheaded woman had passed out of his life. He was never certain whether she condemned or was secretly pleased by his success. He rather suspected the latter. He would never have asked - it would have spoilt the game, the relationship they had. He looked up as Moira carefully opened the door. The void filled with love and light. There, looking tired, in pain and still beautifully strong was his goddess. He kissed the top of his aunt's forehead. He closed the door and left the room with the future in his hands. But what did the future hold?

CHAPTER TEN – STRENGTH

Strength – Compassion – Patience – Soft Control

What the future held initially was bureaucracy. There were repairs to be made; claiming on the insurance of a deceased person, until probate had finished, many things were impossible. Leo's cousins and Blodwen's other great nephews had taken it upon themselves to fix it up. Leo's own grandfather, Blodwen's son, had passed on a few years ago. Her daughter, Cathy's mother, was too distraught to do anything and begged Leo to make all the arrangements. The day she entered the house, Moira had the feeling she was staring into Blodwen's younger face. She was taller, slender like a lily and her long silver hair hung in luxurious tendrils. The spirit there was the same and the same light danced in her eyes, albeit now dimmed by grief.

Moira noticed with a degree of irony that the whole family expected Leo to cope. It was only at the end of the day, when he lay in bed beside her did the pain and weariness show. He did not want to touch her body in an intimate way; he just clung to her, like a drowning man would to a piece of driftwood. Instinct told her not to push it; she held him close and was there in the day to support where she could, making sure he ate and rested when he would. He ploughed through paperwork, he made funeral arrangements and before long the day came.

The weather had no sense of occasion. The morning dawned bright and clear, promising to be a hot day. What was it they said? Sun for a wedding and rain for a funeral? Certainly not what was promising to be the hottest day of the year so far? Liz, from the pub, volunteered to put on the wake at cost. She was fond of Blodwen and had known her many years. The tiny church car park was full and vehicles were parked either side of the road. If any traffic had been passing that day, it would have struggled to get through. Most of the village turned out to watch the coffin move away, drawn by horses on a rough farm cart, Blodwen's specific request. She had been quite emphatic about not a hearse. She wanted to be buried in the same way her mam had been those many years before. No one was going to argue, especially not today.

The church too was packed and people waited outside the doors to listen to the service. The church with its high ceilings and pointed church spire was usually cool, but today it seemed to keep the heat. The vicar stood before the lectern, sweating visibly, the sun streaming through the stained glass windows of some scenes from the Bible. People fanned themselves with hymn sheets to try and keep cool. Cathy read a poem in Welsh. Out the corner of her eye, Moira could see the astounded look on Leo's face. He had forgotten that she was born and had lived in Wales until she was twelve. Moira knew Blodwen spoke Welsh, even if she never used it much. The emotion behind the prose was understood, even if the words were not. There was something about hearing it spoken in the language of the native land, to which Blodwen was now to be returned, that stirred the soul.

It was not until Blodwen's coffin was being borne out, that the crying started. Not one tear until that point had been shed. The coffin was born to a freshly dug pit, under one of the great yew trees. Moira later found out that Blodwen had purchased the plot when her husband had died twenty years ago, in order to be laid at rest beside him. There, she was lowered in the rich dark earth as the sun beat down relentlessly on the mourners.

As the resounding splatter of earth hit the coffin, Cathy keeled over and sagged to the ground. Moira carefully stepped around her and knelt on the grass. The vicar looked on, and Cathy nodded as he finished the service. Blodwen's bones, made on Welsh soil were returned to the same Welsh soil. Moira looked into Cathy's eyes, but had to stifle a gasp: Cathy was pregnant! She doubted yet whether she knew it. She gently helped Cathy to her feet as her distraught husband looked on. Like most men in that situation, he felt helpless.

THE FOOL'S JOURNEY

"Come on, Lee. Let's give her some support. It's probably the shock and heat. She's fine," Moira chimed, as if she was talking to a shy child.

Hesitantly, Lee put an arm around his wife's waist and was reassured as she smiled into his eyes.

They walked back towards the pub, Leo with a protective arm around Moira. His was feeling irritated. His poor little Moira was there, giving everyone support and gently encouraging people onwards. He could tell her back was hurting; she too must be feeling pain. Even though she had known his aunt only a year, they had grown very close. He was not impressed, he later confided to Moira, that that great oaf of a husband of Cathy's had let Cathy deal with it all. He felt so fiercely protective of her. His aunt's words came back to him. He lessened his grip a little and gently held her, trying not to stifle her in any way. Now with his aunt gone, without this woman he held in his arms, he would not be able to be strong.

Thankfully, Moira sat in the shade of pub garden, under the bows of a weeping willow tree, its long boughs and silvery green leaves, dancing in the gentle breeze. She was a little apart from the main party, but the heat was intense and her fair skinned burned. However desperately she wanted to be by Leo's side, he now needed to be with his immediate family, to share their grief. Cathy came and sat beside her.

"I feel sick," she complained. "I thought I could take the heat, but today … She pulled a face that conveyed a hundred words.

"I feel I'm melting! How do women wear black in hot countries?"

"I don't know, that's probably why they're so thin, they melt!" They roared with laughter. Somehow that sound fitted. After all, Blodwen had outlived all her siblings and one child. She had made old bones and beyond. The sound of laughter carried and must have lifted other people's hearts. The mood changed and became lighter and merrier.

Cathy and Moira sat and chatted for a while. Then Cathy got up and was sick.

"Oh God. What's wrong with me?"

THE FOOL'S JOURNEY

"You been feeling like this for long?" Moira asked, in what she hoped was a casual voice.

"A bit queasy for the last few weeks…."

Cathy looked at Moira, her eyes twinkling like stars.

"Do you think I'm…no, it's been five years and three cycles of fertility. We'd given up all hope. Are you sure?"

"I would say so." Moira grinned.

She watched as Cathy ran across the grass to where Lee stood. She knew it was physically impossible, but she could have sworn Cathy flew.

It was the day after the funeral when everyone had gone home and Leo was next door when she found Archie slumped almost lifeless in the middle of the stairs. Screaming, she ran to him. He was hardly breathing and what breath did come out was labored. His silvery form looked bloated and swollen. She heard a voice – she couldn't hear where it was coming from, but she clearly heard the word, 'Poisoned.' She cradled Archie in her arms as she rang the vet and then Leo. Moira was out the door and was putting Archie into the foot well of the passenger's seat by the time Leo came out.

"I think he's been poisoned! I can guess who. I'll ring you when I have news. She briefly kissed his cheek. She fastened her seat belt and with wheels spinning, they headed down the hill.

The vet pumped little Archie's stomach and ran blood tests and hooked him up to drips. Time was all he needed now. Feeling more sedate, Moira drove back home. Her mobile rang, but she ignored it. It rang again and she still ignored it. It was only as she turned onto the driveway of her house when it was ringing for the third time that she looked at it. It was Amber!

"Are you OK?"

"It's Archie. Someone has poisoned him. We don't know if he's going to make it," Moira bellowed at the phone. If she could have breathed fire, the mobile phone would have melted. There, out of the corner of her eye, a couple of doors up, she could see someone laughing. Then she knew.

THE FOOL'S JOURNEY

Moira became vaguely aware of a voice, then remembered Amber was still on the phone.

"Moira, control the rage, stem it and use it. Now listen." Moira did so. Leo was at the front door, looking worried. She walked into the cottage while talking to Amber.

"Who?" she said.

"Oephebia. She is a good friend and an animal healer. She is the best I know. It is a rare talent. I'll ring her and then ring you back."

Moira brushed Leo's caress off and went and sat outside in the garden. Sensing when it was best to leave well alone, he went and busied himself in the kitchen.

Moira quietly sobbed into her hands. Tears trickled through her fingers and she fell onto her knees. Shaking herself, she walked to the end of the garden and there, nestled under the hedge she found a saucer with what smelt like fish in it. She was now certain. Some inner sense told her not to pick it up without a glove or something. Carefully, she used the flap of her skirt and moved it. As she looked up, the neighbour who lived next to Blodwen was making his way down the inside of the field behind, creeping along the hedge. Moira put down the saucer on the edge of vegetable borders, pretending she had not seen him. She spun round on him.

"I call on the powers of earth, air, fire and water. May he shrink and become green, may he croak than speak, may he live in a pond and sleep in the weed. He is no man now, he is a frog."

She pointed her finger and closed her eyes. She could visualize him as a frog, croaking. When she opened her eyes, he was still human. What was the point of being a witch if you could not turn a low life into a frog! He would pay for this. Oh, he would pay. Carefully picking up the saucer again, she went back inside.

Her anger was dissipated by the site of Leo curled up in laughter.

"Oh my god," he gasped. "His face, oh my god..."

Despite her torment, Moira grinned. "He left this, probably with his sticky finger marks all over it."

THE FOOL'S JOURNEY

Leo stopped laughing and gazed in wonder. They stood there transfixed, as if studying some previously undiscovered species. The ringing of Moira's mobile broke the spell.

"I've spoken to Oephebia, and she's willing to take the case on. I've given her your number. She'll ring you in a while."

"Thanks Amber. I owe you." With that, Moira pressed the red button. She then rang the vet surgery to tell them about the saucer.

Moira was tired to the bone, her body ached, her mind ached and her heart ached. Leo took the saucer down to the vet whilst she awaited the phone call from Oephebia. She rang Moira within the hour. Leo was impressed to find that the vet's onsite lab, which not only served their own surgery and those of vets in the surrounding areas, was ahead of its time. Seconds ticked by, and soon they found the cause of the poisoning. They said it would be touch and go whether Archie would recover from the effects as it might have damaged his organs. With this information, Oephebia asked for a photo and started sending healing immediately.

Moira hardly slept that night and ended up sitting by the range in the kitchen, attempting to do a crossword. When light dawned, she went outside and pottered around in the vegetable garden whilst talking to the goddess. She was dimly aware of a phone ringing, but her heart was too heavy. She couldn't face it. Not even trying to strain her ears to hear the muffled conversation, she went further down towards the end of the garden, gazing at the cows in the field beyond as they munched happily at the grass. Slowly, she turned around as she heard the tread of a step on the gravel. One look on Leo's face told her all she needed to know.

She ran up to meet him and threw her arms around him.

"He's not out of the woods totally. He survived the night and seems stronger this morning. Your friend's friend must be good. I didn't want to tell you, but they thought he wouldn't last the night."

Moira just clung to him, tears trickling down her face and onto the back of Leo's neck. He did not shrug her off. He just held her, a little scared by her weakness and vulnerability. It only served to remind him even the strong are sometimes fragile.

THE FOOL'S JOURNEY

Over the next few days, Moira stayed in regular contact with Oephebia and the vet. By the end of the third day after he had been taken to the vet, he was well enough to go home. When Moira went to pick Archie up, the vet asked her about the healing and how it worked. Moira explained that animal healing was a therapy that could be effectively conducted remotely. As with animal communication, there was no barrier of time or space. It was sometimes the only way to reach an animal on a deep level and to help the animal to recover. Energy healing worked hand in hand on the physical and/or emotional level. The healer connected with the cells of the body and worked from "within" the organs, muscles, bones etc, kicking the body's own healing process. It was like putting on a switch, then the body started its own healing process and improvement would occur in the animal. The vet was impressed. He took the details of Oephebia's website and her contact phone number. He would be recommending that others might wish to consider it in line with traditional therapies.

The dust had settled. Archie was back to normal. The day when the glaring blue and white sign appeared outside what had been Blodwen's house, Leo went into the boxroom where Moira was working.

"We've got to move from here. I can't take it. I can't take the fact someone is going to be living in the house where I spent so many childhood and teenage holidays. Some adult ones too, when times got tough."

Moira's heart sank. She felt the whole world was falling down around her ears. Unwanted tears trickled down her cheek.

In a strangled whisper, she asked, "You're leaving me?"

He strode over and held her tight, almost smothering her. "If you only knew how much you mean to me. No, no and no. I am merely going back to my old house to see to things."

Moira's ears pricked up at the use of the past tense. "Old house?"

"We knew we would not be able to stay here once Aunt Blod had passed on. I've instructed the agent to sell my house. It was only when I

THE FOOL'S JOURNEY

went to check the house next door--" Not his aunt's house, Moira noted, "I found this letter from my solicitor on the mat."

He handed the letter to Moira. As she read it, her eyes grew wide.
"How much?" Leo just nodded. Moira read again. "That soon?"
"That's why I have to go back. Will you come with me?"

Moira considered this for a while. She looked out of the window and she could hear the logs being thrown around the kitchen - a sure sign that Jimmy was upset about something. She almost wanted to be near him. When she thought Leo was going to leave her she may as well have died. Yet, what was the saying? Oh yes, 'If you love someone, set them free.' But would he return?

THE FOOL'S JOURNEY

CHAPTER ELEVEN – THE HERMIT

Introspection – Searching – Guidance – Solitude

Moira watched as Leo's sleek black BMW rumbled out of site. The feeling of loneliness hit her like a hammer. There on her drive was her car; it had seen better days. The paint was showing signs of rust around the wings and the exhaust had started to rattle. She doubted it would last the next MOT. Driving away, was not only the love of her life, but the life of her love. His existence was fast cars, expensive suits and high-flying business events. Her existence was this small cottage in the middle of a remote Pembrokeshire village, trying to make ends meet. Could she really integrate in his world? Could she accept she would gain what she sought by relationship and not by her own work? Would she ever find out? Would he come back? With these thoughts twirling around her mind, Moira went inside. Just as huge drops of rain began to fall, echoing the tears of her heart.

Moira sat on the back doorstep, sheltered from the worst of the rain by the porch. Archie looked at his owner in puzzlement. Her man had left, taking clothes and things in bags. He had kissed her and promised her he would be back in a week two at the outside - however long that was - but she was sad. He head-butted her, but she did not seem to notice. She was too caught up in her own thoughts to pay him any notice. With a cat's instinct for trouble, he went off to seek the unseen presence that liked to fuss with him.

When the rain startled to trickle under the cover of the porch and the light in the sky begin to fail, Moira went back inside and lit the fire. The last few days of summer before the September harvest seemed to be a barren time for her. She was in turmoil. Part of her so desperately wanted to drive flash cars and wear tailored suits, to have a choice of shoes and bags. Yet it felt like they were not the most important things anymore,

THE FOOL'S JOURNEY

and she did not know what was. This move to Pembrokeshire had sparked something else, perhaps a need to be in contact with the divine.

Later that evening, Leo rang and chatted on about the house and how he was organizing storage facilities for some of his stuff. He would stop with his parents for a few days to oversee the final arrangements and attend a few meetings. He promised to be back soon. Moira felt like she was being stabbed. She should be happy; he very much seemed to want her to be part of it all. She just wasn't certain whether she wanted to be part of it all: not as the arm candy. Which is how she thought Leo saw her. She was too beset by gloom to acknowledge the real reason. It was almost as if she was scared. The thought brought her up short. Scared, but scared of what? It was too much for her. With the rain still relentlessly drumming down, she went to bed.

The sun rose from somewhere behind the black clouds and the pouring rain. Moira, feeling like her life force was being washed away with the rain, despondently tidied the house. She put Leo's remaining stuff in drawers, trying to keep hold of that part of her that wanted him back. She binned his magazines and was about the throw his books out too, when the pressure that had been building up inside her broke. She sat on her twirling office chair and sobbed. Her sobs were not those of a broken heart, but those perhaps of a spoilt child who hadn't got its own way. She cried at the unfairness of the universe, shouted out at whoever was up there, but as swiftly as the torrent had started, it stopped. She questioned what it was she was crying about. She didn't have the answer. Drying her eyes and blowing her nose in the most unladylike fashion, Moira caught sight of the chest wiggling out of its blanket.

Transfixed, she watched as it tried to edge towards Moira. It shuffled then stopped. The process was a little eerie to watch. This inanimate object had a life force of its own. In her reading, she hadn't known anything like it. It was as if it was an inter-dimensional portal, if such a thing existed. She decided the best thing to do was to meet it. Sitting carefully on the floor, Moira stifled the scream that was threatening to burst out and stroked its lids gently. The box giggled. Biting so hard on her lip it almost drew blood, she decided better of it. Moira took a deep breath instead.

"You like that," she managed to say in a nearly normal voice.

This was, after all, the first time she had seen it make active progress towards her: a little unsettling to say the least. Reaching out with a shaking hand, she again stroked the lid gently. The box giggled again. Moira tried tickling it on the main body of the rough wooden box. The box wiggled. Moira had grown used to this level of activity and was feeling a lot more comfortable. Inadvertently, she found herself becoming more open. She had been too afraid to actively try this. From afar, she could hear the cry of gulls and clinking of sailboats' rigging. She could smell the scent of wood and something else, but she could not work out what. In the distance, she heard the word 'sailing.' Blinking, Moira came back to reality and realised the box had opened its lid, giving the impression it was waiting expectantly for something. Inside, Moira found another note. This one was penned in the same careful childlike hand. It said 'I like you.' A warm feeling surrounded Moira and with the information she had just read, it was time for her to embark on a personal quest.

The rain cleared later that day. Moira sat out in the late summer sunshine reading through the scraps of information that she had gleaned from the chest and the books Blodwen had given her. She planned a visit for the next day. She had never been over the mountains and into Cardigan. While she waited for the pieces of her life to fit into place, this seemed as good a time as any to start find out more about where the Albion she had read about, had sailed from.

The sun was bright, the sky was blue and fluffy white clouds hung lazily in the air. The day was warm but not hot. As Moira's car passed over the mountain, suicidal sheep decided to try and jump in front of it. By the time she had met the third lot attempting such a feat, she had nicknamed them the 'woolly jumpers.' Following the signs into Cardigan, as she approached the town, she came across a stone bridge over a river.

THE FOOL'S JOURNEY

To the left, as she looked at it, was an older bridge. In front of her was Cardigan Castle. She had remembered reading that the first eisteddfod was held by Rhys ap Gruffydd in 1176. There had been a Norman castle somewhere along this river too. Cardigan was once a rich and prosperous town thriving on the river trade, but as the decline in shipping hit and the river silted up, the town's wealth diminished. From the boarded up shops present now, it seemed not even in modern times to have regained its heyday advantage. After finding the car park and backing into a parking space, Moira walked up the hill and headed down towards the river, visiting one or two places along the way. There was a newly refurbished area, which used to be the quay.

 Moira settled herself onto one of the white stone benches that now stood alongside the quay. She looked over at the warehouses on the opposite bank. As she gazed, the air around her changed. The quay was different. It was a thronging place. Goods were being unloaded and people were shouting. Babies cried and women gossiped. The smell of fish filled the air, mixed with the smell of smoke from coal fires, burning from warehouses and chimneys. Gulls cried, scrabbling for any fallen fish. Moira even felt a cat brush against her leg. Looking down, she saw it was a mangy-looking creature with glinting green eyes. She bent down to touch it, and the sensation was gone.

 Moira pulled out the map she had picked up. She tried to get her bearings. From somewhere near here in 1819, two hundred members of this society and that of the surrounding areas embarked for what they hoped would be a better life beyond. What had caused their desire to flee Welsh soil? From her time here, she knew how fiercely patriotic the Welsh were. It was as if the land itself was in their bones. Even those who grew up elsewhere still returned here to their Welsh roots, often never staying long, just feeling the homeland beneath their feet. Feeling a sense of renewal. And then, they went back to their daily lives. How must have these passengers felt, knowing that the return trip to kin would likely never be made. Moira read again where they had embarked, and returning to the car, she tracked her way down to Poppit sands, past St Dogmaels on the Pembrokeshire side of the river.

It was the last few days of August and the beach was busy. Moira managed to find a parking space. With her emerald green bag slung over her shoulder, she went to join the holidaymakers enjoying the last few days of the summer. She passed rough sea grass clad dunes and nestled within these was the lifeboat station. She peered through the windows at the big sea faring lifeboat, ready and primed for duty. As Moira stepped off the wooden boardwalk onto the soft sand, she felt her cares dissipating. She sat to one side and took off her shoes and felt the soft cool sand under her feet. She felt at peace. Although the beach was busy, Moira found that if she walked a little way towards Cardigan she was able to find a little niche between two sand dunes to settle. Lifting out her thermos and sandwiches from her bag, as well as the books she had brought along, Moira leaned back against the grasses of the dunes and began to munch and read.

Looking up from her reading, Moira realised it was a point a little way up from here where the rig Albion must have lain, riding high on the current as it waited for its cargo from Cilgerran Slate. The passengers and their families and friends would have looked on at the splendour of her form, bobbing in the Teifi River. Here, two renowned reverends had preached and blessed a voyage. The passengers and families, along with many residents from St Dogmaels and Cardigan, traipsed down through St Dogmaels to where she now sat. It was from here they had embarked upon their journey.

Moira watched as a family walked towards the car park, the children carrying brightly coloured rubber rings and their dad laden like a pack mule with bucket and spades and assorted beach items. Mum was carrying a cool box and couple of half empty carrier bags. The children ran ahead shrieking with laughter as they chased each other. Smiling, Moira looked on, but they weren't there anymore. There were Welsh voices raised in song and much joviality by the sound of it. Women wore tall beaver hats like small chimneys and long, red, checked material bed gowns known as betgwn. Wrapped around their shoulders, were shawls; square shawls doubled over for warmth to make a triangle, spun and knitted from natural local fibres. They wore aprons of creams or whites all made from local material. Some women wore nursing shawls with babies cocooned inside. Children had red shiny faces, as if they had been scrubbed with brushes until all ingrained dirt had released its hold. Men strode along wearing breaches and brightly coloured waistcoats, overworn with either a soft blue or grey overcoat. Neckerchiefs were tucked into shirts, giving the appearance of a church outing to the seaside. It was the children that struck Moira. Some clung to their mothers' skirts, wide-eyed, looking at this great ship sailing down the river to meet them. Others ran on and shouted. One girl looked over to where Moira was sitting in the present; she had huge grey eyes and jetblack hair. Her cheeks were tear-stained and she clung tightly to a roughly carved wooden doll in her hand. A man behind her gently nudged her on, saying some words in Welsh to her. The tone was one of encouragement, yet by the haunted look in his eyes, the encouragement may as well have been for his own benefit.

    Moira watched the scene as people made their way up the gangplank from the water's edge towards the waiting ship. They carried small packs with them, all their worldly goods in small bundles. Some children started sobbing as they waved towards those left behind, some women too. In all, the air held one of promise and hope. A brightly coloured beach ball came flying over towards Moira, breaking the image in an instant.

    Laughing, Moira threw the ball back to the children running up the beach towards it. The children apologised and they beat a hasty retreat leaving Moira to her solitude. Moira gazed on, hoping to recapture that moment. The eyes of the child and the haunted look of the father stirred Moira. There was something strong and determined about his step, but his face told another story. What had happened to this family? Why did leaving cause them so much pain? Was the life they were leaving behind too hard to endure?

THE FOOL'S JOURNEY

As Moira sat watching the scene on the beach, someone was running, trying to launch a red and blue kite. A dog barked happily as it chased a stick that was being tossed for it. Deep in thought, she looked back over the last several months of her life. Soon, it would be a year since she had taken the step to move down and take the job at the pub. So much had happened in such a short space of time. She let the past months play in her mind like a movie: the renovating of the cottage, the discovery of Jimmy and the chest and meeting Leo. Today had been about a personal quest she realised as she examined her thoughts. She was just leaving the hermit phase of her life. It had been only a few days, but it had been necessary to take stock and restore balance.

Moira shook herself and before she left. She determined to find out what had caused the suffering. She picked up another book and found the explanation she sought. The Napoleonic wars had left Britain destitute and financial instability lead to recoinage to try and stabilise Britain's fortunes. The farmland in Wales had been over farmed during the wars and proper crop rotation to ensure healthy lands had not been followed. In 1816, the crops failed and many faced starvation. Landlords persecuted them for their religion and many people died of illness and hunger. Whooping cough was rife amongst people and for those who had food, it was not enough to stave off the illness. Many children died, some of them infants. Death was heartless and indiscriminate, although it could be argued he was merciful. They did not have to endure the ravaging pains of hunger, with nothing more than a thin gruel to satisfy. They were not riddled by illness or tyrannised by landowners. Perhaps they were the lucky ones. Stretching her back, Moira looked up from her book.

Clouds were bubbling up on the horizon and the air began to buzz, just like before a thunderstorm. Moira wanted to be back over the mountains and home before it hit. She left the beach with a strange feeling in her heart, one she couldn't yet put words to. When she reached the car park, her mobile beeped indicating she had received a message. Before she could look at it, the phone rang.

THE FOOL'S JOURNEY

"Thank God you're OK!" came the exalted voice of Leo. "I've been worried sick. I could not get you for over an hour and..." His voice trailed off.

Moira smiled warmly. Sunlight lifted the clouds that had been hanging over her for the last few days. She knew what she wanted; she wanted him wherever their lives were destined to be. If those families could leave for another continent, leaving their families behind, then she, who had only dwelled on the soil for a year, could move on too.

"I'm fine! I was just out of signal. I've been trying to track down a few things. I'll ring you when I get in."

"Don't bother." Moira could feel Leo grinning down the phone. Before he said it she knew.

"OK, I'll tell you all when you come back then."

Moira walked back to her car and drove back home. There may have been storm clouds on the horizon, but her heart felt sunny and she was happy. Where would life take her from here?

CHAPTER TWELVE – THE WHEEL OF FORTUNE

Destiny – Turning point – Movement – Personal Vision

Summer went out with a bang. The last day of the meteorological summer ended with thunderstorms and hailstones. Leo eventually returned. Later than he had expected, due to accidents and flash floods. Wearily, he got out of his car and glared at the sky which was threatening another deluge. He opened the door to the cottage and was greeted by the smell of baking.

Baking? Moira cooked but never baked. The luring smell of chocolate cake, wrapped its invisible tendrils around Leo's senses and pulled him into the kitchen on unbidden feet. There was his goddess, covered in flour, with cake mix on her nose, washing dishes in the sink. His heart melted. He had wondered how he would feel being away then coming back, now his aunt had passed on. Here were all the reasons in front of him. Wrapping his arms around her waist, he kissed the back of her neck making her jump. Moira had been so engrossed in what she was doing, she jumped. She twisted around in his arms and kissed him warmly. Nothing else mattered.

Over the next few weeks, Moira and Leo tried to narrow down where they were going to live. Leo needed to be central with easy access to the road or the public transport network. Moira did not want to live anywhere too built up. Both of them felt like ships without an anchor. The cottage was already beginning to feel transient. A port in the storm. Moira had been so transfixed with sorting out her future, she had forgotten to tell Leo and Amber about her experience on the beach. The chest had been quiet. She worked in the room for a few hours every day, doing the occasional bit of typing or a VAT return for someone. The money was greater than she received working in the pub, but it was not exactly what she wanted.

   Moira gazed out of the lounge window watching the dark clouds scuttle across the sky. Both Helix and Archie had curled up there too. An unfamiliar van pulled up outside what had been Blodwen's house. A man stepped out, lifted off the 'for sale' part of the sign, got back in his van and drove off. Moira's stomach lurched. She felt like something had cut them loose, even the cottage felt more like a rickety shack than the stone-built house it was. She went upstairs with a pounding heart and tears pricked at her eyes. She knew it was going to happen, but so quickly? They had planned to move out before the house next door sold and then lease this cottage as a holiday let. That had been very important to Leo. He wanted to make sure that Moira felt she still had a handle, a degree of control on her life and destiny. Standing outside the boxroom where Leo was currently working, she took a few deep breaths and walked in.

   Leo was staring out of the window watching the same clouds Moira had. There was something heavy weighing on his heart. Maybe it was the honk of the geese as they flew past to warmer climes. He had an almost irrepressible urge to sweep Moira up, pack their suitcases and kiss goodbye to this backwater. He felt like he was slowly suffocating here. Where was life? He felt he existed here, existed but didn't thrive. He wanted to feel blood pumping through his veins, the sensation of the hunt being on. He barely noticed the door being opened; Moira would often pop in and out. There was something, perhaps an offshoot of the primeval sense of wanting the chase, which made him feel something was different. Was this how Moira felt when she said she just knew about something? He turned round slowly and took one look at Moira's face and guessed his instinct had been right.

   Moira did not know why she was in such a rush to tell him. She was not even certain why this felt like a door shutting. Right now, she wanted to run, she wanted to get away. She wanted, had she been aware, the same thing Leo did. The wheel was turning. Common sense told them they couldn't just leave and run away in the night like eloping lovers.

THE FOOL'S JOURNEY

Things needed to be put into place. They needed to be established. But now felt the time to action it. Discussion time had passed; decisions needed to be made. She took one look at his face and knew he was expecting something, even if he didn't know what.

"The house has gone under offer."

Well that could have been said better, she mused, but it seemed to do the job.

"Why was I not told?" Leo agonized.

He reached into his pocket and pulled out his mobile phone. It showed a black screen; he pressed a button and still no life. Catching sight of his actions and his horrified gaze, Moira threw back her head and laughed.

"Would help if you had charged it yesterday, when you said it needed it."

Leo turned and grinned sheepishly and sauntered out of the room, giving her a kiss on the way past. Downstairs, he put it on charge. Moira too went off to make a phone call or two, leaving Leo pouncing around the dining room, on the end of the cord of the phone charger. She went out for a walk.

The wind whipped Moira's hair around her face. She could feel the first spits of rain being blown against her skin. There was a smell of wood smoke being carried in the air. As she headed down the hill towards the sea, she could hear the waves crashing against the rocks and could taste the salt in the air. There were a handful of late season holidaymakers walking their dogs along the beach, huddled into their jackets against the wind. At that moment, Moira felt more alive than she had in months. The wind invigorated her; it fanned the fire within and made her feel alive. She knew she must leave this place; perhaps she had always known this was only temporary. What she didn't know was where she wanted to settle. Several months ago the idea of moving seemed preposterous. Her plans had been to settle here within this Welsh village. She had known there was something about her that was unsettled, but she had been determined to see it through. Now the universe had turned her on her head and was showing her another path and an open door. All she had to do was to step through.

The rain started to fall in big heavy blobs as Moira walked back up towards her cottage. By the time she reached the door, the blobs had become a deluge. Even her highly waterproof jacket was beginning to struggle; the rest of her clothes clung to her, and the material of her jeans was heavy. She opened the cottage door and stripped off in the hall. Leo came out of the dining room with a harassed look on his face, which was soon replaced by a wide wolfish grin. He went over to caress her and got dripped on by her hair.

"Urgh! You're soaked."

"Funny, that's what rain does," said Moira's fleeting form as she hurried upstairs for a shower to get warm.

Whilst she dried her hair by the fire a little later, with a steaming mug of coffee at her elbow, Leo talked to her about developments. A family from London had made an offer of the full asking price. They wanted the house as a second home. They planned to live in it for six months and in London for six months. It would have been folly to refuse the offer. They would not be moving in until after Christmas but wanted things completed swiftly. Moira gazed into the fire. It brought them some breathing time to make decisions of their own. Part of her felt that the house was being cheated in some way. There were enough locals wanting a property, and then the thought hit her.

"Leo, instead of renting this out as a holiday let, why don't we rent it out to local people on a long-term let?"

He looked at her in wonder.

"It might make things more complicated long-term. Are you sure about this?"

"Absolutely. A good solicitor will sort out the pitfalls, if we write into it a three-month notice period. That should do well enough."

Grinning at her he said, "Not just a pretty face!" He leered at her and made to make a move when the landline phone rang. "Thwarted again," he said roguishly.

THE FOOL'S JOURNEY

Moira answered the phone and spoke in depth to Amber about their plans. Leo left the room with a head full of ideas of his own.

Several days later, with the threat of storm force winds following them, Moira and Leo set off in the direction of Cathy's, leaving Helix and Archie in the care of Liz, who promised she would pop in and feed them twice a day. Moira felt as giddy as a schoolgirl. This was going to be their first night away together. As she watched the miles of the M4 motorway zip past from the leather-lined interior of Leo's BMW, Moira realised this was her first trip since she had moved to Wales a year ago. She reflected on what had happened in that year. Now they were going to be using Cathy's home on the edge of the New Forest as base to explore potential areas to live. On the way, they passed through Bath, where Leo's old house was. It was a beautiful stone built building, not far from the canal that ran through there. Its mid-terrace position made it feel closed in. There was something brooding about the building that made Moira uneasy. Leo turned to look at her.

"Do you know, I am actually relieved to see the back of that place? I was pleased to have purchased it, it was a good investment opportunity, but I should have realised it was not for me to live in."

She smiled at him, not knowing what to say and squeezed his hand. He turned the car and headed towards where Cathy lived.

Moira had not been down to the New Forest before. It was quite a shock to have to negotiate forest ponies straying across the roads, sometimes just standing there like they owned the street. Leo effortlessly negotiated around them like a racing driver would slalom on a Grand Prix circuit. They pulled up outside the gates to Cathy's house as dusk began to settle. The wind, which had been strong before they left, had whipped up to a crazy tempo. It was as if it was trying to dance a cross between a Scottish jig and the Charleston. Things were being picked up and tossed about. The gates swung out electronically and were nearly caught up in a spiraling gust. They closed behind them. There stood the tall red-bricked house, clad with ivy that swayed in the wind, giving the house the appearance of an old man wagging his beard. To the left was a series of low buildings which Leo informed Moira were the catteries. Lottie flew out the oxford blue front door wearing pink flower wellington boots. The wind bowled her over and Leo was out of the car in an instant to pick her up. Holding Lottie by the hand, he helped Moira out and they all went inside.

The hall was tiled in black and white with pillar-box red walls. Moira noticed some of the pictures that had adorned the hall of Blodwen's house were now hanging in Cathy's hall. There was a good-sized wooden staircase in the middle of the hall and closed white doors to the left and right. From one of these came Lee, grinning.

"Cathy is having a lie-down. It's been a busy day. I've got the coffee on."

He led the way into the kitchen at the back of the house. There was a range cooker nestled in an alcove on one wall. There was a cat basket next to this, in which slept a mother and several kittens. There was a more modern element to the kitchen with flat, smooth, shiny surfaces and an oven, which looked almost space aged to Moira. As Lee poured coffee into hand thrown pottery mugs, Cathy entered the room, looking a little dark under the eyes, but the happiest Moira had ever seen her.

She walked over and hugged Leo and Moira. Turning to her husband, she asked, "Have you told them?"

Lee shook his head and grinned. "I was waiting for you."

Turning back to Moira and Leo, who were standing there with puzzled looks on their faces, she said, "We're having twins!"

Another round of hugging and whoops of joy ensued. Cathy led them into the lounge and they sat around a huge log fire.

The evening wore on and once they had eaten and Lottie had been safely tucked up in bed, they started to talk about plans, past and future. As the fire crackled in the hearth and the wind wailed outside, Cathy and Lee explained how they had built the house and business, his one as well, from scratch. When they bought their house fifteen years ago, it was nothing more than walls and a roof. The windows were cracked and there was even plant life growing in what was the spare bedroom. They

THE FOOL'S JOURNEY

had to have plumbing installed and have the house rewired. That had taken all their available funds. They were living in two rooms and seriously doubted their ability to make Lee's business work and pay for the house. That was until Blodwen had stepped in. It was a year after her husband, Cathy's grandfather, had died. She had sold his flat in London and split the proceeds between Leo's grandfather and Cathy's mother. It happened that Blodwen was down in the area visiting Hillier's nursery and gardens in Romsey. Getting bored with the coach tour, she had booked herself into a hotel nearby and paid Lee and Cathy a surprise visit. It took her back, the fact they were living in two rooms. The rest of the house had boarded windows, as they could not afford to replace them yet. Blodwen had taken pity on them. She rang Leo's uncle and arranged for him to come and get them back on their feet. She paid for the windows and if the truth were known, Blodwen had a whale of a time organising it all.

   The few days' stay ended up a few weeks' stay. It was only when Cathy was driving Blodwen back that they stopped in the village where Moira now lived, to buy the local paper. Flicking through the paper, Blodwen had pointed out an advert by a cat breeder selling her business due to ill health. Before Cathy knew what was happening, Blodwen had phoned the woman and driven Cathy to see her. Blodwen sealed the deal and bought Cathy the business, which comprised three pairs of breeding cats; several outside runs and all the advice the woman could give. Cathy had driven back home the next day ready to set up and receive the new arrivals. Lee thought she was out of her mind. Cathy was sure she was out of her mind, but in the toiling heat of summer, they constructed the runs in the garden and later collected the cats. When the first litter born raised more than Lee had managed to earn that month, the insanity of the situation metamorphosed into logic. Although a cat litter did not sell every month, it made a difference. A year later, they were converting outbuildings to run as a cattery alongside the cat breeding business. Lee's business bucked the recession of the eighties and started to grow. As it grew and Cathy's success grew, they became more secure. He gleefully informed them they had been mortgage free for a year. If it had not been for the surprise arrival of Blodwen, they would never have been where they were now. As Moira sipped brandy, nestled in Leo's shoulder listening to the tales, she felt the beginning of what she wanted from her life with new clarity. It needed nurturing, but like the life growing in Cathy, it was there with a beating heart.

Morning dawned too early with a sound of a tree crashing down somewhere nearby. The sun had not fully risen in the sky and the world was shrouded still in shadow. The power had gone and in the semi darkness, Moira, Leo, Lee and Cathy came out their rooms at the same time, each in various states of undress. Cathy had a fleecy dressing gown wrapped around her against the early morning chill, Lee and Leo stood in nothing but shorts shivering and Moira wore fleecy pyjamas. Cathy took charge of the situation.

"Lee, get dressed and check the cat pens. Leo, Moira, get dressed too and please. Could you check the driveway and road. I'll check the back of the house and get the coffee on. Diving back into their rooms, they got dressed and went about their allotted tasks.

It was Moira and Leo who found the fallen tree. It was across the road just down from the gate. Although the branches rested on the gate and the fence, mercifully nothing was broken.

"That's scuppered today's plans," mused Leo over coffee sometime later. "We'll have to see what the full light of day brings."

With a degree of trepidation, they awaited full light.

What full light brought was a scene of devastation. There was more than one tree down on the road. The forestry commissioner, a good friend of Lee's, had knocked on the door and enlisted his and Leo's help, grateful that another strong pair of arms was available. With a hastily thrown together lunch, they went off to help. There were tiles missing from the roof of the cattery, but nothing pressing. There were one or two fence panels down in the garden. Moira and Cathy put them back up; otherwise the forest ponies would come in and trample the garden, potentially doing more damage than the wind. After lunch, when the

THE FOOL'S JOURNEY

boys had not returned, Moira, Cathy and Lottie decided to go for a walk in the forest to see for themselves what had happened.

The girls had a fantastic time, chasing through piles of autumn leaves, picking them up and throwing them all over each other. They found conkers. To Lottie's annoyance, Cathy had told her that the conkers had to stay in the forest to make new trees. She sulked for a good part of the way back home, kicking sullenly at piles of leaves until she found one hiding a hedgehog. They carefully piled the orange, red, yellow and russet leaves back over the slumbering creature, which helped to improve her mood. All of them chattered about hedgehogs having to go to sleep all winter. As they neared home, they saw Leo and Lee coming out to meet them. Lottie ran on ahead. It became clear to Moira in that instant she knew where she wanted to live and what she wanted from her life. Would Leo agree?

CHAPTER THIRTEEN – JUSTICE

Justice – Responsibility – Decision – Cause and Effect

Sitting in the dwindling light of the afternoon around the log fire in the lounge, sipping mugs of hot chocolate, Lee and Leo told Moira and Cathy about their day. They had had to round up pigs and mend fences to keep livestock out. They moved logs and shifted small fallen trees. There was a ring at the doorbell and the same Ranger as earlier was standing there with a couple of bags in his hand.

"Thought you guys deserved some venison. The wife's baked little Lottie some gingerbread biscuits - her favourites, I understand," he said, winking at Lottie who giggled.

"Thanks, Chris," Cathy said. "Tell Margaret she'll have to bake even more soon. There are going to be two more mouths joining us in several months."

"Oh Cathy! Lee! Oh, congratulations to you both. We know how hard you wanted this. Two though! She'll enjoy baking. Wish our Denise would get her maternal instinct, but alas, she wants to be a lawyer."

"She's young, Chris, give her time," said Cathy, softly, knowing how they hankered after more children, Denise being their only child. Grandchildren seemed a fair substitute.

"Better be off. My dinner will be on the table. Have a safe evening, folk, and thanks."

They stored the venison in the freezer now that power had been restored, and Lottie munched on her biscuits. Leo then announced, "I now know why you like it here so much. It's always felt remote to me, but after spending months in Wales, it's positively cosmopolitan!"

"Would you think about living here, then?" Lee asked.

THE FOOL'S JOURNEY

Leo exchanged a look with Moira. Moira's heart leapt. As easily as that, the decision was made. Her world had been turned on its head and back round again, Moira mused, as the wine was being poured to celebrate. The Wheel of Fortune had been compressed into a few weeks. She did begin to wonder what was coming next!

Over the next couple of days Lottie returned to school, having been on half term. Lee went away for a few days on business and Leo and Moira spent a good part of their days driving around different areas and visiting different estate agents. Nothing yet was available in an area they wanted, but decisions had been made. Having made those decisions, things felt lighter for them. Cathy and Moira had become firm friends over the last few months. Lottie, in the grown up way of children, announced that Uncle Leo and Aunty Moira had better get married; otherwise they would be living in sin. No one had the heart to say that they already were what old fashionably might be considered 'living in sin'. It had delighted them all so much that she called Moira 'aunty'. The thought of being a big sister and starting school had matured the already mature Lottie into a grownup young lady with the naivety of childhood, which made her a delightful person.

After dropping Lottie off to school one day, Leo and Moira headed back to Moira's cottage. They had made an appointment with Leo's solicitor, who was in his Bath offices, to write up the contract for the rental of Moira's cottage. They wanted everything in place, so that when they found their house they could buy it, and as soon as things were completed, they could move in. They did not want the extra stress of trying to sort other contracts out.

Moira found her self-stepping into a whole new world. This was not the stuffy solicitor's office she had seen before, smelling of old musty paper and big, heavy, polished wooden desks in small rooms at the top of rickety stairs. This one had big glass windows overlooking the canal. The main office was open plan, with small neat meeting rooms and stylish leather chairs and glass coffee tables. This office gave the impression the staffs were there to help, rather than the client imposing on their time. A few people greeted Leo with familiar calls and waves.

"You're well known," Moira teased.

"One of their best customers, aren't I, Tristan?" he said, slapping a fair-haired man in his early thirties on the back.

"Leo, the lion, as I live a breath. So this is the lovely temptress that's lured you to the depths of the never beyond."

"Pembrokeshire has a lot going for it, not just the lovely temptress as you put it."

"If beaches in the rain are your thing. Give me sun, sand and exotic beauties bringing me large glasses of something cool and alcoholic."

"Still a confirmed bachelor then?"

"Yep! I thought you and I would be seeing out our later years playing golf and sipping malt whisky in a gentleman's club."

"Sorry, but Moira's got more luring attributes than you."

"I can see," Tristan said, leering at Moira.

Moira shook her head at the pair of them. Sometimes men never grew up. From what Leo had said, they had known each other since they were young boys.

Once the friendly sparing and greetings were over, Tristan stood up and became Mr. Lawyer, all at once. Beneath the bonhomie, Moira saw a shrewd and calculating brain. When the secretary had brought freshly brewed coffee into one of the meeting rooms he proved it.

"OK Moira. I hear you want a contract that means only locals can rent the cottage, but have to maintain it in the standard it is in now; plus have a three-month notice period either way. Three months' arrangement is fine, the local only and no social is shrewd."

"People move in from away, like I did and it forces the locals out. I guess I am just doing a small bit to ensure I restore the balance again."

Tristan scribbled down notes and listened to what Moira's questioned, never once turning to Leo for confirmation. Moira warmed to him. She had the feeling behind it all, he was lonely and work, for him, as for many others, filled the gaps. When the meeting ended, Tristan suggested lunch in the nearby pub. Everyone agreed with enthusiasm.

It was a little bit later than they would have liked to have left, but Tristan obviously relished the company and Moira was feeling content and in no hurry. As they pulled out of Bath and were heading towards the M4 motorway back to Wales, Leo remarked, "Traffic's a bit heavy."

A little while later, with a little over two miles to go until they joined the motorway, they ground to a halt. After they had been sat there for about quarter of an hour, Leo loaded the traffic app on his iPhone and groaned. "Jackknifed lorry, blocking both carriageways. Perhaps we better turn around and overnight in Bath?"

Swinging the car round, they headed back towards Bath. They kept the radio on for regular traffic updates. As they approached the last roundabout, as fate would have it the only way out, a car accident was reported blocking the main Bath roundabout closing off the road into the town centre.

"Time to let the satnav earn its keep then. Find us a detour out of here," Leo grumbled.

Moira was not feeling best pleased herself. She had a growing sense of unease.

They sat in relative silence whilst Leo concentrated on negotiating the winding unfamiliar roads. Eventually they were over the Severn Bridge and back on Welsh territory. They stopped at the motorway services for a break. As night was drawing in, Leo suggested, "Let's overnight somewhere in Cardiff as it is getting late?"

"No, I've got a funny feeling. I don't know why, but we really need to go home."

One quick glance at Moira told him not to argue. With greater urgency, they pushed on towards home.

Leo knew that Moira's feeling was justified, the moment before they pulled onto the drive. Liz's car was there; she should have been in the pub by now. A light was on in the house.

"Something's wrong!" Moira exclaimed. "Leave the car here."

THE FOOL'S JOURNEY

Leo knew it was wiser to obey. Down the road by the light of the street lamps, they could make out one of Liz's regular customers approaching them.

"Liz is not back? Owen is worried," Sean uttered.

They all approached the cottage; they all seemed to feel a sense of unease.

"Leo, go around the back," Moira commanded.

Before he could do so, a wail came from the house. Then the sound of a crash, the three of them stood there momentarily transfixed. They continued to stare, shrouded by the darkness, as wails and crashes came from the cottage. Leo broke the spell.

"Sean, ring the police. Moira, let's go and see."

Furtively, they crept on, using the deep shadows to hide their progress. Light spilled from the front room of the cottage, inside they could see the coffee table levitating and gently spinning around.

"Jimmy," Moira whispered. "But he knows Liz."

They crept down the side of the cottage and around to the back. Light too spilled from there. The door was wide open. With racing hearts and dry mouths, they carefully popped their heads into the kitchen. No one was there. With cautious footsteps, they entered. They jumped out of their skin when Helix brushed himself against their legs. He then walked towards the door that led into the hall and repeated the process, as if urging them forward. Moira grabbed the heavy skillet that hung on the wall near the range. She never used it much, but Blodwen had bought it for her for Christmas. With vague encouragement, she had learnt how to make Welsh cakes. Now the solid weight of the cast iron felt like a girl's best friend.

They opened the kitchen door with trepidation. Moira felt like time had stood still. They were greeted by silence. Not a whisper, not a breath. The silence was more eerie than the background noise of crashes and things being moved. Leo stood immobile. Moira felt herself being drawn as if being pulled by unseen hands towards the handle of the lounge door. Leo tried to speak the words 'wait for the police' but the

THE FOOL'S JOURNEY

words stuck in his throat. He was unable to utter anything more than a whimper. Moira reached for the door handle. The air around her swirled and the handle felt like ice. Ice so cold it burnt. She took a few steps back. Leo made a grab for her and shook his head. He heard the sound of a wailing siren in the distance.

"A little noise please," he whispered to the world at large.

Something answered his request as a wail whipped up. The wail threatened to freeze blood and ran fingers down the blackboard of the soul.

"Jimmy's hurting? How can Jimmy hurt?" Moira whispered, her warm breath against Leo's ear was the only warmth in the hall. Something unnatural was happening. It was drawing all available energy from the area. From inside the door, Moira heard someone vomit.

Leo and Moira sat on the bottom step, clinging to each other like children. Tears were flowing down Leo's face. The utter raw energy that had been flowing around the place had tweaked something within him. He felt lost, scared, lonely and abandoned. He clung to Moira even tighter. She had gone white, almost porcelain in colour. She was muttering something under her breath; the words couldn't be heard above the din. Then there was the sound of footsteps - human footsteps, heavy and fast. Some came from round the back and some from the front. Moira leapt up and opened the door at the front. Without saying a word, she let the waiting policemen in. She pointed to the lounge door, when they were greeted by the sound of someone retching again. One policeman opened the door, whilst the other waited on the other side to go into the room. A moment later, he entered. He came out backwards almost immediately. His hair was standing on end and he looked like he had seen a ghost. He ran out the front door and vomited in the border. His colleagues who had come around the back looked on at this spectacle. No one seemed able to move. Moira edged forward. She fought the wave of nausea that swept over her. There was Jimmy; well, she presumed it was Jimmy. A semi-translucent, rotting corpse. Maggots were crawling from his eyes. His flesh hung off his bones and his white skeleton could be seen. Spiraling around was her coffee table; her best vase was already shattered on the floor. The television looked like it had been shot. The curtains were torn and the sofa and chairs were tumbled and upended.

"Rest, Jimmy." Her words hung frozen for a moment, crystalized in the freezing air. Yet, like fire they burned. Jimmy's apparition faded. Her coffee table came down with a crash, breaking as it fell. A policeman put his hand on her and drew her back. She had seen enough.

There, bound but conscious, was Liz. Next to her like a guard dog was Archie. The image that had burned into the fabric of Moira's existence was a man. A big burly man. He had a shaven head, with a death's skull tattoo on one arm and an inverted pentagram on the other. A scar was evident on one of the hairy forearms. He had a sawn off shotgun lying at his feet in a puddle of his own vomit. He had scratches down his face, which had now clotted. He was a jabbering wreck. He rambled nonsense, rocking himself backwards and forwards. When two solidly built policemen grabbed him, he didn't move.

The next few hours were long and hard. There had been police interviews and forensic teams were crawling over the cottage. Leo had gone, at Moira's insistence, to the hospital with Liz. Someone should have been there for her to bring her home if necessary. A young female police officer had taken quite a shine to the cats and was keeping Moira good company, so Leo went, albeit reluctantly. In the lull between making tea and waiting for news, Moira went upstairs to the boxroom. The chest was there, wrapped in its blanket and safe. Reaching for the deck of cards she kept on the table, she shuffled them, more to keep her hands busy whilst she tried to piece together what was going on, rather than for a particular reading. A card slipped and fell to the floor. Justice. Moira reflected ruefully it had certainly been a day for things related to justice and the day was not over yet.

It was nearly eleven o' clock when Leo rang from the hospital to say that he was bringing Liz back home. She was badly shaken and sore, but had discharged herself when they threatened to admit her for the

THE FOOL'S JOURNEY

evening. He also said that she had requested that they stay the night at the pub with her, including the cats. Secretly, Moira was pleased. She still didn't know the full story and felt vulnerable. She left the policemen inspecting and making notes; they promised they would lock up and take the keys to the pub.

Owen and the pub's chef, Jennie, stayed on. Neither of them felt quite happy to go home until they were sure their boss and friend was OK. A pale, tired and hungry Liz arrived shortly after Moira had got there. Jennie had taken one look at Liz, whizzed back to her kitchen and knocked up some steaks, with chips, mushrooms and onions, for Leo, Moira and Liz. She refused to hear any arguments. Owen begrudgingly went home, and Jennie went to hers shortly after. It was only when the pub was empty and the doors firmly locked and barred, that Liz began to explain things to them. They sat around the inglenook fireplace, Leo stoked the fire and it burned brightly in the hearth, warming the stone around it. Moira went behind the bar and poured drinks.

"The man arrested is my ex-husband. We were married very young and I was a rebellious teenager. At first it was great fun; we'd go out on his motorbike and go to wild parties. Then one day in a drunken rage, he knocked me down the stairs. I broke three ribs and my arm. Of course, he was full of remorse and promised it wouldn't happen again." Liz took a sip at her pint. "Yes, you've guessed, it did. It was then he started getting into bad company. Before he'd just been a bit wild. He came back one day; I'd just got in from night school, which I had to do in secret as he did not like me going out without him. He came home earlier than usual. He was covered in blood. He'd told me what he'd done. He had stabbed one of his work colleagues as he'd caught him selling company stock out the back door."

For a while she stared into the fire.

"I was scared; I was scared he'd do the same to me. I promised him I would not say a word to anyone. He went up the stairs and showered. Whilst he showered, I stowed the blood soaked sock in a bag and hid it under the sink. I don't know why I did, but I did. After he'd showered, he went out and burned his clothes. He then went on the run, promising he'd come back for me soon enough." Again a period of reflection.

"The next morning, it was all over the news. A mystery man had stabbed a policeman and shot two other passers-by, when he'd got disturbed trying to rob a bank. My world fell apart," Liz said, matter-of-factly. "I decided to shop him. Yes, the bloodied sock under the sink proved it. I was given protective custody. Then, I set up with a new identity. I've lived here in peace ever since. I don't know how he found me, but I'd heard he was out of prison; he threatened to kill me. Tonight, I believe that was his aim. Your Jimmy and little Archie saved the day."

Eventually, speaking as if from a long way off, Moira asked," How? Why my cottage?"

"How? Well Archie leapt at him, claws scrabbling down his face as he tried to shoot me. I owe you a new TV," Liz said with a smile. "The shot missed and hit the TV. He then decided to tie me up and I guess take me elsewhere. But little Archie fought on and Jimmy worked himself up into a frenzy. The rest you pretty much know. As for why your cottage, I guess he'd been watching me and saw it as a perfect opportunity. I would go in the back door and leave it open whilst I sorted the cats' tray and made sure they'd not demolished anything. I don't know for sure, but maybe he'll tell. Whatever happens this time, I hope they throw away the key."

They spent a little while talking about things; the heavy burden of post-stress weariness fell on them. They slept long and late. Where would things go from here? Only time would tell.

CHAPTER FOURTEEN – THE HANGED MAN

Letting go – Reversal – Suspension – Sacrifice

    Liz had gone to the police station after they had finished breakfast and Leo and Moira went back to the cottage. Everything was a mess. Whilst the vomit had been cleared up, the cottage still held the smell, mixed with sweat. Despite the cold and threatening rain, Moira made sure every window in the cottage was opened. Leo was putting the larger bits of TV and coffee table outside the front door, ready to take to the dump. Moira was starting to wash all the floors with disinfectant, when her phone rang.
    "Chick–a–dee, are you OK?" came the voice of Amber booming concern. "Maggie woke me from my sleep last night to tell me that you needed help."
    Despite her weariness and the dreadful mess that the cottage was in, she smiled with pure delight. Maggie was one of Amber's spirit guides. Moira still had to work out the principle of this, but she never doubted spirit guides existed. She explained to Amber about the night's before events. About what Jimmy had done and Archie.
    "I think Jimmy needs to move over. You said you could feel his pain. In which respect, pain?"
    "He was hurting. I can't describe it more than that. Also a sense of heaviness, and today I can't feel him apart from a weak pulse. Does that make sense?"
    "Perfectly. I think what you describe is a pain that comes from a spirit when it wants rest. He's obviously feeling his task here is nearly completed. Hang fire for a bit. I'll bring Michael across. It'll do him good to do something more down to earth."

THE FOOL'S JOURNEY

Moira giggled. She knew Amber only tolerated Michael's TV appearances because she got to travel with him. That satisfied her wanderlust.

"I'll look at his schedule and ring you soon. Take care, chic." Amber hung up, and Moira went about tidying up.

Once things were organised and cleaned up, windows shut up against the fine drizzle that permeated everything, Moira and Leo sat in front of the wood burning stove on the floor. Even the furniture had been damaged by random shot gun activity and Jimmy's fit.

"What do we do now?" Leo asked, despondently.

"Wait I guess. There are no properties available yet where we want. I guess I'll put a claim in on the insurance for this lot." Moira gestured to the now empty room. I don't honestly know whether I want to live here anymore or even whether I want to own it. I just don't know."

Moira's voice echoed the frustration, the emotion and the dogged stubbornness not to crawl under a rock somewhere and hide. The part of her, which had clung desperately to the notion of being independent, was losing its tenuous hold on her. Perhaps this was the sign she should let go of the cottage once and for all. Cut ties and move on.

"I'm going to have a look at the cards on this."

Leo nodded. Whilst he knew she had the ability and often got good guidance, he still questioned her sanity about using pieces of cards for advice.

Moira went upstairs and into the boxroom. She glanced at the chest; it was all quiet. She was glad she had had the good sense to put her special box containing her tools of the craft, as Leo referred to them, up out the way. It would have hurt her more to lose this than the rest of her goods, even though the loss of her favourite vase stung. She retrieved the velvet emerald green reading cloth, but instead of reaching for her usual deck, she brought out the box set Cathy had given her. It was called Druidcraft. The images were Celtic in influence and the pictures told more of a story than the Rider Waite deck she owned. Shuffling the cards, she thought

THE FOOL'S JOURNEY

about her life, where it was and where she needed to go from here. Without asking a specific question, she laid three cards face down.

Turning over the first card, she saw the Hanged Man. A man hung upside down by one leg, the other was crossed behind. He had a look of serenity; the tree appeared to be supporting him. From his mouth grew oak leaves, signifying the connection to the Green Man, suggesting that his words could not describe the experience. Behind him a Sickle lay next to ripe corn, signifying it was soon time to sacrifice rural traditions to the Corn King. Moira smiled at the card. Letting go. Was that not what she had been thinking about. Perhaps here letting go was even more in depth, surrendering to the cycle of life in order to gain the information sought. It was a time of harvest in the card, reaping what had been sown and preparing for the winter ahead.

She turned over the next card. The Ace of Swords. From a calm lake up in the mountains, a hand emerged holding a sword. The leafless trees and light in the sky suggested it was still cold and winter had not yet ended. Yet on the shore, the first snowdrops grew, suggesting spring was near. Moira knew from her course that swords were representative of air and air was associated with thoughts. Aces were new beginnings, the beginning of a phase. Perhaps she had to use the power of thought to cut through the binds and see things clearly for what they were.

She turned over the next card. Death. A crone stood cradling a skull in her hand, cradling it lovingly. She held it over a steaming cauldron, the cauldron being a sign of rebirth. In the background the sky was at evening and the sun was setting behind a stone burial mound. The eagle soared up high. Sighing, Moira held the card in her hands for a while. She had trouble working this card when she did the tarot course. Whilst it did not signify a physical death, it signified the end of an era. It was a time of change. Sometimes things have to end in order to move on and start anew. Not all endings were easy, but they had to be made in order to clear the way for the rebirth, the new.

Right now, Moira felt like the crone depicted in the card: old, haggard and world weary. What she needed was time for reflection. Her eye caught the small collection of items on the shelf, which had come out of the chest. Perhaps sitting back and concentrating on something else would be beneficial. She knew now the chest could be moved, it was now in her care. That is why Jimmy now wanted to go to the other side. She did not know whether she would ever get to the bottom of the questions, but she knew she would try.

Deciding that there was nothing to do now and that she was in no fit state to make decisions about her own life until things became clearer, she decided it was time to kick back and perhaps just be a couple. Her work was going through a lull - something else she needed to look at. She needed time to reflect on the answers and a long walk on the sand might just be the ticket.

By tacit agreement, Leo and Moira dined in the pub that evening. Neither yet felt comfortable to spend long in the cottage. Moira made a mental note to talk to Amber about this, in case there was something that could be done. In the meantime, they enjoyed the company of the pub locals, who bought them drinks in appreciation of saving their beloved landlady. Later in the evening, Liz came over to join them. After discussing the day's events she announced, "I'm not running. I'm not going to leave this place. I've worked hard at making this place work. What I think I need is a big dog or a decent man!"

They chuckled. The statement seemed to be frivolous but there was cast iron intent. Liz had spirit. Sometimes, Moira felt, her's had dwindled. Perhaps this period was needed for reflection.

Moira did not get her planned walk along the beach for nearly a week. Insurance surveyors had come out and declared everything 'an utter mess.' To Moira's surprise, they agreed to pay up without a fuss. Leo had to go away for a few days on business to sort out a situation. One of his directors had had a nervous breakdown and was found in his underpants, crying like a child, in the middle of the fountain outside the offices. It would have been most comical were it not for the fact that he had lost his wife the week before in a hit and run accident. She was away on business when a drunk driver ploughed her down. He carried on normally until the day after her due return date. It had hit him desperately hard. Leo had gone down to offer what support he could be. Although he seldom dealt with the day-to-day running of his businesses, everyone knew him as a firm but fair hands-on type of guy. Until a temp could be brought in, Leo manned the position and kept things working. Moira, in her own turn, enjoyed the peace, which gave her time to reflect.

    It was a cold, blustery day approaching the end of October when Moira eventually got to return to Poppit Sands, the beach on which she encountered the image of the immigrants on their way to new pastures. As they walked along the beach, she told Leo about her experiences again, pointing out the place where she sat. They were in the process of walking past it when they heard the sound of sobbing. As they got closer, they could see the shape of a figure in a threadbare blanket, head on its knees crying. Crying so hard that its body shook violently. Leo tried to pull her past. Moira escaped his grasp and went over to investigate. Something about the figure pulled at Moira's heartstrings; she knew she had to go over.

    Leo stood back a little whilst Moira sat herself quietly next to the figure. Upon closer inspection, she could see that the shoes the figure wore were worn through. The feet were red and sore; which was the only way to determine that they were living feet and not those of a skeleton. The clothes were like the shoes: worn to the point where they would fall apart if washed. The figure seemed to sense Moira sitting beside it and lifted its head up. It was a female, a young, thin female hardly out of her teens. She looked as if she had been living rough and was at the point of starvation. Her eyes were sunken hollows. She turned to look at Moira. They were so full of hurt and misery that Moira felt like she had taken a physical blow. Swallowing hard, Moira asked, "What's up?"

    It sounded feeble to Moira's ears and not the most original thing to say, but perhaps the meaning and warmth behind the words had done more. The sobbing ceased to just a flow of tears.

THE FOOL'S JOURNEY

"You really want to know?" The voice was weak and embittered but held a flicker of hope. "I usually get kicked and told to move on, or I'm ignored."

Moira glanced up at Leo and glared at him. He shuffled his feet in the sand and looked embarrassed.

"I've walked from Cornwall, after my boyfriend kicked me out. I ran away with him when I was 16; that was two years ago. Mum and Dad said I was a disgrace and never want to see me again. You see, he was older than me, almost double my age. He did not have a proper job and was a bit of a wild boy. So in the middle of the night, I packed my bags and left."

The frail body shook, as the wind whipped around them. Moira put her arm around the bony shoulders.

"I walked here to leave my baby at the door of my parents' place. They live a short way from here. I use to come down here as a child and picnic here, in this spot."

The wail that came next pierced both Moira's and Leo's hearts and rendered their minds useless.

"I've now got nothing. No one. Now I may as well die. But I don't want to die. I want to see my baby girl grow up. I want to go home. I want to go home."

"Do you want to call them?" Moira asked, offering the girl her phone.

The girl shook her head. "I don't know what to say."

The two girls sat there together for a while, united by an uncommon and unseen bond.

It was Leo who had the idea as he looked on. Before he said anything, he waited to see if any more information was forthcoming. When the girls sat quietly, he took control.

"Do you want me to go to the house?" he said as gently as possible.

The girl started, either by the suggestion or his presence, he couldn't tell. She treated him to the same look that Moira gave and whilst it smote his very being, it held a glimmer of hope, a very weak glimmer, but it was there.

THE FOOL'S JOURNEY

"Yes. My name is Star. Yes, that's my real name."

After Leo took down the address, he went back up the beach at a swift pace. Star would not go with him, and Moira stayed to make sure the girl remained, as she looked too weak to go anywhere. Whilst Leo was away she related her journey to Moira. She never dared to hitchhike, in case someone tried to hurt her, and then what would her baby do? She slept wherever she could, in barns, on farmers' lands, under hedges, selling everything she could as she went to buy baby milk to keep the little one alive and well. She even confessed ruefully to Moira, that she had sold her body on more than one occasion, whilst her baby slept hidden nearby, always using a condom. Moira found this child, for she was little more than a child, a strange creature. She was obviously not naïve. Perhaps what she had done had been born out of pure love for her child. She obviously felt she had nothing to offer her and didn't try to find a house and claim benefits. It seemed that she sacrificed everything for the child. Moira held back the tears that threatened to fall from her eyes. As it began to rain, she took off her jacket and draped it around Star's shoulders. It was like this that Leo and an unfamiliar man found them a short while later.

The man was running up the beach and Leo had to run fast to keep up. He shouted something, not quite clear enough to reach Moira's ears, but Star looked up. The man who had been running was very red-faced and totally out of breath; he slumped to his knees in front of them. Reaching out, as if coaxing a scared animal, he held his hand out towards Star.

"We've found you."

"You've been looking for me?" Star asked, amazed and enlightened all in one go.

"Since the day you left."

Star tried to push herself up, but was too weak. Having got his breath back, the man got up.

"You're coming home," he said.

"What about Summer?" Star asked, hesitantly.

THE FOOL'S JOURNEY

"She's with your Mam. I left her cooing over her and fussing. As soon as we heard you were here too, she started fussing about nursery furniture and all those things I'll never understand."

Star sagged, smiling now, but her energy spent.

"Come, let's get you home. We'll get Doc Roberts out to have a look at you and get you warm and fed." He stooped and lifted her up, carrying her like a babe in arms. He turned towards Moira.

"I cannot thank you and your husband enough." It was hard to tell if he was crying because the rain splashed his face, but his voice was choked with so much emotion, it felt that his soul was crying for joy instead of his eyes. He gave Moira back her coat with a smile. She and Leo watched as he walked back up the beach, clinging to his daughter like a drowning man a life raft. Leo turned with glistening eyes towards Moira. "Thank you." Then with a hint of humour he said, "Wife. We better sort that out before too long; don't want anyone getting the wrong idea." Moira responded by wrapping a sodden arm around him. She was chilled to the bone, but the sacrifice of her coat to Star had been worth it.

"We'll pop into town and get you some warm dry clothes, then some lunch."

Moira felt in no mood to answer. They walked back up the beach towards the car. A little while later, once Leo had bought lunch and Moira had changed into new dry clothes, they sat in the Flat Rock café, a restaurant attached to a hotel overlooking Poppit sands from the other side. Moira felt she never wanted to go there again. Too much had happened in the last two visits. As she watched the tide sweep up the shore to where they had been, she reflected they were just footsteps in the sand of life, washed away by the sea of time, just like those who had gone before.

THE FOOL'S JOURNEY

CHAPTER FIFTEEN – DEATH

Ending – Transition – Elimination – Inexorable Forces

With one hand, she clung onto the hat she wore and with the other, held Leo's arm. They walked towards the pub from the cottage. The subdued light from the street lamps fell onto Moira's emerald green dress. The flaps of her cloak were teased apart by the unseen force and then let fall back again. From doorway to doorway Pumpkins, Wizards and Fairies flew, carrying bags and buckets full of brightly wrapped delights. The smell of wood smoke was in the air. Clouds raced across the gibbous moon. They reached the pub in safety. Light spilled out from the pub door; a skeleton nearly collided with them, as they were about to enter.

"Great night for a Halloween party," Liz boomed. "It's early and the back rooms are already filling up. Bit breezy for flying though," she said gesturing with her head at the broomstick Leo held. "I would've thought you'd make more of an effort to dress up," she teased Moira. "After all, a witch dressing up as a witch."

They all laughed, for tonight it felt like all recent cares and worries had flown away, carried off by the wind, and all that remained was the lightheartedness, which came from relief.

Stepping through a low door into a long room beyond, Moira and Leo shed their coats and put them in the makeshift cloakroom at the end of the hall. Moira's dress clung to her, emphasizing the shape of her breasts and the curvature of her hips. The neckline was low, but not enough for everything to fall out. The waistline was V shaped and finished in a point at the top of the skirt. Her fiery red hair tumbled loosely in curls down her back. She wore the stereotypical witch's hat. This though was made from the same green velvet as her dress. This was no costume shop outfit. Moira had commissioned this from a local seamstress who was just setting up in business. Leo looked on at her as she walked into the main part of the hall ahead of him, carrying the broom. He knew what he would be doing later; in fact he would quite happily do it now, just not in front of everyone. Feeling his already skintight trousers that constituted his Dracula outfit get a little tighter, he put such thoughts out of his head and concentrated on socialising instead.

At the far end of the room was a makeshift stage. On the stage, a band had set up. The positions were currently empty and low background music was being played instead. Moira and Lee headed towards the bar, which was half way up along the left hand side. They joked with a Frankenstein and laughed with a fairy. Moira had worked behind the bar a year ago. Words washed over her from a myriad of voices as she thought back on how she felt last year. She had newly purchased a house that the locals refused to go near. She had completed the renovations. She was determined to set up and live her life here. But rather than a home, it had proven to be a safe haven in a passing storm. Now that was coming to an end. And it was not without a little sadness. She really had no friends here apart from Liz. She knew people, but not to the extent that she could pop around for coffee and cake, or invite them to dinner parties. She also missed the hubbub of living somewhere less remote. The heartbeat was slow here and Moira preferred living her life to a faster tune. Knowing that, she could step back and recharge if necessary. She heard someone calling her name and came quickly back to the present.

"Moira!" It was Kate, dressed as a fairy, "You were off somewhere else."

Moira tittered. She did not think much of Kate. It was not a dislike. There was just something about the woman that was so false and it grated on her nerves.

"I was asking whether you wanted the punch, it is rather good."

"Yes please. That sounds great."

As soon as was polite to do so, Moira steered Leo off into the room to mingle further before Kate's self-righteous whining turned her into a

THE FOOL'S JOURNEY

metaphorical frog. For the umpteenth time, Moira still reckoned that if you were a witch you should be able to turn people into green, croaking frogs, even for a few minutes. Then she reckoned they would have to be big frogs, or there would be lots of spare body parts and that might be messy.

The party went well. There was apple bobbing and pin the tail on the donkey, except that this game had a twist. The donkey was not a paper version stuck to a wall, it was a man dressed up as a donkey that moved around. So, whilst the person was blindfolded, the man in the donkey suit was allowed to move around but not outside the square that had been drawn. This had caused so much amusement that there were people clamouring to be the donkey and be the one blindfolded. Even the band members wanted a go and had gone on performing for much longer than originally planned. There was a splendid buffet and the band played on right up to the witching hour. Everyone was sent home with a goody bag full of Halloween treats. Walking a little unsteadily back to the cottage, Moira reflected that this was the best way of seeing in this festival. No lone ritual would have felt the same.

October turned into November and brought the first really sharp frost of the year. Leo fretted about burst pipes in the house next door. The people were dragging their heels on exchange and completion. Moira began to look at other job options. In the present economic climate, people were trying to do everything themselves and work was bringing in enough for her to live off frugally, but not what she wanted. Apart from anything else, it was giving her no satisfaction. All the customers seemed to do was whine. Things were either not done quickly enough or done too soon or they delayed in paying. It was one day after a particularly trying conversation with someone who had failed to pay that Moira decided to stop this. She pulled the advert out of the local paper and took her name off the websites that she had subscribed to. She would work with her existing customers for now, until they either gave up or she found something else. It was this same day that she received the phone call that the buyers of Blodwen's old house had exchanged and completion was set for the week after next. Leo was relieved. However, it did raise the question of their having to find a house. No new houses had come onto the market this side of Christmas. All they could do was wait. Moira knew there were things to be attended to before the right one would come up. One of those was helping Jimmy across to the other side.

December heralded two things: the first snow and the phone call from Amber that she and Michael would be coming up to help move Jimmy on. Michael felt it would be easier if they stayed nearby, so Moira booked them into the pub's rooms. Almost immediately, word went round the village and beyond, that Michael Stewart, the famous psychic medium, was coming to stay. Moira had not heard the rumour, so when she went to meet Amber and Michael when they arrived, she was not prepared for the pub to be totally packed. Michael was very graciously smiling and talking to people. Amber stood guard behind him, like a scarlet haired avenging angel. After a short while, Michael whispered something into Liz's ear, which caused her to blush. She rang the bell for last orders and asked for silence. Michael stood up.

"The day after tomorrow I will be holding a book signing in the back room which the beautiful Liz assures me will be available. So please feel free to come back then, and we will have more space."

This caused the pub to empty to its more normal level of business. Eventually managing to sit near them, Moira asked, "Can you get the books here in time?"

It was Amber who answered. "We get this a lot. The publishers have a good courier company, so I'll go and put a word in now so that they'll be here tomorrow ready for Friday's book signing." Seeing the momentary look of concern float across Moira's face, she added "We'll deal with Jimmy on Saturday, as promised. We find it's best to get the hype over and done with, then the rest of our stay should be relatively groupie free."

Moira noted by the glint in her eye and the tone of her voice, she enjoyed this as much as Michael obviously did.

THE FOOL'S JOURNEY

Saturday evening arrived. After dinner in the pub, Liz excitedly told them that she had had such a wonderful time on Friday and that Michael had agreed to come back with the film crew, because he felt this place had a resident spirit. Moira had cast a furtive glance at Amber who nodded and purely added to the dialogue, in the out buildings. Michael told them how he thought it was a milkmaid who had hung herself when she found out that she was pregnant and the father of the child didn't want anything to do with her. She felt such remorse at ending her own and the child's life, she could not move on. Moira secretly felt that he could have helped without the glare of the cameras; but then, she mused, that was how he earned his living. Moira felt a change within Michael and Amber as they progressed down the road towards the cottage. The mood became more somber and even though Moira knew Jimmy wanted to move across, she would be sad to see him go. Mornings would not be the same without having to clear up logs or re-hang moved saucepans. Yet, she knew too that she was moving on; perhaps that was her part to play here.

In the velvety darkness of Moira's lounge, Michael lit a solitary pillar candle. It spluttered for a moment, then the light grew steady. He secured it in the middle of the room on a black mirror. He lit a taper from the candle and then lit the fire Moira had prepared earlier. Sitting down cross legged on the floor, he calmed his mind and softened his breathing. When he felt himself in perfect balance, he lit a bundle of dried sage, known as a smudge stick. Walking slowly to each corner of the room, he let the spiraling smoke drift. He set the smouldering bundle on a saucer near the mirror. He proceeded to place a white candle in a simple candleholder at each of the compass points in the room.

"You can come in now," he called to the others waiting in the kitchen.

With varying degrees of apprehension they all walked into the dimly lit room. The air was heavy with the scent of sage. After Michael had made sure they were sitting in a vague circle around the dark mirror in the middle of the room, he ground up some dried herbs in an antique pestle with a mortar. As he ground the herbs, the smell of garlic,

THE FOOL'S JOURNEY

spearmint and rosemary filled the air. Moira snuffed the air, her nose twitching trying to pick up the scents that filled the room. There were unfamiliar smells mixed in with the ones she recognised. It felt like she was no longer sitting on the floor of her own lounge, but somewhere else: a temple or wooded glade. Each waft of fragrance brought about a changing perception.

Michael stood up after he finished grinding. Using the herb mixture, he traced a circle around the outside of the candles; carefully making sure the line was solid. Placing the pestle and mortar back on the floor, he relit the taper from the pillar candle that stood in the middle of the dark mirror. Lighting the first candle, the one placed in the north aspect, he called out in a clear and commanding voice, "I call upon the guardians of the north to watch over us and protect us. I evoke the element of Earth to and protect us."

Moving onto the East candle, he lit it with the taper and with the same commanding voice, this time he called out, "I call upon the guardians of the East to watch over us and protect us. I evoke the element of Air. For air brings us life and thought."

With an almost rhythmic swaying motion, rather than a walk, he made his way to the South candle. "I call upon the guardians of the South to watch over us and protect us. I evoke the element of fire. To warm us and give light in dark times."

He lit the final candle."I call upon the guardians of the West, to watch and protect us. I evoke the element of water to quench thirst and allow emotional release."

Striding with purpose, Michael quickly came back to the centre of the room. He stood with his arms aloft. Moira could see in the glowing light that he wore a dark purple gown over his clothes, not dissimilar to a smock. As he held his arms up, the sleeves fell back. In the dancing candlelight, Moira could see that around each sleeve were embroidered various symbols of protection. His voice changed tone, becoming gentle like the sighing breeze.

THE FOOL'S JOURNEY

"I call upon the Spirit who unites all, to hold together the elements and protect us. Please hear our call."

He lit a second candle, which was also on the mirror, a shorter squat one, a smaller version of the first. Sitting in his position to complete the circle of bodies, he fell silent for a while.

When he spoke, his voice sounded like it was coming from a distance, perhaps from the next room or out in the hall. "Jimmy, Moira tells me you would like to move over to the other side. Can you not find your way?"

Michael sat there with his head cocked slightly, as if straining to hear something distant.

"You've protected her well. Are you being called back?"

The monotone conversation carried on for a few minutes, until Moira realised she was being called, not by one of the members sitting around the circle but by someone else. Michael looked over at her and nodded.

Moira stifled an urge to scream and run from the room. She had chosen this path or the path had chosen her, she wasn't sure. Once the plough to the furrow had been set, it had to be finished. Although the metaphor needed some work, she felt now that she must complete here what had been started.

"I'm listening."
"Who is she?"
"Where did they go?"
"Why did they do that?"
"That's OK."
"I understand. You've done well. You are a brave lad."

Eventually, feeling like she was experiencing a whole lifetime, when in fact only a few minutes had passed, she handed Jimmy back to Michael.

"He says there's one task left to perform."

With that the room's atmosphere changed, it felt less inhabited, but Moira could sense Jimmy moving around upstairs. In the next moment, the lounge door flew open, causing the candles to dip and then recover.

THE FOOL'S JOURNEY

In floated the chest. Out of the corner of her eye, she could see Amber reaching out to stop Leo from jumping up. Her gaze fell firmly on the chest as it floated through the air. Her heart thudded in her chest, but she didn't feel scared. Slowly, like a feather falling, the chest settled into her lap. She felt what could only be described as a kiss on her cheek. In an audible whisper, the words 'open the door' could be heard. The room gained an extra dimension and shadows moved. Then he was gone.

Michael sagged. The atmosphere of the house changed. For one thing it felt emptier. It had also lost that feeling of oppression, which Moira sometimes felt. Of course, there was the act of closing the bedroom door and telling Jimmy to stay out, when they were making love. Now a sense of calm befell the cottage. She could feel the love that owners of the past had put into the place now seep out. Oddly, it no longer felt like her home. Moira watched Michael get up, weary now it had been done. His face seemed older, the lines deeper and in the flickering candlelight, his skin looked pale. Amber handed him a brass-hooded candlesnuffer. Walking to the North candle, he snuffed it out.

"Thank you for your protection and service here today. I release the element of earth to go whence it came."

With heavy footsteps, he made his way around the circle in turn snuffing out the candles and releasing the elements he had evoked. He came back to the centre of the circle again and extinguished the smaller candle.

"To the sprit we thank you for your protection."

Turning to the group, Michael said, "He has gone now. He was scared and needed encouragement, but his mother was there to welcome him. I must rest now. We will talk some more tomorrow." Turning to Moira, he added. "Sweep the incense with which I created the circle and bury it in the garden. Send thanks to the universe. Leave the mirror with the pillar candle burning while you do so. When it is done, extinguish it and go to bed. Don't be tempted to work this further tonight."

Amber carefully took his arm and led him away.

THE FOOL'S JOURNEY

Moira set about the task of clearing up and settling the chest back upstairs. She did not speak a word to Leo for some time until he snapped impatiently.

"What did he say to you?"

"Not tonight, dear heart. Lie with me. I need the comfort of human flesh. Tomorrow we will discuss it all."

He grumbled, but in the way of a man who knows he's going to get something out of the situation that might just be better than what he had asked for. She snuffed out the candle, closed the door and went to bed. In the morning Moira thought, would I really tell all?

CHAPTER SIXTEEN – TEMPERANCE

Temperance – Balance – Health – Combination

The smell of coffee, bacon and freshly baked bread greeted Amber and Michael when they arrived the next morning. Although Liz at the pub ensured all her guests had a splendid breakfast, this morning she knew they had things to discuss.

"What is it with me and snow?" grumbled Amber, hanging her coat in the hall and putting her snow covered boots by the range in the kitchen to warm through. "Have I a message on my soul that says, 'I'm in Wales that means snow on me'."

Michael laughed. "She's been like this since she woke for a pee in the small hours and found that the world was now under a white blanket."

"Ha! Not all that time. I slept until you woke me with your gleeful remark of 'it's snowed', then leapt about the room like a kid," Amber retorted. There was no malice behind the remark.

"Give her a coffee, and she'll become near human." Michael said grinning.

Moira did note the change in him. He seemed to be back to normal, with his unbridled energy and boyish charm. In fact, it seemed snow agreed with him much more than it did Amber. Who, Moira remembered from the last visit, actually quite liked it, remembering when they were outside making snow angels. Amber caught Moira's eye and gave a huge roguish wink when Michael's back was turned.

It was sometime later when bacon sandwiches had been consumed and mugs refilled with coffee that they set about discussing what had gone before. It was Leo, his impatience not totally abated, who said, "You lot are acting like nothing has happened. What did he say? Why could he not move on and why was he a brave lad?"

THE FOOL'S JOURNEY

Michael grinned at him. "Did you not hear or feel anything?"
"Half whispers and feeling eerie that's all."
"Jimmy, as we already know, died here within the cottage. I think he died from tuberculosis or some sort of lung disease. He told me he could not breathe properly. He had bad lungs for a while. But the death of his mother came as a shock and it got worse. He does not know why his mum died. He told me that she used to take in washing, do odd jobs and sometimes the landlord would come and make a noise with her, like Moira and Leo do." Michael looked across at Leo, who blushed splendidly. "His mum was getting very breathless and very tired. He thought she had bad lungs too, but she shook her head in the spirit world. I think it was probably her heart." Michael stared out at the falling snow for a little while, then said, "He was also feeling a bit guilty. He'd promised his mum he would not leave the house, but one day after she'd lain with the landlord he spied through the keyhole. He felt an urge to do the same to a girl. He snuck out one night and took a girl. He said he liked it very much and wanted to do it again and again. He said he paid the girl some money. He went out and did this for another two nights; he said he did it lots. Then the girl screamed at him that when he was doing that he hurt her, but he couldn't stop. He said the devil took him and he wanted to hurt and to have pleasure. He went home. Then, the next day his Mum died. After that, he would tell me no more."

They all looked at Moira, who was staring out of the window. She was not certain she wanted to talk about this. She felt a degree of sadness and a sense of responsibility now.

It was a little time before Moira decided and would answer. Amber had laid a restraining hand on Leo's arm. "Give her time," she whispered. "The first time is hard on a soul."

Then, clinging to her mug, like she was clinging to the fabric of reality, Moira started to speak.

"He did tell me about himself, but he wanted me to know more about Annie."

"Who's Annie?" Michael queried.

THE FOOL'S JOURNEY

"The girl whose belongings were put into the chest," she said gesturing towards the upstairs room, where it now lay at peace in its blanket.

"From what I know and from what Jimmy was told, Annie's parents were booked to go on a long journey. He said there was a great hunger in the previous years, when people died because they were cold and hungry. I looked this up this morning and the year was 1816, and the northern hemisphere was plunged into a volcanic winter. There was no summer and crops failed. It hit Wales particularly hard because their lands were already diseased and under fertile, due to the intense farming to supply the Napoleonic wars. They had lost three of their children, Annie's mum had lost her father and Annie's dad had lost virtually all his family. The all lived in a cottage with Annie's mum, Annie's sister and husband and their four children. They had two remaining children, Annie and her sister, May. A few days before her parents went on a long journey, Annie got really sick. She was too weak to travel, but they promised they would come back for her. They never did, and she died only a few days later. They put all her belongings in this chest, which her uncle had made and was, kept in safekeeping in case someone returned. The chest was passed down to Jimmy's mum when she was old enough. Jimmy says that his mum could remember Annie, because they were about the same age."

Looking around, Moira noted there was not one dry eye in the room. There was a sadness that seeped into the soul through the ears and was burned there by the words.

Leo gulped and forced out what was on his mind. "What about the other questions and remarks? Why was he a brave lad?"

Moira looked at Leo with a degree of amusement in her eyes. "I need a refill." She pointed at her empty mug. "But first, there is something I want to do. It's snowing, we're alive, and so who fancies a snowball fight?"

Moira was not certain who jumped up quicker Michael or Leo. Amber lingered and said, "You're doing fine." They then joined the boys who were already pulling on boots and coats and making a beeline for the garden.

In the gently falling snow, Moira, Leo, Amber and Michael ran and played, throwing snowballs and building snowmen. After completing this task, they all decided to walk down to the beach to see what it looked like covered in snow. Before they went, Leo ran without a word to the storage shed in the garden, where he unearthed a huge red sledge.

"I stored it here in case Lottie came..."

"Yeah, I believe you," Amber said, managing to convey that she did not, not one iota.

Jumping on the sledge at the top of the hill that led down to the beach, he whizzed down, before failing to take the bend and implanting himself into a beech hedge. The snow still clinging to brown leaves spilt all over him. Moira and the rest laughed long and hard at the figure that emerged. Slipping and sliding, they made it down to the beach. Here, snow clung to the rocks and the sand. The approaching incoming tide was trying to restore the beach back to its natural state, whilst the sky seemed to take objection to this and started snowing harder. They soon became cold. They slipped, clung and gingerly trod their way back up the hill. This was accompanied by hoots and catcalls as one or the other would end up on their bottom or fall flat on their faces. Exhausted but happy, they went into the cottage and collapsed into armchairs and sofas whilst they ate cake and drank coffee, still giggling softly.

After the plates and mugs had been cleared up, they returned to discussing the night before. The pure joy of living had balanced out the sadness, but now Moira felt it was time to tell the rest of the tale.

"The girl who Jimmy had taken I think was the local girl of easy virtue. He said that she made him feel good. When he could not stop and he had hurt her, he left her half asleep, he said. There was a bit of a hue and cry, for it seemed he nearly killed the girl. But when the locals found out who it was, no one would go near him, for they feared him. When he told them that his mum had died, shouting in tears from the gate, they barred the doors and locked him in. They were too afraid he would do them harm and too afraid to go in and retrieve the body of his dead mother to give her a proper burial. It was several weeks later, when the landlord had returned from London that he discovered what had happened and from what Jimmy said, he heard him shouting and screaming. It was then he knew he was a ghost. He knew he'd failed his mum and felt a lot of remorse. He said it was the landlord who made sure they were buried and with all honors due to the dead. He seemed to think that his mum and the landlord were sweet on each other, as he put it."

Moira wiped the tears out of her eyes.

"He was brave, because some time later when the house had new owners, he did not like them. He said he made lots of noise and often hid upstairs with the chest in the attic. They got a priest in to try and get rid of him. But he said it hurt him, and he was so afraid of going to hell, he tipped a boiling pan of water on the priest. He said he could not leave Annie. After that, he said he was weaker; he couldn't do the same things he could do before. He was dreadfully upset that he had done wrong, but he wanted reassurance that he did the right thing by protecting Annie." Leo went to speak. She glared at him. "Who are we to judge what we would do? Now all that is left is to try and find out where the family went, although I do have a good idea and perhaps what can be done to settle Annie."

"Alas my friend," Michael said. "I don't know the solution either. This child clings onto the chest in the spirit world, because she wants to be with her mummy. Her mummy is dead, defined by the passing of years. We don't even know a surname to work with. This case makes my heart bleed. What child does not want to be with its mother when poorly and sick? The heart wrenching anguish that her family went through leaving the child. Maybe they really did believe that she would get better and then join them."

All sat there in silence for a long time, thinking their own thoughts. Then suddenly, they all began talking at once, giggling. Someone grabbed some playing card games and they contented themselves with silliness. It did not take long for their bellies to remind them they needed

THE FOOL'S JOURNEY

feeding. Michael suggested that he treat everyone to one of 'lovely Liz's lunches'. No one argued with that suggestion. Over lunch, they talked about happy times and the Christmas that was fast approaching. Moira and Leo bade Michael and Amber farewell. The forecast was for more snow so they planned to leave shortly. Moira and Leo went back to the cottage and enjoyed their first evening of natural peace.

Over the next few days, Moira and Leo found the cottage wonderful. The cats were less impressed as the invisible presence that had been so content to fuss over them had gone. As clever felines, they had felt the temporal shift and were not quite so happy to see the back of it. They were curled up on their humans' laps one evening, whilst they discussed moving. The cats wondered if they would move to somewhere that had another invisible friend to fuss over them. Or perhaps there were more small furry squeaky things to catch? They contentedly dreamed cat dreams.

The snow cleared and the weather was dull, damp and cold. Moira felt her spirits drop. She had been out for a walk, feeling her back grow less painful and stiff. This had not shifted the gloom. She came through the front door to see Leo talking animatedly on the phone whilst sitting on the stairs. An odd feeling crept over her. It felt like someone had shut a door. She went into the kitchen to warm herself by the range, but the kitchen felt wrong. It felt oddly empty. Sitting in the chair by the side of the range, she sipped hot tea, feeling it warm her through. She could still hear Leo on the phone; he sounded excited. With growing impatience she waited until he had finished. He burst into the kitchen like a one-man whirlwind. He was the total opposite of her gloom.

"My Mum and Dad have invited us down for Christmas and your Mum and Dad too. We're going to have a big family Christmas, won't that be nice? Mum's ordered a huge tree, which she says we've got to decorate. Your mum's asked if you would ring her back, and oh, I am just so excited! I feel like a school kid again. Oh, and the cats have got to come. Family Christmas, Mum said, everyone!" Leo said excitedly.

THE FOOL'S JOURNEY

Despite her earlier gloom Moira laughed. Although the idea of such a big Christmas get together scared her a little, it sounded exciting.

When Moira got through to her mum a little time later, she heard how she and Leo's mum had become firm friends. Her dad had started playing golf and bought some new snazzy clubs and…Moira felt she had been lifted up and placed somewhere else. Her life seemed to be getting back some of the vitality it had lost. It was still tempered with a degree of stress and sadness, but the early stirrings of the enjoyment of living were returning.

Christmas was a joyful affair. The Christmas tree was huge. Moira decorated it with the help of Leo's dad. Leo himself had been closeted away with her dad for hours. On Christmas morning, she found out why. While they were unwrapping presents, there was a knock on the back door. Leo raced out of the room to answer it. He came back with a brightly coloured box in his arms. The box was wiggling. Setting it on the floor in front of Moira's feet, he grinned.

"Surprise."

She undid the bow and lifted the box lid off. Out jumped a chocolate-brown and white puppy, with big doleful eyes and long ears.

"A Cocker Spaniel. How did you know? I mean I've never discussed having a dog with you, never. I've always wanted one." Tears were streaming down her face as her tongue tripped over the words.

"Your parents," Leo said simply. "When I asked them what special present I could buy you, a new car, designer clothes anything you really wanted, they suggested all you've ever wanted was a puppy. With them both working, it was the one thing they could not give you. Now I have."

Archie took this moment to saunter into the room to see what the fuss was about. He saw the small dog, went over to it and batted it with its paw. He made sure there were just enough claws showing to make certain the puppy knew who was the boss. Then he snuggled down by Moira's side. Moira hugged the puppy, hugged Archie and Leo in spontaneous and random turns, until her mum put a present in her lap. Moira opened it. There was a bowl with a name on it, 'Bruno'. This time

THE FOOL'S JOURNEY

she openly sobbed. She had a toy dog as a child called Bruno; it was the name she dreamed of calling a dog if she ever had one. Years and years later, her mother had remembered.

After Christmas, they went down to Cathy's for New Year's, taking the cats with them and little Bruno too. Lottie was delighted to see the puppy, which by this time had learnt a very healthy respect for cats. but that lesson did not stop him from chancing his luck when he could.

It was a couple of days after they had arrived that they were in Cathy's kitchen, preparing for the following day's New Year's Eve party. Bruno had chased one of Cathy's cats into the kitchen. The cat had jumped up onto the work surface and knocked the bowl of trifle all over the dog and the floor. Moira was horrified, but Cathy was bent double in laughter. She was laughing so hard, Lee and Leo came in to see what was going on and started laughing too. In the end, Moira could not help but join in. There was Bruno wearing the mask of innocence covered in jelly, fruit and custard. The cat that had jumped up out the way wore a feline grin: a sniggle wrapped up in a purr.

Cathy and Lee talked Moira and Leo into staying a little while after the festival celebrations were over. In truth, though neither said it, they weren't in any great hurry to go back. They decided instead to have a drive by of some properties and have a look at the few new ones that had come onto the market. They were a little over what they had set themselves as a budget, but as Leo said they were buying their family home. It had to be right, but did more expensive mean better?

CHAPTER SEVENTEEN – THE DEVIL

Bondage – Materialism – Ignorance – Hopelessness

    The soft cream heated leather seats of Leo's BMW warmed them. They were protected in their plush comfort from the icy chill outside. As they drove through the forest, frost clung to gorse bush and grass alike. Forest ponies huddled together; sharing what little warmth they could muster. The car rolled smoothly over the cattle grid that held off the wild creatures. Parking in front, the gravel crunched under their feet. Up at the stable-style front door they were shown into a cream carpeted hall, where they were politely but firmly asked to remove their shoes.
    The wood-paneled walls made the hall feel closed in and the large chandelier style lampshade gave the impression of the ceiling being low. Moira felt like she was walking down a tunnel not a hallway. Doors led off the passage, firmly closed against prying eyes. They entered a huge kitchen. In the centre of the room was an island counter. It most likely served as an eating area, as tall white leather, chrome-legged bar stools stood in regimented positions. The women who had shown them in, enquired in her most undressing tones, "Would you care for coffee?"
    They both respectfully declined.
    "Well this is the kitchen." She stalked off leaving Moira and Leo to follow in her wake. "The utility room contains the dogs. We won't go in there. They'll trail mud through." Leo looked at Moira in astonishment.
    "This house is over a million pounds, she's treating us like we're muck"
    Moira gently put a hand on his arm. They were shown into the lounge.
    More cream, Moira could not help noticing. Huge deep-seated cream sofas and the deep-piled cream carpet almost felt as if they were walking

THE FOOL'S JOURNEY

through treacle. "This room is for entertaining," she announced in a braying tone. "We don't light the fire often - too dirty."

Moira and Leo had toured through the dining room and into the master bedroom. It was one through one of the closed doors off the passageway they had entered. Moira was getting fed up and frustrated. Doing her best to try and set things on a more even footing, she enquired, "Why are you selling?"

"When the dogs go for a walk they get covered in horse muck! I thought the forest would just be trees and such. My agent chose the house. He's now not working for me. You see my husband and I moved back from living abroad. Do you know how expensive and selective servants are over here?"

Leo made a noise between a snort and cough. The woman showing them around the house looked down her long, equine nose at him. "The agent informed me you're a cash purchaser. Rob a bank did you?"

"I run my own businesses," Leo answered through gritted teeth.

The woman said no more. She showed them four further bedrooms. Each furnished with white bed linen and cream carpeted floors. When they were back by the front door, she announced, "That's the house. Outside is a swimming pool for summer and tennis courts. You can go and look if you want."

"I think I've seen enough thanks," Moira said in her sweetest tone.

By the time they were safely closeted in the secured environment of the car, Leo was fit to explode.

"Was that woman real? Does anyone really feel that way? I think what she needs is a talk with Harry!"

"Who's Harry?" Moira enquired.

"Good friend who is a shrink in Harley Street," Leo chuckled.

Turning the car back out onto the main road, Moira noted with a degree of despondency that all the houses had the same manicured look, all with similar cars. She said nothing to Leo. To her, the area seemed to be the land of keeping up with your neighbours. She felt strongly this was not for her. Yet from the look of Leo's last house, this was his world.

THE FOOL'S JOURNEY

She was silent for a while whilst he negotiated wandering cows and the occasional flight of a deer. It was early for their next house viewing, so they stopped in an open tearoom for some refreshment.

Moira felt she had entered a time warp. This tearoom had been carefully decorated to incorporate the natural rural charm of the building with contemporary art deco design. They were served tea in proper bone china teacups, decorated with a black and white art deco pattern. A choice of bite-sized cakes was brought to them on a cake stand. The waitress was dressed in a black dress with a white apron and a lace cap perched on her head. Her good humoured face did not quite fit the formality of her attire and probably would have had her confined to 'below stairs' had she been serving in a house in the 1920s. Once they had had all the delightful cakes they could eat and drank enough tea to march an army on, Leo got up to pay. Behind the till was an older version of the good humoured face that had served them.

"That was incredible!" Leo exclaimed, before the woman could ask.

"Really?"

"Absolutely! Have you got a business card?" Leo asked as he handed over the cash for the bill.

The woman flustered. "They have just been delivered this morning. They were due to have been delivered before Christmas, but the company blamed the snow. Hold on, I'll get you one." She turned towards the kitchen area. As she walked towards it, the girl that had served them came out.

"Here we go, Mam. I'll pop some by the till."

"We only opened a few days ago. I guess wrong time of year." Her gaze fell on the empty tea room."

Moira, who had joined Leo, caught the tone behind the words.

"How come you decided to open now?"

"Our John was medically retired from his job after a car accident left him with back problems. With the payout we set up this place. We sank all we had into it. Our eldest daughter gave up her job as a chef in London to help. Mary here," indicating the girl, "is helping us man this

THE FOOL'S JOURNEY

place while studying for her law degree. We pull together as a family. It's just a pity money is needed."

"I feel sure it will work," Leo said. "This is charming. Have you considered functions? Tea dances, that sort of thing?"

"That'd be a hoot, Mam!" declared Mary.

Leo handed her a business card. "Think about it, and let me know. I think some of my employees would enjoy it. In the mean time, I'll put the word about with this place."

Moira gently nudged him and indicated the clock above the counter. They left with the thanks of both the women.

Moira was in a very reflective mood as they drove onto the next property. She thought of that family who had struck out anew, supporting each other and breaking the mould. The feeling of everyone keeping up with the neighbours returned. Similar cars were parked on gravel drives with well-manicured lawns abutting them as they traveled up the road to the next house. Leo pushed the button by the gate; it swung open, admitting them into another pristine world.

This time, it was a tall, red-bricked house with the stems of wisteria clinging to it. Bare of its leaves and sweet smelling blooms in this the depth of winter. A smiling woman, dressed in the height of fashion, opened the door. Soft silk slippers donned the woman's feet. Moira was sure that they were handmade and very expensive. Again, as at the last house, the removal of boots and outerwear were taken care of by the door. Leo stifled a cringe as another cream carpeted expanse opened up in front of them. They were shown into a lounge where a fire burned merrily within a stainless steel modern wood-burning stove. The curtains were heavy and embroidered with gold thread. The furniture was exquisitely made and as they were invited to sit down, they found it to be of the softest leather. Again, coffee was offered and again declined. After some small talk about the coldness of the weather and the general selling of the area Moira asked, "Why are you moving?"

THE FOOL'S JOURNEY

"Oh, we've had this house for five years now, time for a change. The kids are growing up and want bigger horses than the two acres we have here will allow."

Perfectly normal explanations and genuine warmth from the woman. Something irked both Leo and Moira; neither could explain what it was.

The kitchen was a custom fitted one, with oak cupboards and doors and white marble tops. An expensive range cooker stood against one wall, a modern gas one, and not solid fuel like Moira's. A man came out the utility room, dressed in cord trousers and a check shirt under a mohair jumper.

"Tristan." he said holding out a hand.

Leo shook it, but it was not proffered to Moira. Leo snuck a side-on glance. Moira shook her head slightly, so he left it.

"A beautiful house you have here," Moira said.

"Only the best for our women." Tristan said, addressing Leo. "Jane here makes sure the cleaner does her job, the nanny takes care of the twins. The older two are now in boarding school during term time. I don't want my beautiful woman to be tired and soiled at the end of the day. She's great at tennis, you know. Only the best instructors!"

"You're good to me," Jane said with perceptible fondness in her voice.

They were shown the rest of the house. The older two children, also twins it appeared, were in their rooms playing computer games. They gave a cheery wave and went back to what they were doing. The master bedroom was something out of a magazine. There was a hand carved, four-poster bed with rose-pink Italian silk hangings. The ensuite bathroom held a double Jacuzzi and a huge shower. Everything was the best money could buy. Moira was getting tired of this opulent splendour. It was making her itch. Still, they had to look, they could not leave too soon. The third floor was a nursery where the twins slept. Moira felt a pang of pity; these two beautiful, blonde haired girls, asleep in their cradles could wake up crying, without the compassionate touch of a mother. Always under the care of a girl younger than she was. They

THE FOOL'S JOURNEY

made their way down a second staircase; different to the one they had gone up. This one was curved with a carved banister and supports. Leo mumbled into Moira's ear, 'we're in a film set.' Moira had to bite her lip to stop herself visibly giggling.

They all donned boots and jackets and made their way out into the still lingering frost of a January afternoon. They stomped their way to two ponies grazing contentedly in warm rugs, their breath hanging in the air as they snorted their greetings. Next to an all weather tennis court. The gardens were mature with a mixture of shrubs and herbaceous plants, now dormant. Outside the triple garage that flanked the driveway, the men shook hands.

Moira was in a black temper by the time they got back to Cathy's. She took herself out for a walk in the dwindling light, adding an extra layer for warmth. Her warm boots crunched along the grass; Jack Frost was returning to mend his handiwork the weak winter sun had destroyed. After half an hour walking and the sun hanging low in the sky, Moira sat down on a log and began to cry. She loved Leo more than anything. But, the level of materialism of this area and the houses they had viewed felt so wrong to her. There was nothing wrong with having nice things and even the level of luxury they had seen. What was wrong to her was that it was at the expense of more natural things, like a mother's love. She could even understand it if the woman worked. All she did was swan around in expensive clothes, drive goodness knows what car and be slave to money. Yet, she seemed happy in her world. Moira's head ached. She could understand what was wrong and why.

The light was fading fast. She had obviously sat for longer than she had intended. She felt lonely; alien in a world she had long craved after, yet now she felt she was uncertain of what she really wanted. It was almost like she was afraid. As if she entered this world, she would lose the person she had become. Lose her connection to the higher power; lose the values which she held dear. Would she survive as an independent soul in a pond of average people leading the lives they wanted to? She was not even certain what she wanted from her life, apart

THE FOOL'S JOURNEY

from Leo. Still the tears fell down her cheeks. The cold was making her back ache.

Slowly and stiffly, she got up from the log and walked with heavy footsteps back towards Cathy and Lee's house. It had seemed such a good idea all those months ago. Her soul felt it was the right thing. So why were things not coming together for her? The sky was now pink with the setting sun, the air was bitter and despite the warmth of her coat and extra layers, it seemed to be penetrating her, like knives stabbing into her flesh. The scent of the fresh air's crispness wafted up her nostrils and down into her soul. She began to feel alive again, being out in this winter evening, knowing that the days would soon get longer and before too long, spring would return. With spring, hope.

Moira was about five minutes away from the house when she heard a high pitched voice. The voice was young and carried a worried note.

"Aunty Moira. Aunty Moira." It was Lottie.

"I'm here," she answered. Running towards her was Lottie in her pink snow boots and pink coat, wearing the pink, flapped hat that Moira had bought her for Christmas. She threw herself at her to be hugged.

Moira hugged the child's warm body to her. Over her shoulder, she could see Cathy. She wore an expression half of relief and half of consternation.

"What happened today? Leo's been like a bear with a sore head. We came back from ballet class to find him grumbling all over the house and you gone! We thought you two had had a blazing row. Lee said you were fine with each other and didn't understand. Leo's getting worried, which made him even grumpier, so we came and looked for you."

As they walked back Lottie clung to Moira's hand. Moira explained about the day. About the teashop and about the feeling she had. Cathy said nothing for a while and just let Moira talk. By talking and walking, Moira began to feel better. By the time they got back into the house, she felt calmer and happier. Leo hugged her so hard she could scarcely breathe. No one felt much like cooking, so they ordered a Chinese takeaway and ate it on their knees whilst watching Friday night TV.

THE FOOL'S JOURNEY

After they had settled Lottie into bed Lee had opened a bottle of wine. Cathy was sitting in a corner, quietly embroidering a blanket when she looked up. "I know what you two need to do to solve this situation."

"What!" they exclaimed together.

Cathy looked up and smiled. "Make a home together."

Was it as simple as that?

CHAPTER EIGHTEEN – THE TOWER

Sudden Change – Release – Downfall – Revelation

Leo and Moira sat and looked at each other. Was it that simple? Had they been looking at this from the wrong angle?

"What you are suggesting is that instead of looking for a house that has had everything done and has been made someone else's, look for one that we can make into what we want it to be?" Moira spoke as if exploring an uncharted piece of land.

"That's what we did. You two are in a more fortunate position. Leo's got the money to do it. So you won't be at the point of starving, like we were. I would not recommend that to anyone! If you don't feel right here, explore a different part of the forest. Tomorrow I suggest we take the people carrier out and go on a family adventure. Lottie would like that."

Indeed, Moira, Leo and Lee liked the idea a lot. They all went to bed happier and had to wait to see what the next day brought.

Lottie was delighted when she was told they were going on a family adventure. She made sure her favourite bear, Honey, came along too. Everyone was in high spirits as they set off into another frost-covered morning. Today though, the sun was not quite so bright and there was a hint of dark clouds looming in the distance.

Lee drove them into a part of the forest Moira had not explored before, not too far from where Cathy lived; a village called Burley. It was a little village, nestling at the bottom of a winding hill where ponies roamed freely. They pulled into the car park and to Moira's delight, there were ponies standing in a few of the parking spaces. People just seemed to work around them.

"Mummy, can I have some fudge please?" cooed Lottie.

"Oh, chocolate fudge from the fudge shop, yum. Mummy, can I have some fudge?" Leo teased.

THE FOOL'S JOURNEY

"Pair of you! What hope have I got?" Cathy laughed.

Lee added, "If I'm a good boy, can I have some too?"

With a twinkle in her eye, Cathy said, "It's you being a bad boy that got me into this mess." She said patting her swollen stomach. "Thanks, you two," she added talking to her belly.

"They want fudge too!" Leo suggested.

"OK, OK! We'll go and get some fudge."

Laughing happily, they walked across the car park and through the little gate, which led to the courtyard area where the fudge shop was situated.

The sweet smell of fudge greeted them as they walked through the doors. The girl behind the counter smiled warmly and greeted them. However, after a few minutes her expression took on a flustered look. As the orders were mounting up she was becoming confused on who wanted how much of what. Having decided that vanilla and chocolate fudge was the one for her and given Cathy the money for it, Moira wandered out of the shop to have a look around. There were a couple of gift shops, one that sold clothing, a tearoom and an estate agent. As the others still had not come out, Moira treated herself to a pair of gloves from the tiny little clothes shop. She stopped to pull them on, gazing with only vague interest into the window of the estate agent. Then she saw it.

Excitedly, not caring what people thought, Moira ran the few steps to the fudge shop. The rest of them were coming out with a carrier bag laden full of fudge.

"I've found it!" she gasped. "I've found it!" she said, emphasising the words as they stood there looking at her agog. Light dawned on Cathy first.

"Show me." Almost pulling her over, Moira showed Cathy the house she had seen in the window.

"There. That one."

By this time, Leo was standing behind her.

THE FOOL'S JOURNEY

"That's over half the price which we've been looking at. It quite clearly states it's in need of modernisation. My gosh girl, you might have it."

Before even Moira could move or speak, Leo was pushing the door of the estate agent open. Cathy looked across at Lee, who was last to realise what was happening and smiled. "Remind you of anyone?" he whispered and held Cathy tight. Lottie looked on bemused by her aunt and uncle's apparent loss of senses and munched a piece of fudge.

A short while later, Leo and Moira came out the estate agent smiling broadly. "We've got a viewing in half an hour. It's vacant possession, as the lady that lived in it passed on a few months back. Instructions have only just been issued," they explained excitedly. They wandered around the rest of the shops, passing time until they found one called The Witches Coven. Of course they were almost made late by Moira spending so much time pawing over decks of tarot cards and wistfully looking at the assortment of witch type stuff they stocked. Leo dragged her out, and they ran back to the car. Leo gave them directions, and they arrived at the house, just as the estate agent drove up.

A red-bricked house stood in front of them, with tired windows that needed replacing and guttering hanging off at an angle. The paint on the front door was peeling. The garden, although overgrown, was just about manageable, its growth halted by the winter. There were well-organised borders, with some stunning evergreen shrubs with variegated leaves. The estate agent let them in to the house. The house had not been given the same love as the garden. Yellow, large floral print wallpaper hung peeling from the walls. The original floorboards lacked polish or wax but were structurally sound. They were shown into a lounge area, where an open fireplace housed some plant life, hastened on by the relative warmth of the room.

The kitchen was large and old. Half the cupboards were missing doors. Those that did have any were screwed shut. There was a solid fuel range cooker, standing forlornly in an alcove on one wall. Lottie drew close to her mum as they wondered around the house. The dining room

THE FOOL'S JOURNEY

looked out onto a terraced garden. The patio was flanked with balustrades with steps down to formal borders and beyond were well-tended lawns. Inside, the plaster had fallen away, leaving exposed latticework beneath. There were a couple of other rooms on the lower floor, one with an ancient bathroom. The agent explained this room had been locked and boarded over. The suite looked like something from the Victorian era.

The house comprised three floors. The second floor had four large bedrooms and a more modern and functioning bathroom. One room was well decorated. The room's walls were sound and were painted in a milky coffee colour. The colour of the walls could be barely seen behind the bookshelves that flanked two sides of the room. Although a lot of the books had been removed, a few, on horticulture remained. The third floor was an old nursery. The one eyed, broken legged rocking horse discarded in the corner made Lottie cry. Cathy led her from the room and out into the hallway.

"Why is the house so unloved, Mummy?"

Cathy looked down at her daughter inquisitively. "Why do you say it is unloved, darling?"

"Because it feels sad."

Cathy just held Lottie close. Words did not express the emotions she felt.

A short while later, they were all back out under the increasingly grey sky. The agent did not try to sell the house to them. Moira wondered why.

"We'll make you an offer," Leo said, after exchanging a look with Moira, who nodded almost imperceptibly. The estate agent looked like a rabbit caught in the glare of a vehicle's headlights.

"You want to buy it? Can you afford it?"

Moira could not help herself. She burst out laughing.

"Yes." She and Leo answered in unison.

Moira saw the calculating look in the agent's eye and added, "With the level of work that needs doing, including re-wiring and plumbing, we won't be offering you the full amount. That would be pushing our budget a bit." She suggested a figure.

Cathy started to cough to hide the laughter she felt spilling over. Lottie kept a very straight face for a five-year-old.

While they looked around the house again and some hurried conversation into his mobile, the agent came back and said, "The solicitors responsible for selling the property have suggested they meet you half way on figures."

Leo looked at Moira, and Cathy hid herself from view this time.

"Subject to survey, we will meet you there."

It was done. After months of heartache and frustration, on a whim they had just made an offer on a house that needed a lot of love. Moira and Lee held hands and looked at the green in front of them, at the trickling brook and enclosed woodland beyond. They knew they had come home.

Moira and Leo found themselves being picked up and dropped down again, as if swept up by a tornado. The house they were buying was structurally sound, but the wiring and plumbing were in a shocking state. Contracts were completed and they took possession of the keys of their new home. Standing in the hallway once again, despite the chill wind of the late February day, the house felt warm. They walked around the house making notes whilst Leo phoned his various contacts, including his cousins. Within a few days the first of them visited, made assessments and scheduled when to start work.

It was one day in early March, daffodils had started blooming in the garden, and the house did not know what had hit it. Plaster was stripped off walls, electrics were strung and new pipes were installed. Dust and debris were everywhere. Amid the chaos, Moira wondered what the heck they had done.

At the end of March, when Leo was away on a business trip, she drove herself down to the New Forest to talk to the local tradesman they had chosen. He was to fit a bespoke kitchen in keeping with the character

THE FOOL'S JOURNEY

of the house. She had just turned off the main road when her car disgorged a puff of smoke. She had just pulled it to the edge of the road when her bonnet burst into flames. Choking on the smoke, Moira managed to grab her handbag and phone and leapt out of the car. Her clothes that were in a holdall in the boot had gone up in smoke as the car burned and smoldered on the edge of the road. Her beloved little car was gone. She had had it since she had started work all those years ago. It had only been serviced earlier this week and now, along with some of her clothes, was gone. It felt that her last connection to the woman she was and the life she had led before was gone. Part of her felt sad. All that she had strived for, she had cut loose, yet still tried to retain certain elements. She tried to hold onto her financial independence, her aspiration to be an astute businesswoman and her car. Now it was gone, including the laptop that held those ideas. Shaking from cold and shock, she first dialed the fire service, not wanting a forest fire to start, as March had been unseasonably dry. She then rang Leo.

It was only a few minutes before she heard the wail of the siren of the approaching fire engine. Moira sat, feeling lonely with part of her world up in smoke in front of her. She let tears fall; holding them back would only sharpen the pain. It was like this that the firemen found her, her face blackened from the smoke and the tracks of her tears evident for all to see. One of them, a big fellow who dwarfed his fellow firefighters, put an arm around her.

"Hey up. At least you're safe."

Moira looked up at him with tear-reddened eyes.

"Thankfully, yes I am." She added with returning humour, "Well I better ring the poor carpenter who's coming to measure up today for my new kitchen."

"You're Moira McNally?"

"Yes," Moira answered with puzzlement in her voice.

"Then, I am he. I'm Chris. Burley fire station is manned by reserve fire fighters," he explained.

THE FOOL'S JOURNEY

"Oi, Chris, stop chatting up the birds and give us a hand," one of the other firefighters shouted, grinning.

Moira watched as her carpenter and the rest of the crew covered the remains of her car and the flames in foam. All that was left was a blackened shell. Moira recognised the black people carrier haring up the hill towards them. It drew to a halt and out jumped Cathy, moving more like a waddling duck than a running woman, heavy now with two children and only a month or so away from her due date. With a hefty sigh, she sank to her knees and hugged Moira.

Moira rang Liz, who was looking after the cats and Bruno, despite Moira offering to put them in kennels and cattery. She firmly disagreed, saying that it was the least she could do after causing such a hassle last time. Moira explained what had happened, explaining that she was going to be away longer than overnight. Liz cheerily agreed and said that Bruno was so adorable she wanted to get herself a dog just like him. Leo rang to say he was flying back from his meeting a day early and that he was too worried to concentrate despite Moira's insistence that she was fine. Once Lottie had finished school, they had gone shopping in the nearest town, so that Moira could buy replacement clothes. Whilst she was there, they visited a bear factory where she bought Lottie a special pink bear to celebrate her becoming a big sister. Lottie named it Candyfloss. Despite feeling shocked and still a bit wobbly, Moira felt she had changed as a person, perhaps a stronger one, but she certainly felt more centred.

When Leo arrived the next morning, he took her out car shopping. They had driven straight to a BMW garage. When they got there, Moira protested that she could not afford one of these. Leo had given her a look, the one that suggested she was fighting a losing battle and she succumbed in silence. It was as they approached the showroom that Moira's dream changed.

There on a ramped stand, all pretty in cherry red was a Mini. It had a white roof and white bonnet stripes, lovely five-spoke alloy wheels and when she walked around the front, its spotlights mounted on the front grill and the scoop on the bonnet for the turbo made it look so cute, she fell in love with it immediately.

Quite some time later with Leo shaking his head with the fickleness of women, they had bought the car and arranged for collection a few days later after the paperwork had been processed. Moira could not wipe the grin off her face, in spite of the weather turning foul and wet. If she closed her eyes, she could feel the sensation of speed as she eased the gas pedal down; the car did not drive, it flew.

That was it. The kitchen had been commissioned and fitted. The bathroom upstairs was refitted, an ensuite added to the master bedroom and a further bathroom was added to the attic rooms. The bathroom downstairs had been stripped out and was now Leo's home office. A lot of the house still needed decorating and the windows and door replacing, but today was the day. Moira stood outside what once had been her cottage, watching the last of her furniture and boxes being loaded onto a removal van. Leo had already gone with the cats and Bruno chased his tail at Moira's feet. Bruno was uncertain what was going on, but sensed that it was something exciting. The clang of the removal van's door signaled the end to what once was. Liz came up the hill from the pub, carrying a large box.

"Phew, I'm not too late. I overslept. I had to run an errand," she said, lowering the box to the floor.

"I wouldn't have gone without saying goodbye," Moira stated, hugging her one time boss and now friend.

"What do you get your favourite girl, who's going off to marry Prince Charming himself?"

"Prince Charming who does not empty his pockets before putting his trousers in the wash. Prince Charming who has a habit of discarding his socks willy nilly."

"Yeah, that's the one," Liz said, grinning. "So I got you this." She stooped down and opened the box. "Bruno's outnumbered with two cats." She lifted out a blue roan Cocker Spaniel, wearing a very large pink bow. "I heard of a breeder in Pembroke with a litter ready. I went down

THE FOOL'S JOURNEY

there to get myself one, which I did, but there were only two left and I couldn't choose between them. So I bought them both. This one is for you and Fang is being entertained back in the pub as we speak."

"Fang? You called a Cocker Spaniel, Fang!" Moira said with amusement. She looked at the grin on Liz's face. "What have you called this one?" She asked, indicating the puppy now in Liz's arms.

"Twinkle! But you can change it. I could choose their registered names."

"I like the name Twinkle, although I have a funny feeling Leo will twist it."

"You bet he will, "Liz said, handing over the puppy. "You don't think I didn't think of that when naming her?"

Moira hugged Liz tight. "Come down and see us. Bring Fang to play with his sister." Bruno was greatly interested in this new arrival and pawed at Moira's legs for a closer look. Moira bent down and Bruno gave Twinkle a lick on the nose, indicating his approval.

"I'll miss you, Liz. You've been fantastic to me."

"Go now you daft sot, you'll have me blubbing like a baby. Be sure to make sure you get the guest room sorted. I've not been down to the New Forest, so as soon as Fang has had his last jabs, we'll be down."

Moira loaded her two dogs into the back of the Mini, thankful she had bought the Countryman with at least some boot. She waved at Liz and with a mixture of emotions drove off and onto her new life. What that would hold, would be anyone's guess.

CHAPTER NINETEEN – THE STAR
Hope – Inspiration – Generosity – Serenity

With the dogs asleep in the boot and the chest nestled in its pink blanket behind her seat, Moira crossed over the Severn Bridge with only a small pang of sadness. She patched a call through to Leo, grateful the car came with a hands-free kit.

"You're in England then, I take it," Leo boomed over the radio speakers.

"Yep, just crossed the bridge. Err…Liz stopped by with a present for me."

"That's nice, what did she get you?"

"A friend for Bruno."

"Oh God alive, not two weeing little tikes!" Leo chuckled

"Yes, she's named this one with you in mind."

"Go on, deal it. What's she called it?"

"Twinkle."

The laughter that burst from the car's loudspeaker stirred the dogs in the boot. "We've got ourselves a widdling winkle."

Moira grinned. "Yes, funny, that's the association I thought you would make. I'll stop at Warminster services for a coffee and give the dogs a stretch. I should be with you in a couple of hours. I passed the removal van on the motorway, I should be there before them. Did your stuff come out of storage OK?"

"Yes, it did. It should be here tomorrow as arranged. Wait until I tell Lottie about the new dog. She'll want to see it right away."

"Leo, you promised."

"True my love, I did. Today is just for us. I'll let you tell her later, when it'll be too late to come over."

THE FOOL'S JOURNEY

Moira clicked off, smiling. The late April sun was warming things up a treat and leaves were bursting from the swollen buds on trees. Spring, the season of new life and hope.

She turned down the road that led to her new home. She drove through the ford and shortly after, turned across the cattle grid and onto her driveway. The garden was alive with daffodils and tulips. Herbaceous plants were rising and the deciduous shrubs were bursting into leaf. After Moira got out of the car, she stretched, taking a deep breath. The scent of the garden and the gorse out in the forest filled her senses. Letting the dogs out, she made sure the side gate was shut. From nearby, she could hear the neighing of a pony and the stream babbling along its stony bed. Birds sang high up in the trees. In front of her was her new life. The dogs tumbled and played at her feet. She waited impatiently for Leo to make the short drive from Cathy's with the cats. As she waited, she wandered around the garden. Plucking at a stray weed here and there. She happened to glance up at the window in one of the rooms upstairs. For a moment, she could not be sure, she thought she saw an old woman looking out, smiling. She decided to keep it to herself until she knew completely.

Before long, Moira heard the distinct sound of Leo's car. She picked up the dogs and watched as he swung onto the roomy driveway, his music playing; he wore a grin that filled his face.

"Come then, Miss McNally, time we enter our abode." He held his hand out and Moira took it. She put Bruno down, kept hold of Twinkle who was trying to wiggle out of her arms. They went inside their home, now empty of all trade people.

Sunlight filled the hallway. Dust motes stirred and glinted in the sun before falling back in the wake of their footsteps. The two dogs, both now down with their noses pressed against the floor, snuffed up the smells that only they could sense. Moira heaved a contented sigh.

"The house is happy. We're meant to be here. The future is ours; within this blank canvas we make our home."

THE FOOL'S JOURNEY

Leo looked at her with affection. If he had the way with words that Moira had, that would be the gist of what he thought. Instead, he said, "Fancy a quickie!"

Moira lightheartedly clouted him. "Cats in car. Two small doggies running around!"

"Worth a try," Leo conceded with a grin. He walked back towards the door. "Later?"

Moira threw her head back and laughed. She felt hope rising like the sap in the trees.

The moment of calm only lasted a short while. The animals had just been securely shut away in separate rooms when the removal van turned up. After a frantic moving of cars they squeezed the lorry onto the drive, not wanting to totally block the road. Before long, beds, boxes, sofas and saucepan racks were being carried off to their various destinations. The sun was beginning to sink lower in the sky and the chill of a spring night start to make itself felt.

Moira was upstairs making the bed and from the garden below, she could hear Leo calling, "Widdling Winkle" and "Boisterous Bruno." She smiled to herself; she had not heard him this happy in months. He had grown serious, like part of him had died when Blodwyn had passed on. There was less of the boyish enthusiasm. Here and now, it seemed to have returned. She did wonder though what the poor neighbours must think. She was soon to find out.

Moira had just come downstairs to try and get the lounge into some order, so they could at least sit down that evening, when she overheard Leo chatting to someone. Slipping on her jacket, she went out to investigate. Leaning on the gate was a man in his mid-forties, a well trained Springer Spaniel sitting at his heels. The spaniel was looking on with mild amusement as Twinkle tried to leg it over the cattle grid to see him and got herself stuck.

"Come on, Widdling Winkle," Leo said, fishing her out from between the struts. The man leaning on the gate threw back his head and laughed.

THE FOOL'S JOURNEY

"I thought I was the only one to give my dogs silly names. This here," indicating the spaniel, "is Silly Simon."

"Twinkle here was given to my fiancée from a good friend of hers as a house-warming present. Which reminds me," Leo said slapping his head, "I clean forgot to pick up a bed as I was asked."

Moira had walked over to the gate by this time.

"Looks like you're sleeping in the shed tonight then," the man said with a rough grin.

Leo flushed red when he saw Moira. "Sorry love," he said sheepishly.

"Is there a pet store around here that is open till late?" she asked the man.

"There is down in Bournemouth, but don't stress. I breed these hounds," nudging the dog with his foot. "I've got a bit of bedding and a bowl spare. By the way, my name's James. I live a couple of houses up," pointing up the road.

"Thank you," they both said in unison.

"I'm Moira, this clot is Leo. We will gratefully accept the loan and I promise himself will get some in tomorrow."

"Consider it a house warming gift to your hounds from Simon here. Tell you what, why don't one of you come up with me now?"

Moira looked down at the slippers on her feet and said, "Leo, you go, I've only got my slippers on."

That was it. Arranged. Leo walked up with James, chatting happily, and Moira took the dogs inside and introduced Twinkle to Archie and Helix.

The cats were amused by the arrival of the new puppy and took great delight in tormenting her in only the way a cat can. They let it chase them, only to find what it was chasing was wiley, devious and had sharp claws. Moira drank a cup of coffee watching the goings on of her fur babies with amusement. It was only when she returned the empty mug to the kitchen did she realise Leo had not returned. She stood in a quandary by the front door, wondering whether to ring him or go and look for him? Whether that would seem like he was hen-pecked. In the growing

THE FOOL'S JOURNEY

twilight, she saw a figure staggering down the road like a laden pack mule.

Leo saw Moira watching him with a look of puzzlement mixed with amusement on her face. She went out to greet him by the gate. Once he was inside he explained.

"James kindly gave us a nice vet bed, which can be easily washed when she wees all over it. Here is a bowl for her and a couple of days' supply of puppy food." He deposited said items on the floor. "I was then introduced to his wife Elaine, who insisted I came in for a cup of tea. She then packed me off with a cake, fresh out of the oven. Also some squeaky toys for the fur bags. I've invited them over tomorrow evening for some drinks to say thank you."

Moira laughed. "A good job that your furniture is coming in the morning, otherwise we would look like poor hosts!"

Leo smiled at her; his heart felt as light as thistledown. He himself felt a new kindling of the fire of life. What was the saying? Oh yes, that was it; hope springs eternal.

Days ran by in a semi-exhausted blur. They had visits from all the surrounding neighbours. They were given cakes, homemade wine and a host of other delightful little things including chutneys and jams. They had not met their immediate neighbours on the right yet. They were told they worked away for several months at a time, but were endorsed to be 'utterly divine'. It was one night after a busy day when they were woken by the phone ringing.

"'Ello," Leo answered sleepily.

"Cathy's gone into labour! She's a week early."

"Take her to the hospital," Leo suggested drowsily.

Moira took the phone from him. "I'll be there in under half an hour. Do you want me to stay?"

"Lottie's awake. She woke up despite us being quiet. Astute child has packed her own little case and is waiting for you."

"Clever girl. I'll be there quicker then." With that they disconnected.

THE FOOL'S JOURNEY

"Of course, Lottie!" Leo said sitting up, now semi-awake.

"I'll get her. You make sure the bed's made up."

With that, Moira threw on some clothes, ran down stairs and out the door.

When she arrived at Cathy and Lee's house, there was Lee waiting in the hall looking panicky.

"Thank god you've arrived. The contractions are coming every three minutes and an ambulance is on its way."

A bleary eyed Lottie came out from the lounge.

"Mummy's said I've been a good nurse but can go with you now."

"I'll get Lottie into the car," Lee said. "Cathy wants to see you."

Moira entered the lounge where Cathy was pacing around sweating. Then as another contraction hit, she clung to the back of the chair. Moira went over and rubbed her back. When the contraction had eased, Cathy asked, "Will it be OK?"

"Yes!"

"If I don't make it and the babes do, will you help Lee?"

"Yes, but it won't come to that."

"But..."

"Cathy, look at me." Cathy did. "Everything you fear might well happen. Are the babies moving?"

"Yes."

"Do you think the higher power, after years of barrenness would have granted you two lives, would let them or you go now?"

Cathy looked at her and said nothing.

"Trust me, everything will work out. Be brave. Be strong. Instinctively, all will be well. Now, I have your little princess to take to her castle bed Uncle Leo has had made for her."

Laughter flickered in Cathy's eyes, which passed as the next contraction hit and returned as it eased. "He'll make a great father one day."

"You concentrate on getting these two bairns out and give him something else to dote on until I'm ready!"

THE FOOL'S JOURNEY

Cathy squeezed her hand and smiled into her eyes. Moira drove back with the droopy-eyed princess, installed her into her castle bed and collapsed herself, exhausted into her own and slept like the dead.

Moira woke with a feeling of unease. She knew childbirth was not a thing to be rushed, but labour had been advancing at a fair rate. She busied herself around the kitchen, making coffee, kneading out some bread she had left to rise over night, and then once it had rested a little more, she put it in the oven. The scent of freshly brewed coffee and baking bread lured the two sleepers from their beds.

Lottie came down with tousled hair and dangling her pink bear by one leg. She was very subdued over breakfast and ate the fresh bread and drank the juice without any apparent enthusiasm. It was only when Moira was helping her get changed did she say what was up.

"I had a dream Mummy nearly died. But Granny Blodwen saved her."

Moira thought for a moment before answering. Her initial reaction was to reassure the child all was fine, but then this girl was too astute to take flannel. Instead, she said, "If Granny Blodwen did save her, then she'll be home with your brothers or sisters really soon."

"This is true," Lottie said, her smile lighting up her face. "I hope I have a brother, well at least one. Then he won't try and wear my makeup or pinch my clothes when I am older."

Moira laughed, "Why do you think they'll do that?"

"Aunty May, Uncle Leo's mummy said she use to enjoy pinching her sisters' clothes. They seldom minded, but Mummy said pinching things is wrong."

Moira hugged the child to her. "It's not quite the same thing. It's different between siblings. As long as you tell them you did it, if they ask," she added as an afterthought. "I expect if you have a brother, he might borrow your music or your iPod or something like that."

Lottie grinned. "Maybe you can then put an anti boy spell on my bedroom door?"

"Hmm, you might want it removed when you're older" she teased back.

THE FOOL'S JOURNEY

Soon Lottie was nearly back to her normal self. She seemed to have one other thing on her mind however.

"Aunty Moira, did you bring the chest which belonged to the little girl who died."

"Yes."

"Can I see it?"

Moira had glossed over a lot of the details when Lottie had asked her about what happened; there are some pains a child should not endure. She questioned now whether she should let her see it. But she decided she should. She had never asked before, so this must be related in some way to her dream.

After Lottie was dressed, they mounted the stairs to the attic rooms, where Moira had installed the chest. She had periodically checked it, but it seemed quiet and content for now. Moira unwrapped the folds of blanket and gently stroked the lid.

"I've brought a little girl called Lottie to meet you."

The chest wiggled slightly. Lottie gasped and moved back fractionally. Moira kept on talking.

"Lottie's Mummy is in hospital having a baby."

Lottie moved forward and sat quietly by the side of the chest. She looked up at Moira and asked, "May I touch it?"

Moira nodded, Lottie then stroked the lid in the same way Moira had. Bravely, she did not jump when she felt the chest quiver beneath her exploring fingertips. Moira moved a little way down the room to where her desk stood in this makeshift office.

She heard Lottie chattering gently about the weather, what she did at school, who her friends were. In fact, all the things that a little girl would talk about to another little girl, who she hadn't met before. Moira could see the chest gently moving, not making any of its mad leaps or movements. Perhaps it sensed it would scare Lottie. Could it really understand? She shook her head and focused instead on the deck of cards she picked up. She thought of Lottie's dream and Cathy in the hospital. As she shuffled a card fell. Putting down the deck and stooping to pick it up, she noticed it had fallen face up. The Star. She smiled to herself. The Star was a card of hope. In the card a naked lady poured water over rocks and into the stream where she was. Behind her, there were stepping stones, and the light of dawn could be seen. She was tranquil and calm and perfectly poised. The ringing of the phone downstairs interrupted her thoughts. Lottie had heard the same noise and ceased her chattering to the chest.

They both listened for a while with strained ears. In a short while, Leo called up. "Safe delivery of two boys! Ralph and Richard. Lottie, Daddy wants to talk to you."

Lottie said bye to the chest and flew from the room on wings of joy. Moira took her place by the side of the chest and breathed a huge sigh of relief.

"I think she was worried she would be without a mummy."

The lid of the chest opened and there in the same hand as before was a note.

'My mummy went away. Where did she go?'

The chest lid closed. Moira stared at the words. "I don't honestly know. I am trying."

The lid opened again, taking Moira by surprise. 'I like it here. I like the girl.'

The chest fell silent and inert. Moira wrapped it back in the blanket, placed the two pieces of paper on her desk and went downstairs.

Over a cup of coffee a little time later, while Lottie played in the garden with the dogs, Leo explained that Cathy's heart had had problems with the delivery and they thought they were going to lose her. Moira explained what Lottie dreamt about. She looked at Leo who had gone pale.

"Lee said that once Ralph, the eldest, was born Cathy's heart started going really fast and in odd rhythms. They started talking about an emergency C-section to save the life of the second child, but they were uncertain what effect it would have on Cathy. He said he stood there with tears streaming down his face, holding his first child, praying to

THE FOOL'S JOURNEY

whoever or whatever was up there. He said when he looked over to the bed where Cathy was drifting in and out of coherency, he saw Blodwen standing there, soothing Cathy's brow. A few minutes later Rupert was born. It surprised all medics. Cathy is very weak, but oddly, the heart complications have not worsened."

Moira looked at Leo, "You doubted she was still watching over you all, like she had in life?"

"I don't think I doubted that, I think I doubted there was anything beyond the grave."

"Now?"

"Now," Leo smiled. "Now we are going to go shopping to buy our nephews some gifts and then head to the hospital in time for visiting hours. Cathy wants to see Lottie."

"You didn't answer my question," Moira prompted gently

"Now, I have you looking after me in life and her looking after me up there," Leo said, gesturing to the sky. "I've got no hope."

Moira kissed him. She called over to Lottie and once the dogs had been put away and everyone had put on their shoes and coats, they went shopping and onto the hospital. Moira mused as they drove through the forest and onto the motorway how life can be full of despair one moment and hope the next. Whilst you had hope, you had life. She now had hope, she had a good man, two newborn surrogate nephews, one surrogate little niece. Now she wondered with wry amusement, what card would be next?

CHAPTER TWENTY – THE MOON

Fear – Illusion – Imagination – Bewilderment

It had been a hot day for May. Moira had spent time digging, weeding and planting out the herb garden. It had been too nice to spend the day indoors. The sun had burnt her pale skin, despite wearing sun tan lotion and she felt stiff and sore from the exertion. She was unable to settle in the early evening. It was too early to cook dinner and Leo would not be back from work for another hour. She decided a walk in the cooler air of evening would be ideal. She scribbled a note for Leo and left it by the kettle. Calling the dogs to her, they set off.

Overhead early swallows dived in the evening light, grabbing at the buzzing insects that circled the running stream. As she passed the forest ponies, they whinnied in recognition. Moira kept the dogs on the leads until she entered the enclosed woodland at the end of the green. When they were let off, they bounded through the leaf mould, kicking up the earthy smells warmed by the day's sun. There was a light, refreshing breeze, which teased the curls of Moira's hair, enough to be refreshing but not strong enough to be a nuisance. As she walked, the aches of the day started to ease and her skin cooled by the movement of air. From side to side the dogs wove across the paths, content in their search for new scents to smell.

They walked on for about half an hour, the rhythmic motion helping her think. From out of nowhere a dear bounded across her path. Before she could call the dogs back they were off following it with great enthusiasm. Their genetic code telling them to chase, obeying the call of the hunt. Moira pursued them as quickly as she could, tripping over fallen logs and snagging her light clothes on dried branches. Her pursuit was not as graceful as theirs. She was not aware of how long she had been chasing them when eventually she found herself at another fence. The dogs were panting and whining, unable to get through where the deer had clearly leapt. She clipped them back on the leads as a way of reprimanding them for running off and did her best to find the path and the way back.

    Moira walked in one direction for a while and found that she was moving further into the woods and no sign of a path could be found. Wracking her brains, she tried to remember all the lessons she had learnt as a child about finding her way back home if she got lost. She was supposed to use the position of the sun and the time on her watch. Except in the tall pine forest she had now entered, she could not clearly make out where the sun was. The time was seven o'clock and she had been out for well over an hour already. She was thirsty after the chase and was weary from the come down after the adrenaline shot. Standing very still, she could hear the babbling of a stream over its rocky course, but could not see where it was. Walking on in a different direction, she eventually struck a path.

    The light now was dim in this forested environment, long shadows lay across the path. The scuttling of forest creatures going to their night's rest added to the eeriness she felt surrounding her. A sudden flash of inspiration struck her - her mobile! If she could ring Leo, he would be able to track her on his phone, patch that into the computer and find her way out for her. Lifting it out of its holder on her belt, she saw with dismay she had no signal. For the first time in years, Moira felt scared.

    She started jumping at the slightest sounds in the undergrowth. Twinkle was getting tired so Moira picked her up. Her warmth against her skin reassured her and settled her nerves a little. On they trod in the darkening gloom. How can she have gotten so lost?

    In the last glimmers of light she spotted the stream she had heard a while back. Thankfully, she scooped a few handfuls of water out. Not caring, Moira drank enough to slake the worst of her thirst. The dogs drank for a long time and appeared much revived by it. She sat for a while trying to gather her thoughts, trying to remember in which

THE FOOL'S JOURNEY

direction the stream that was down the road from her home flowed. Every time she tried to remember, fear welled up and drowned common sense in its wake. Leaning on her hands, she started to cry. The two dogs nuzzled their mistress in reassurance and insisted she get up and get them home. In an instant, their nuzzling stopped.

Bruno set up a low growl, the hair on his back rose. Twinkle slunk close to Moira, trying to hide under her legs whimpering. Moira felt her skin try and creep off and run away. She attempted to stand up, but her legs had turned to jelly and would not support her. On the path on the other side of the stream, from the direction she faced, she heard an odd sound. Was it the cry of an animal? Was it something else?

With her heart pounding and a cold sweat breaking out on her brow Moira ran blindly on along the stream edge, in the direction she thought was towards home. Around her, screeches and hoots drove her half mad with fear. With the dogs dragging on their leads, she ran on until she had no breath left. She leant forward, trying to calm her racing heart and get air into her burning lungs, breathing in through her nostrils and out through her mouth. Within a few minutes, her heart was beating nearly normally and she was breathing freely again. Her only hope lay with following the watercourse. Around her, the darkness had crept in, making it difficult to see. She would have been at risk of breaking something if she kept up this mad pursuit. She was just succeeding in steadying her nerves when from a distance she could hear the thudding of hooves. Instead of giving her hope she might be near the open, it filled her with a sense of dread.

The thudding of hooves passed, but was replaced by a lashing in the bushes, just behind her. Moira had got to her feet again by this time and was about to set off again, when a deer leapt out from behind her. This was not an ordinary deer, but the ghostly shade of a great red deer, his magnificently antlered head semi-translucent in the dim nightlight. Moira felt the wind as it leapt past her and over the stream to disappear into the same instant as landing. She was not in a position to see any more, as the shock had knocked her back and into the water.

THE FOOL'S JOURNEY

Moira sat there in the shallow stream wet through. Ironically she started to laugh. She was a witch, someone who was naturally psychic and she was jumping around being afraid of ghosts. Hadn't she a haunted chest at home? Didn't she recently help a poltergeist move across? She looked at the two dogs, with their heads to one side, looking at her with canine bemusement, wondering why their mistress was sitting in the stream laughing. Getting up and dripping with water, Moira decided it was time to get a grip of her senses and stop blundering about blindly in the night.

Although the night was warm for the time of year, she felt chilled by the wetness of her clothes and by something else, an extra dimension to the surrounding environment. The act of sitting there in the water had not only brought her to her senses regarding getting a grip on her fear, but also returned her sense of direction. She realised she had been following the stream the wrong way; the water flowed in the opposite direction. There was no choice but to retrace her steps. Now she was not jumping at every little creature noise nor rustling branch; her progress was smoother and better paced. Before too long, she found herself back at the ford where she had started. Finding the path, Moira followed the stream within a few feet for as far as she could make out. With a little more speed, she walked onwards. The breeze dried her clothes slightly and the action returned warmth to her limbs. Despite the fact she was still cold, tired, wet and hungry, she found herself with a greater degree of calmness and a second wind of renewed energy.

As she walked, Moira noticed the trees changed from just pine, to the mixed broadleaf species in the woods near where home was. She still did not recognise where they were, but the scenery was changing. She must have passed through a broken fence or something somewhere, she mused, as her senses settled. The trees were normally segregated. Just as she was pondering this, she heard the distant thud of horse hooves again. The dogs slunk in behind her, their hackles up and they growled softly at the path ahead of her. There was nothing perceptible, but as she edged forward, she could feel a distinct cold spot. In the instant she recognised

THE FOOL'S JOURNEY

it, the sound was immediately gone. Fear had now been replaced by curiosity. Her curiosity soon was to be hammered out and remade on the anvil of experience.

Moira was certain she was getting closer to home. When she checked the time again, it showed it was just after eight o'clock. Probably outside this wooded darkness, twilight still lingered. The dogs too, seem to sense they were getting closer. They perked up their ears and picked up their step. Moira looked down with anxiety at Twinkle, but the pup seemed to be doing OK, perhaps keen now to get to her warm bed and bowl of food. She wondered how long she had chased around after the dogs. Noticing that her mobile now had a signal, she called Leo, but as she selected his number from the memory list, the phone's batteries died. She knew it had been fully charged when she left, she had removed it from the charger and remembered checking. A strange sense crept over her; it was not quite fear returning but a degree of something unsettling about where she was headed.

The sound of galloping hooves came again, this time more than a single set, perhaps two or three, but no more. Through the silent night air came the distant sound of a hunting horn being blown. The dogs, instead of pricking up their ears, shrank back and closer to Moira. On the breeze that stirred, Moira could make out the faint sounds of hounds baying. Not liking the feeling, she hurried forward. In front of her, on the path, was a hound, a single ghostly hound with red eyes. Moira screamed. The hound disappeared. She fingered the pentacle she wore round her neck and uttered a small prayer to the Lord and Lady for protection. She hoped it was just black hounds that were the harbingers of doom and not brown and white ones.

The sound of the hunting horn and the baying of hounds drew closer, Moira thought she could hear the distant shout of 'Tally ho'. The distinct sound of a whip being cracked tore the night apart. The thudding of horses hooves could be heard louder now, too many sets to distinguish the exact number. The horn sounded like it came several hundred metres along the path in front of her. Unsure what to do for the best, Moira moved to the side, onto the soft turf edge that bordered the hard gravel. The sensation beneath her feet seemed to unsettle her; it was like the feeling of stones beneath her feet gave her some reassurance and a link with reality. The sound of horses' hooves thudding in gallop approached her.

    Moira could now hear the baying of the hounds upon her. As they passed her by, she couldn't make out any sound other than their voices, their padded feet made a muffled noise. An unearthly shout. 'Tally ho, there she goes' and the baying hounds changed direction and ran into the woods on her left. She could make out the thrashing of bushes and the lolling of tongues; it seemed the hounds where close to their prey. The sound of horses was upon Moira; she could hear their snorting breath, thudding hooves. She could smell the horse sweat and feel the texture of the air change, like a rushing wind, yet nothing could be seen. There was a jumble of cries around her, blood was up and they were near the kill. She stopped. As they passed her by, the dogs pressed close to the ground and whimpered. The feeling passed. She was about to step back onto the firmness of the path, but the dogs would not move. A lone horseman riding a spectral image of a great big cob came galloping up and reined in by her. She saw him stand up in the saddle and with the twitch of the reins, spun his steed around and leapt straight over her. Instinct had made her duck, but as she did so, she slipped and her arm struck something hard in the turf. Dimly aware of the shape of the girth and the horse's belly, Moira lay there and watched. Although there was reminiscence of primeval fear, it was the main emotion of curiosity that now had shaped itself into firm fascination.

    A flood of weariness swept over Moira, everything hurt, and her evening walk to ease the stiffness of doing the gardening had gone wildly astray. Through all the other pain, like a fiery lance, the pain from her arm where it had hit something hard, came piercing through. She plodded onwards, tripping over her own feet from time to time. She was beginning to give up on getting out of here when the dogs' ears pricked up and they started to wag their tails.

THE FOOL'S JOURNEY

Moira stared into the gloom, unable to see what had caused the dogs so much joy. She then heard her name being called by an unfamiliar voice.

"Moira."

"Here," she croaked. She cleared her voice and started again. "Here."

Then the familiar voice and the weaving of lights could be heard and seen.

"Thank God!"

Moira was aware of running feet and the panting of dogs. James and Leo came into view, with Simon the Spaniel running on ahead of them.

Relief consumed Moira and she began to cry. She stumbled forward with the dogs straining at their leads.

"How did you find me?"

Before he would answer, Leo hugged her close. She yelped as he squeezed her injured arm. Releasing her, he took the dogs from her and held her good hand. It was James that answered.

"Leo came up to us saying that you had not returned from your walk and asked if we'd seen you."

"I came back later than expected," he explained. "There was an accident on the motorway and you weren't back. At first I thought nothing of it, but there was no dinner on, nothing to show you'd been in for a while. I know James walks his dog about this time of day so I went to ask him."

"Elaine grew worried," James explained. "I've learnt to listen to her. As it was, Simon had not had his walk because I was caught in the same traffic chaos as Leo. He caught a sound or a smell of something a little while back and we had to hasten as much as possible to keep up with him and not trip. I wondered at first whether he was on the scent of a deer, but he did not deviate from the path."

"Are we far from home? I am cold, wet and ache all over, and my arm hurts."

"Ten minutes walk at most. Not far now."

THE FOOL'S JOURNEY

They all headed back towards home. The reassuring warmth of Leo's hand in her's gave Moira the strength to carry on. She really wondered what they would make of what had happened to her.

CHAPTER TWENTY ONE – THE SUN

Enlightenment – Greatness – Vitality – Assurance

It was only as they left the woodland, that all the dogs seemed to relax. Twinkle kept tripping over her own feet with weariness. James scooped her up in one big arm and got an approving nod from his dog Simon. Bruno with all the enthusiasm of a puppy, but with the added stamina of being nearly a year old, ran circles, quite literally, around them.

"He's a game young fellow. Good sturdy stock that," said James when they were crossing the green heading towards Leo and Moira's house. "Have you had him done yet?"

"No," Leo replied. "We never got around to it."

"He'll be good for breeding, given a bit more maturity."

"Maybe," Leo conceded "For now, like me, I bet he's ready for his supper."

With the thought of food and warmth, they hastened the last few hundred metres to the gate of the house.

Moira stretched out to slide the bolt back on the gate with the arm she had hurt and winced. She tried to stifle it, so neither of the men saw, but James had caught it.

"I'll take Simon home and let Elaine know you're back safe and sound. I'm sure she'll want to see for herself. Then she can have a look at that arm of yours. You know she's a trained nurse?" James grinned at Moira, barely perceptible in the dim twilight, but she caught it, smiled back and merely said, "Thank you."

It was a little longer than a few minutes before Elaine came down. Enough time for Leo to feed the dogs and Moira to strip, with a little help, out of wet clothes and shower. Moira could not quite manage to manoeuvre her arm into the sleeve of her dressing gown. Instead she wrapped the shawl she had received from her mum at Christmas around her shoulders. The softness of the wool felt like a balm to her weary soul. She had just finished dressing and was heading back downstairs when the doorbell rang.

Leo opened the door and there stood Elaine, with a bag slung over her shoulder and a pan in her hands.

"I thought Moira would want to get cleaned up and warm," Elaine said, eyeing Moira coming down the stairs. "Men never think of these things."

Leo knew better than to argue with a statement such as this, as it had been Moira herself who had organised such happenings and eased his worries by doing so.

"You look tired girl. Leo, go light the fire, she'll need warming through properly."

"Thanks Elaine." Moira said and watched as Leo sheepishly went about doing what he was told.

"Let's get you into the lounge and look at you. While we do, I'll set this onto the cooker to warm through. I'd made a big pot of stew up. The boys were out at football and rugby. I didn't know what time James would be back. This was the easiest meal to feed three hungry men. Although, I reckon those boys will be hungry again before bed and searching for the apple pie I've made."

Moira went into the lounge, musing how Elaine managed to keep her work up to date, running a home and kennels. Moira had heard that Elaine also did voluntary work at a homeless drop-in centre in Southampton a couple days a week. Elaine's eldest boy was due to go to university in September and had won a place with a rugby scholarship as well as getting his predicted grades. As rough and tough as the lad may have seemed, he had chosen a university only a hour or so drive away from home, so he could be far enough to sow his wild oats, as James had put it, but close enough to run home to Mum when he was hungry and needed his washing doing. No sooner had Leo got the fire lit, Elaine had

THE FOOL'S JOURNEY

bustled back in the room and sent him to watch that the stew did not boil up and just simmered until warm. Moira then realised how she did it. She had a matron's tone of voice, the one that said 'thou shall not disobey!" However, she found usually with Leo it was best to let him think any idea was his own.

Elaine examined her arm and considered it badly bruised but did not think it was broken. She told Moira if it was any more swollen or painful in the morning to go down to the hospital. In the meantime, she prescribed rest and painkillers. She left them to eat the stew she had brought, saying that if she left the boys for too long, they would eat her out of house and home. It was said in the mildly tolerant but fully affectionate way mothers use to describe their offspring. Moira and Leo enjoyed the stew, although not something they normally ate because they never thought forward enough to plan to cook it. Moira noted, as she dozed in the firelight, no one had asked her anything, not even Leo. Apart from how did she get lost. Maybe it was best left unsaid.

The month of May ended in a deluge of rain. Farmers stressed about crops being ruined and wheat prices being high with low yields. Leo and Moira watched with interest as the stream down from them grew deep and was for a day or two impassable by the ford. The twins continued to thrive and Lottie relished the idea of being an older sister. Cathy returned back to full health and fitness, and despite being a little weary, she was again showing what a natural mum she was to her two youngest offspring. Lee lost his worried haggard look. Leo was busy looking at rescuing another business and was feeling great. The only small fly in the ointment of contented life, was Moira's feeling of being aimless. For as long as she had known, she had been driven, with a goal to achieve or something to overcome. In between pottering happily in the garden, she decorated the house, room by room. Something was still lacking though. Being the domesticated goddess was not her cup of tea, and in fact her baking talents were not always well received. But what was it she should do?

THE FOOL'S JOURNEY

June was nondescript. There was neither enough sun nor enough rain to keep various factions of society happy. But for time being Moira was happy. She had planned an outside feast for Midsummer's Day, something she had always wanted to do as a child. Leo, with his boyish enthusiasm had agreed and bounded off to start getting another failing business he had just purchased back on track. For most of the early part of June, Moira only saw him in the evenings. Sometimes he would work late into the night before collapsing into bed. She didn't mind; her own mind was busy with organising a marquee in case it rained, organising caterers and a firework display. She had set up a workroom in one of the attic rooms, the one where the chest was kept. Moira took to making name cards and little favours normally only found at weddings, but she wanted this to be the feast of her dreams. In her dreams, she had little boxes, which contained jellybeans. She doubted whether all her guests would appreciate it, but she loved the idea.

It was several days before Midsummer's Day, when the weather switched to boiling hot. Leo now spent more time around the house, now that he had got, as he called it, his crack team in and was generally back to being his lion-like self. Bouts of energy and enthusiasm returned to his natural laid back attitude. It was one day when Moira had come downstairs from crimping edges and writing people's names in curly script, that she found Chris, Leo's occasional chauffeur, standing in her hallway grinning.

"Hi Chris," Moira said with enthusiasm, she liked his gentle nature and quiet manner. Leo came out from his home office.

"Right, that's sorted," he said to Chris, not noticing Moira at first. "Good timing, love. Go wash the glitter off your nose, we're just going to the cottage we've got Chris," he said winking roguishly.

Moira popped into the downstairs cloakroom and wrestled her unruly hair into shape and removed said glitter. She hummed to herself. She really was going to enjoy this next bit. They had sought tirelessly to move Chris nearer and eventually a cottage had turned up. Good timing

THE FOOL'S JOURNEY

too. She really could use his help in fetching the flowers and things for the forthcoming party.

Leo drove them the few miles into the village on the edge of the forest where the cottage was. It had been a cracking find. They had been tipped off by a friend of their solicitor Tristan, who was in the process of going through probate on it. Leo looked at it. It needed a little décor but all systems were modern. He made an offer and it was accepted on the spot. Moira had popped over to make sure things were clean and tidy. Now the day had come. They would show Chris. This would probably be his home until the day he died. If Chris got married and predeceased his wife, then the widower would still be able to live rent-free. It offered long-term investment potential, so it was a win-win situation all rounds.

It was a charming little cottage, with a red-tiled roof and whitewashed walls. Roses grew around the door, in full bloom at this time of year. The front garden had been planted in a low maintenance cottage style; the back garden had run to overgrown grass. There were three decent-sized bedrooms upstairs, with a bathroom and a kitchen/diner and separate lounge downstairs. As they pulled up Moira heard Chris gasp.

She turned in her seat to see the big man's eyes were glinting with tears. He had both hands pressed against his face.

"It's Gran's old cottage! How did you know?"

"It was a friend of Tristan who alerted us of the fact this was available. Tristan looked through the papers and noticed that the owner prior to the one that recently passed on had the same surname as you. He rang his friend back, called in a favour and made sure it did not hit open market until I'd viewed it. Too good to over look!" Leo explained.

Moira and Leo stayed outside, whilst Chris went and looked around his new abode. He came out a little while later with tears streaming down his cheeks. Unable to say a word, he clapped Leo on the shoulder and hugged Moira tightly.

"Your furniture should be here tomorrow. You can stay with us if you want tonight?"

THE FOOL'S JOURNEY

"No, it's fine, thank you. I've got my overnight kit in the car, I'll bunk down in my sleeping bag and get cracking at stripping back some of the garish wallpaper. I don't think I can ever thank you both enough."

After locking up, they drove back to their home and watched with light hearts as Chris went away to go and live in his gran's old cottage.

The day before the party dawned bright and clear. Moira was up with the dogs walked before Leo had crawled out of their bed. On the whiteboard she had hung on the kitchen wall, she made a schedule for the next two days. The dogs were wandering around, lost at being walked so early, the cats were perched on the bar stools that lined the breakfast bar watching her with intent. Leo shook his sleepy head at the scene and poured coffee.

"I need you to go down with Chris and get the flowers about midday. Before that, I need you dressed. The marquee is coming to be put up in about half an hour. I have to pop to the party store and pick up the helium balloon tank and balloons. I promised Lottie she could help me blow them up, as it's an inset day at school. I will pick her up on the way through. OK?"

Leo's answer was a salute: she threw the board rubber at him, which missed by a mile and was then chased around the floor by Twinkle. The cats, with a feline's instinct for self-preservation, slinked out into the garden to hunt mice.

The day was too hot and the air too still. Moira drove the short way back across the forest with Lottie in the backseat worrying about the clouds building up on the horizon. When Moira got back home, she was relieved to see the marquee was up and the house locked up, despite Leo's car being on the driveway. That meant he had gone to get the flowers. They had only just got the stuff from the car into the house when the black clouds sped up their advancement and congregated overhead. Moira opened the back door to find both cats waiting, looking heavenwards with wary glances. She left the door open as the kitchen was too warm; the cats howled until she closed it. None too soon, rain

THE FOOL'S JOURNEY

poured down, driven against the house by the wind on the edge of the thunder cell. Overhead thunder cracked and lightning stabbed.

"Cool!" exclaimed Lottie, munching at the grapes in the bowl on the counter, which Moira had given her. Moira normally loved thunderstorms, but she watched with anxiety as the winds whipped around the flaps of the marquee making it sway slightly. Rain swirled and gushed; the wind eased but the thunder and rain rumbled on for over half an hour. It stopped with the same rapidity it had started. Moira opened the backdoor and the smell of damp earth after summer rain hit her. The mixtures of scents from leaves and flowers, the rich earthiness of the soil and the damp warm pavements and brickwork made an intoxicating smell. The air was less heavy; whilst still warm, it was not the baking heat of the last few days. The wind seemed to have changed direction. All boded well for the next day. For now, there were balloons to inflate.

Moira set her alarm and was awake before the sun rose. Whilst she waited for the coffee to brew, she shuffled the deck of tarot cards she kept in a carved wooden box on a shelf in the kitchen. She drew The Sun, biting her lip to stifle the laugh that leapt there. She hoped that it was a good omen for the day, but also wondered what the message was. Either way it was an appropriate card for Midsummer's Day. With Helix and Archie following her, Moira went out to watch the sunrise. Sitting there on one of the benches in the garden, mug of steaming coffee in her hand, wrapped in a dressing gown against the early chill, she watched the fiery ball climb slowly into the sky. The weather boded well; she felt the blood coursing through her veins. Life at this moment felt great. Moira went back inside. There was much to do today. Her parents and Leo's parents were coming to stay. There were last minute decorations to sort. But for now, she snuck back to bed to cuddle up to the one she loved. and perhaps, doze for a while. After all, it was going to be a long night.

Moira ended up going back to sleep and was awoken suddenly by the noise of the doorbell. She opened one sleep-encrusted eye and looked at the time: half past eight. She had intended to be up again over an hour and a half ago. Who was ringing the doorbell this early? Nudging Leo with her elbow, she said, "Someone at the door, come on we've overslept."

Before he could answer, she had picked up her discarded dressing gown, covering her short pajamas for decency and went to see who it was this early.

When Moira opened the door it revealed not only her parents standing there beaming, but also Leo's. They had become close friends, to such a degree her parents were selling their home and moving nearer Leo's, as they liked the area better. Shaking her head about the unpredictability of parents, she let them in.

"Surprise!"

Leo was coming down the stairs, his hair tousled from sleep, wearing a pair of boxer shorts. He took one look at who was there, ran back upstairs and came down a short while later in a dressing gown too.

Moira had never been so grateful for the arrival of visitors. Leo's mum made everyone breakfast and while she did so, she explained that Moira's parents had come the night before. They had all gone to bed early intending to rise and see the sun do the same. They did so, and as they were so excited, they chose to drive down to Moira's immediately. Moira's mum went and walked the dogs. Leo's dad and Moira's dad set about moving the cars and reorganising things so the catering lorry could get onto the drive. Just by having them there and the way they shared the jobs and organised things meant Moira was less stressed and enjoyed the process more. When the catering lorry turned up mid-morning, Moira started to worry about the space left for those who were driving and not staying. James came to the rescue and all their cars were moved onto his driveway. A host of small, inconsequential problems kept Moira on her toes until six o'clock in the evening.

The clock in the hall chimed the hour and Moira opened the door to the first guests: Cathy and Lee, the twins in arms and Lottie in her best party dress. They were only coming for a few hours as the twins were

THE FOOL'S JOURNEY

still waking in the night several times. The party would go on too late for Lottie, despite her protests that she was old enough. This was the children's party. The neighbours with children of a similar age soon arrived too. There were jelly and ice cream and cakes and a man called Mr. Magic who entertained them with tricks, balloons and a puppet show. As she watched the show and heard the delightful squeals of the youngsters, she was grateful she had found MKP entertainment on the Internet – they were proving to be a hit. When the sleepy and protesting children were ushered off to their beds and the lawn cleared of their mess, then the real magic began.

The garden was decked with tiny twinkling lights. They were strung around the marquee, over the trees. Nestled in the flowers, individual lights shone, the flaps of the marquee were rolled up and the scents from the bowls of lilies and roses that adorned the tables inside, wafted out into the evening air. Up on the patio, a string quartet played. The haunting strains of Gershwin's 'Summertime' floated in the air. Greeting the guests as they arrived. Waitresses circled with trays of glasses filled with champagne. When they sat down for the meal, a group of medieval music-makers circled and played. Drinks flowed and all had a good time. No one got wildly drunk and many danced their way into the wee hours of the morning. As the last of the guests went home or to their beds or sleeping bags on the dining room floor, Moira sat wrapped in a blanket, nestled against Leo's shoulder.

"Thank you for letting me do this," she said softly.

"My pleasure. Do you know how many people came up to me this evening and said how lucky I was? Not only did I have a beautiful fiancée, but also one who made each person she met feel special. Why don't you do something that helps people feel better about themselves?"

"You're drunk and babbling," Moira giggled.

"Maybe, but think it over. Now wife-to-be, to our bed we go."

As they sunk gratefully into the soft mattress of their bed and into sleep, Moira laid awake long enough to ponder whether Leo did have something there in his suggestion. As she drifted off to sleep, the early

THE FOOL'S JOURNEY

sun rose. Little did she know then, within her an awakening was beginning.

CHAPTER TWENTY TWO – JUDGEMENT

Judgement – Rebirth – Inner Calling – Absolution

The sun had lost its early glare and was riding high in the sky before the partygoers from the night before stirred from their slumber. Moira woke to the smell of bacon and coffee. Leo, too, rolled over and woke.

"Mum," he said dopily. "It's a day after a party, bacon sandwiches will be being made, coffee will be on and a jug of juice on the table."

"This is our home!" Moira exclaimed, but with amusement.

"She'd do it in Buckingham Palace," Leo said, rolling out of bed and struggling into some clothes. "You once asked me whether your mediocre domestic skills bothered me. Can you remember what I said?"

"Yes," Moira said, slipping on her dressing gown. "You worked hard so that you could afford someone to cook for you and clean for you. If the woman you fell in love with could do these things, then fine. But you did not want to marry a woman like your mother, as much as you love her."

"Now you know why. You cook decent, tasty food. Not Masterchef, but I've eaten worse in restaurants. You enjoy pottering about in the home, but you yearn for more than that. I just want you to be happy."

Moira hugged him. "Now, what will make me happy is one of those bacon sandwiches!"

Moira mused as she came downstairs that their conversation had just lifted a weight off her mind. Oddly, she felt she had been brought before a judge and deemed to be worthy of something. She shook her head, reckoning the night before had riddled her senses. Looking around she saw that several other guests were in varying states of consciousness and dress.

THE FOOL'S JOURNEY

Sure enough, on the breakfast bar in the kitchen stood a plate full of bacon sandwiches, a jug of fresh orange juice and already half a dozen people were tucking in. Leo's mum saw them come in and waved them over to her.

"You got Moira a decent set of pans here. Do you think you could convince your dad to get me some?"

"Have I? All I did was put the money into her bank account and she chose her own! I wouldn't have a clue. But I guess I can persuade Dad you need some new pans. But Moira will have to let me know where she got them first!"

"What makes them good pans?" Moira asked in wonderment.

"The weight. They're well balanced, the pan bottoms are good thick solid ones and not warped."

"I just went into a cookware shop when I was shopping for pans and chose the set I liked the look of and felt comfiest to work with."

"There's hope for you yet girl!" Leo's mum laughed. "But hope for what? You are a fine daughter-in-law to be, but no domestic goddess. Which is just as well. Leo needs a firm hand on his reins."

Leo blushed. There were friends from years back who had been invited, including his best friend, Tristan. He could hear a distinct sniggling coming from that direction. Thankfully, the ringing of the phone interrupted any more comments.

After breakfast, a lot of the guests departed. Except their parents and Tristan, who declared they needed a few days off work and liked it here. Moira showered and changed and was being very secretive. Eventually her dad got suspicious.

"What you planning, petal?"

"Jennie's coming! Don't tell Triss, otherwise he'll run a mile and think I'm playing cupid. Jennie could not make it yesterday, so she's coming down this morning and as Triss has decided to stay…"

"You little minx. Not a word shall pass my lips. Does Leo know?"

"It was in part his idea!"

THE FOOL'S JOURNEY

She watched her dad walk off chuckling. She called the dogs to her and went out for a walk, avoiding the woodland this time and sticking to the open forest. She had not ventured in there alone since.

By the end of the weekend, her plan had worked perfectly, better than she had expected. Tristan and Jennie were getting along like a house on fire; the poor dogs had been going on frequent walks. Before everyone left on Sunday evening they announced that they were now a 'couple' and would be seeing each other a bit more. Moira's dad gave her a broad wink and with the departing cars, Moira felt another phase of her life was just beginning. As yet, she could not fathom out what it was but there was something in the air.

June passed into July and before July could pass into August, Jennie and Tristan announced they were coming down for a few days midweek, before they flew off on their first holiday together. Moira organised an outing to The New Forest show. Membership tickets were purchased. The day before the show they arrived.

Everyone got up early in order to get a good parking spot. Moira had packed a picnic breakfast into the hamper. There was crusty bread, still warm from being in the breadmaker - her oven attempts after the first time had failed - also cold sausages, cheese and fruit. There was a thermos of coffee and at the allotted hour they were meant to leave, Chris pulled up in a four-wheel drive Range Rover. The car was wearing a rather large red bow.

"Happy Birthday, darling!" Leo said, coming up from behind Moira.

"I thought we agreed this trip today was my birthday treat!"

"Yeah, birthday treat not birthday gift. I thought as much as you love your Mini and I love my BMW, we better have a car that was at least people and dog-friendly, and I know how much you want one of these."

Words failed Moira. Tears of happiness sprung and trickled down her cheeks. She looked across at Jennie. This car was a childhood dream car; they had dreamt of driving a car like this, wearing floral printed dresses

THE FOOL'S JOURNEY

and hats whilst going to race meetings. She kissed Leo, hugged Jennie, hugged Tristan and even hugged Chris.

"At least you did not say 'kids'," Moira smiled.

"No, I know you want to wait until we're married first and umm…"

Moira looked at him, growing suspicious. She did not quite trust him, but couldn't help anticipating a little surprise. He just handed her an envelope. Inside the envelope was a confirmation of a booking of a wedding to be held on Halloween.

"How?"

"You've often joked I had a finger in lots of pies. Well, you wanted to get married in a castle - a small wedding with a big party at a later date. Well that's what I've organised. Everyone was given a provisional heads up at the Midsummer's Day party, but if you agree, I'll ring the wedding planner and get things firmed up and invites and all that stuff moving."

"Agree!" she exclaimed. "You've been talking to my dad."

"Err, yes actually. He said unless I took control and arranged things, you would probably just drift on as you were." He added with an increasing degree of stubbornness in his voice, "I want you to be my wife, not fiancée, so there!"

"You, cunning, devious little…but I do love you, and of course I agree!"

"That's sorted then. This may not be a race meeting, but Chris is going to drive us to the show, as I understand the Pimm's tent there does a rather splendid mix!"

"Pimm's o 'clock," chimed Tristan, enjoying the spectacle very much and getting a few ideas of his own.

"Coffee o'clock," Moira laughed as she was ushered into the front seat of the car so she could see her present close up; the rest clambered into the back and they headed off. They felt like they were teenagers again, young, carefree and off in an old banger for their first trip without parents, instead of the plush luxury of a chauffeur driven car.

Even at this relatively early hour, they had to join a queue of traffic going into the showground, which only served to heighten the excitement. An orange tag was hung on the mirror to show they were to go to the membership car park and they eased the car into the queue. Moira let the chatter of the others and the periodic phone calls Leo seemed to be making wash over her. She reflected that this was the happiest she had been on her birthday since she was a child. Here she was just beginning a whole new life. She was marrying a man who was rich, but sensible. Even if he did occasionally like to flaunt it. She was being given a chance to do anything she wanted with her life. All she had to do was take the opportunity and make the most of it, whilst remaining in touch with her spirituality. She was brought back from her ponderings by the car moving forward at a greater speed than the snail's pace.

Before too long, they were driving over the grass and being directed to a parking space by a steward in yellow visibility vest, looking half asleep and very bored.

"He better wake up and buck up soon," Leo mused. "From what Cathy said this place gets heaving."

Once the car had been brought to a halt within its designated area, everyone bundled out and made their way to the boot where Chris had installed the picnic hamper. They looked around. There were already a couple of rows of cars and the events in the ring did not start for another half hour or so. The main event was not until lunchtime - at least that's what the programme told them. Here and there, other people were doing the same thing: having a picnic breakfast from the boots of their cars. Once caffeine levels had been topped up and stomachs filled they headed off into the showground. Chris went his way, saying that he had arranged to meet up with an old friend who was running a stall at the event and would be there or about when they were ready to go back.

The first few hours were spent wandering around the various stalls. So many stalls selling a wide variety of things. There were stalls selling coats, hats and outdoor clothing; there were stalls selling equestrian products; there were stalls selling handbags and shoes, which both girls made a note of. There was so much to see, let alone the displays of woodworking, falconry and other traditional crafts. By eleven o'clock

THE FOOL'S JOURNEY

they all declared a much needed rest and went off in search of the membership enclosure.

The two girls were sitting on the seats by the ringside, still available, as the show jumping event had not yet started, while the boys went in search of refreshments.

"I bet Triss will come back with a Pimm's jug," laughed Jennie. "He's been muttering about it for half an hour."

"A cold drink of any kind would be fine!" exclaimed Moira fanning herself with the brim of her hat. "And to take the weight off my feet."

"I would hate to think what this place is like on a wet day."

"Well, where you're going in a few days time, I believe the rain will not bother you. Or if it does then it will be the loving, warm tropical sort!"

"I know, I can't wait. Our own little beach hut! Do you know it has its own little swimming pool from which you look out to sea."

"Yeah," Moira leered. "We know it won't just be swimming you'll be doing."

"Ha! You cheeky mare! Yes, drinking long cool cocktails!"

They both laughed. "But how did you cure yourself of your flying phobia?" Moira asked. "You've always been scared witless of flying."

"Triss suggested I see a hypnotherapist."

"What? One of those people who make you bark like a dog on stage?"

"No silly! This one specialises in phobias. I had several sessions. At the first session, she took me under hypnosis as far as the airport. The second session she took me on the plane, but didn't fly. Third session I was flying on the plane with a feeling of total calmness. I'm still nervous, but she backed it up with giving me some deep relaxation exercises."

"Wow. I never knew hypnosis could do that."

"Do you know, I think you would be good at it? She immediately made me feel welcome and put me at my ease. You do that with people. It must be great to know you can help someone in such a way."

"I'll look into it," Moira said noncommittally. At that point, the boys came back with a jug of Pimms and several bottles of water.

THE FOOL'S JOURNEY

"If we just drank alcohol, we'll be as drunk as lords and seriously dehydrated," Leo said. "So I have got us some water too. I'm not carrying you girls back to the car."

They sat for a while drinking their drinks and watching the class 'best in hand.' A fabulous array of horses, washed, plaited and polished being put through their paces by an equally well-washed and polished person leading them.

At the end of a long and exhausting day, five contented people made their way back home. There were packages aplenty stored in the boot. Tristan had treated himself to the latest style Hunter Wellington boots, a new jacket and an assortment of other things. Both Jennie and Moira bought themselves to new handbags and of course, as there was a show offer on the matching shoes, it would have been folly not to buy them too. Moira and Leo had bought all animals a new bed. Leo himself had bought a radio-controlled helicopter, with the only reason of 'I wanted one.' Cathy's kids had been treated to several little gifts that neither Leo nor Moira could resist. Chris declared he never knew running a stall had been so much hard work and had purchased a couple of things for his new home too.

Before Moira knew it, August had gone and September was halfway through. It was nearly time for the Mabon and the harvest moon would hang low in the sky. Who knew weddings took so much organising? There were dresses to be chosen and fitted. Bridesmaids and even a small guest list seemed to be a huge task. Amber and Michael and Liz and her new man were all coming. Jennie had agreed to be matron of honour if Moira would do the same for her when they got married. Tristan had asked her on a moonlit beach when they had been away. In some ways, Moira felt that she was being carried on the flow of life, surfing the wave it offered.

Then one day whilst she was gardening, Moira reflected on what had gone before. Part of her wondered about what happened to Rupert, to the baby that Claire had. What she was amazed to find, is that she'd so succinctly put it behind her she had not even given it thought until now. Now as she planted bulbs for spring, she laid this ghost to rest as well.

With the early autumn wind blew around Leo and Moira as they walked the dogs by the woodland one day. Leo remarked, "Was it the ghostly hunt you heard?"

Moira stopped in her tracks. "How did you know that?"

"James said it was likely. Locals never go in the woods within an hour of darkness. It just freaks them out too much. Some say there's a hound in there that was a harbinger of doom and all who saw him, died within a month. I just had to hope."

"All cases of grimoire hounds I've read about since were not brown and white!"

It was Leo's turn to stop. "You saw him?"

"Yes and looking back, I think he may have been a rabid dog in life. Red eyes and foaming mouth are rather suggestive." Leo shuddered. "I would love to know more about the history of those woods and perhaps find out who the hunt were. I must look up whether there are any paranormal investigators in the locality."

Leo shook his head. "You're mad, but I love you."

Moira kissed him and now she had put voice to the thought that had been in her head. She now had to see if she could find a group like the one she mentioned. Surely there must be one. Maybe she would join it.

CHAPTER TWENTY THREE – THE WORLD

Interrogation – Accomplishment – Involvement – Fulfillment

With the harvest moon hanging heavily in the sky, Moira mused on the meaning of Mabon, The Autumn Equinox, a time for harvest, for making amends and preparing for the winter ahead. Yet, here she was now just over a month away from getting married. She had decided that after she would start a course on hypnotherapy and then, if it worked out, she would set up an alternative therapy center. Renting rooms to other therapists and having a base receptionist there. She still needed to work through the finer details and run the business model, but she now felt she had a direction. This was a direction where she could not only use her skills in business but help people too. She sipped at her mug of steaming hot chocolate, savoring the sweetness, feeling the cream top and marshmallows against her nose. This, after all, was a special day, which so deserved the special hot chocolate. Leo came out of the house and called across to her.

"Someone called Annabelle on the phone for you."

"Thanks, be in now."

Moira smiled to herself: and now the next phase of things would begin.

Soaking in the bath a couple of days later, Moira ran through her mind the details of that phone call. Annabelle had been the co-founder of a team of paranormal investigators. Moira had expressed an interest in joining them. She had asked Moira to think through a few things. Annabelle wanted to know her motive for joining, whether she was a believer or a skeptic or whether she was neither. She had assured Moira there was no wrong answer, as the team was made up of all of them. She just needed to be clear in her own mind. In a little while, she would be going to meet with them and see if she was suitable to be part of their team. Leo had made circular motions around by his head to suggest that she was going mad, but had not even tried to dissuade her. She thought he would have, after the fear of what she had seen in the woods, but perhaps he had started seeing things from a cooler, logical perspective. Or perhaps Blodwen's words still burnt bright and he was trying not to stifle her. Either way she was very grateful.

Moira drove over in her Mini. It was an area she was not familiar with and she did not want to seem pretentious by driving her Range Rover. She was dressed in jeans, a pair of Ugg boots and a jade green body warmer over a cream turtleneck top. She hoped she had dressed to make the right impression. She breathed a sigh of relief as she pulled up outside a nice four-bedroomed house in an estate of similar looking houses. The Mini had been the right call, as there was one on the driveway of the house she was visiting. She smiled as she got out the car; something about the area felt comfortable. If things had been different, this would have been the life she had envisaged for herself; whether it was fate or luck that played the part, her life was different and definitely more lavish, but no less welcome. Moira pressed the bell and was shown in by a lady probably in her late thirties, it was hard to tell; not much younger and not much older. She introduced herself as Annabelle. With her heart racing a little, she took a deep breath and entered the room.

Moira was introduced to the other people: two other members of the team. They were George and Megan. Both waved a greeting. They were sitting companionably on a brown leather, two-seater sofa, suggesting if they were not lovers, that that was the prelude to it. She was then introduced to a man named Edward, the co-founder of the group. He was sitting in an armchair in the bay window. He reached out and shook Moira's hand.

"Who is Annie?"

"Ed! At least let poor Moira settle down before you start interrogating her," Annabelle said with mild amusement.

THE FOOL'S JOURNEY

"Annie is in part the reason I am here," Moira answered, sitting on the end of a three-seater sofa, in the same style as the others.

"Go on," Annabelle urged.

Moira recalled her tale from the first viewing of the house and the fact she had sensed something there and that someone, had turned out to have been Jimmy. She explained how Jimmy was tasked with protecting a chest. How Moira, on that cold January evening, had been shown the chest after Amber had done a séance to communicate with Jimmy. How an innate object would move or open its lid spontaneously when the rest of the time the lid could not be moved.

Annabelle went out and made hot drinks for everyone. The rest of the group listened, enthralled as Moira showed them the pieces she had got from the chest. Ed had stroked the writing as if it was a rare specimen, an expensive gem. Moira explained what information she had learnt from Jimmy the day he was helped to cross to the other side. About how the girl whose belongings and messages she held was the cousin of Jimmy's mum and about the same age. How all she knew was that her parents had gone on a journey with the only remaining sibling alive and well. Edward had punctuated the explanations with remarks, "Ha, I've met Michael a few times. Not as pompous as he appears on TV." And "You don't say."

The other members of the team in turn had asked a few questions. They had been amazed when Moira explained how Jimmy and the cats had protected her friend Liz when her ex-husband had tried to shoot her. At this point Annabelle said, "Jimmy fancied you I think." Moira blushed. She went on to explain. "I am not as psychically inclined as Edward, but when you talk about Jimmy, I can sense him. He's happy and still watching over you." Moira was not quite certain how to take this. She had not detailed the finer points of Jimmy's life experiences and his wild lust. Moira had finished her tale with moving to the outskirts of Burley.

For a while they asked her more questions. Moira explained how she believed, but was more likely to look for a logical explanation than for a

THE FOOL'S JOURNEY

paranormal one. As of yet, Moira had skirted around the subject of her experience in the woods. She said she had seen the face of an old woman once in the house but had not picked up anything since. Edward explained that she had happily moved on when she knew the house and gardens would be loved.

Edward asked, "You said Annie was part of the reason. Why?"

"Because she wants to know where her mummy went. I think I might know, but I was hoping to learn if there was a way to find out for sure. I had a rather strange experience. It involved me being out late at night, lost in the woods, meeting a ghostly hound, the leaping spectral shape of a Red Deer and a group of noisy hunters. I would like to know why some ghosts choose to remain ghosts; whether they are intelligent hauntings or just shades of what has gone before, ingrained in the fabric of a place."

Edward looked over at Annabelle who in turn looked at the other two members of the team. He then said to Moira, "Well, you seem to be on the same journey as we are, with more practical experience than some members of our team, we would love to have you."

Moira beamed. "Thank you." There was a generalised round of back patting and welcomes and another round of tea. As she left, Edward had a quiet word with her, "Can Annabelle and I come around and see this chest?"

Moira deliberated for a few seconds, torn between her charge and her desire to find out. She would have sworn later she heard the word 'yes,' as if uttered as a breath on a breeze.

"I think so, yes."

They arranged a date for a few weeks from then, and Moira drove home feeling like she had really accomplished something.

Moira had been busy with confirming up with the wedding organiser various aspects of her forthcoming nuptials. She had also started to put together a business plan and start some business modeling for her proposed alternative health centre. She almost forgot about Annabelle and Edward coming over. Thankfully, her phone alerted her to it a few hours before they were due to arrive. Racing upstairs, she vacuumed and

THE FOOL'S JOURNEY

cleaned up her office space of all the detritus of plotting and planning. She asked Leo to walk the dogs as soon as stepped through the door from visiting one of his ongoing projects, explaining briefly and then rushing to throw some dinner together for her and Leo before the guests arrived.

Moira tried not to pace around the floor of the lounge whilst she waited for them to show up. It unsettled the dogs and two hyper dogs were not what she needed. She took to sitting on the sofa, clenching and unclenching her hands or twiddling her fingers. She saw the flash of headlights through the window and heard the tread of two pairs of feet on the gravel. Moira went out into the hallway and shut the door on the dogs. The doorbell rang and she counted to ten before opening it. Standing there smiling, were Annabelle and Edward.

"Wow, what a lovely house," enthused Annabelle as she was shown in.

The dogs started to yelp and scratch at the door.

"I love dogs," Edward said, "We would love to have them, but we are renting the house we met in. We are renovating an old farmhouse not far away and until we get that finished, no mutts."

That explained something about them, Moira decided. Not married, not exactly an item more like two halves of one coin, yin and yang. "Would you like to meet them before we go up?"

"Yes!" they said together.

Twinkle and Bruno were let out and greatly enjoyed the fuss lavished upon them.

Helix had come out from Leo's office when he opened the door. When he saw the visitors he just looked at them with a knowing cat's stare. Moira could have sworn later he had actually nodded at them before sauntering off to the kitchen. After Leo was introduced, with Archie following, they went upstairs and to the room where the chest stood.

"Annie," Moira said, addressing the chest. "You are popular. Annabelle and Edward have come to see you. They are going to try and help me find out where your mummy went. Is that OK with you?"

THE FOOL'S JOURNEY

The chest giggled. Archie jumped up onto Moira's office chair and watched.

Moira carefully lifted the chest into the centre of the room, where they all could sit around it.

"Hi Annie, I am Edward. You know that you are dead. Moira has told me. Do you want to cross over to where the other dead people go?"

The chest made a noise, which to Moira's ear sounded like someone blowing a raspberry.

"I take that as a no then," Edward said, trying to keep the laughter out of his voice. The chest lid flew open without any of its usual preamble. 'I like it here' was scrawled hastily on a piece of paper and was launched from the opened chest.

"I like having you here," Moira said soothingly. "We just wanted to know what you want."

The lid had remained open. Moira looked inside. There was a picture, drawn in chalk. On the picture was a stick figure girl in pigtails, wearing a smudgy blue dress and standing by a box. On the other side of the box was a woman with vibrant red hair. Carefully lifting it out, Moira smiled.

"You shall stay here then. You can stay as long as you like. If I have children, they will look after you. I will tell them the secret of the box, and if you want to move across into the spirit world at anytime, you tell us."

The lid shut and the chest giggled.

A while later, Moira, Edward and Leo drank a..., as Edward phrased it, a pick me up. Annabelle had a large cup of tea, as she was driving. Edward explained to Leo about the conversation with the dead girl's mother.

"She went on her voyage to Canada really believing that Annie would get better and they could come back and get her. But when she was at sea, another little girl on board had whooping cough and died. She was buried there, in a seaman's burial with the captain reading the last rites on deck. She explained how, once she had seen the body go into the water, she had tried to throw herself overboard, but her husband and her

THE FOOL'S JOURNEY

remaining child had stopped her. She explained how she did not eat or drink for days until the captain came to talk to her. He explained that at least if her child had died, she would not be ill, no longer in pain. It was God's will that they were to go and start a new life out here, to forge a better life for their remaining child and maybe with His blessing and the fullness of time have more children."

Leo looked across at Moira who nodded. "She spoke, not like Jimmy in the quietness of our heads, but out loud. Edward seemed to think her soul had not yet been reincarnated as it was troubled. When she spoke about the voyage, you could hear the creaking of the boat timbers and smell the sea. She also spoke of her life when they got there. There was no work for them, as most spoke no English. Only she spoke English, having learnt it to go and work in England before the famine hit. Instead, she and her husband decided to take this trip, away from the persecution of the English."

Edward picked up the tale. "They were eventually given their own settlement, where they were initially supported by the townsfolk, but soon they had to fend for themselves. They lost a few members of their little community to the harsh Canadian winter, but soon they cleared land and fended for themselves. They retained their Welshness for a good while, but eventually they took on the way of life of those native to that land. The settlement was called Cardigan, from where many originated."

"Does that mean Annie now knows where her mummy went?"

"Yes," Moira said. "But for now, she's staying here. She likes it here." She showed him the picture.

After Annabelle and Edward left, asking Moira whether she wanted to attend the next 'ghost hunt,' to which she agreed, she went out into the garden. The stars twinkled brightly in the sky, the air held the metallic tang that suggested Jack Frost was nearby. Moira thanked the Lord and Lady. She thanked them for the life that she now had, the skills she had acquired and mostly thanked them for helping her to bring a mystery to a conclusion. A mystery that one child had for over a century. Within her

THE FOOL'S JOURNEY

hands, she held the future and now a cycle of her life was complete. With her marriage, a new one started and she was content.

THE FOOL'S JOURNEY

About the author:

Kristina Jackson is an avant-garde author with a soulful style of writing. She believes stories should sing, not merely speak. Kristina lives with her husband David, and their two children. She has several pets, one of the cats, Bono, is her writing companion. He is often found sharing her laptop.

"One day you will write your own book, just let your heart guide you."

They were the words of Kristina's teacher in the 5th Year of Primary School. Her short story had just been published in the school magazine. Kristina knew she had wanted to write since she could put sentences together. Twenty-eight years later she is now realising that dream.

Kristina took the hint that she should be writing after her illness POTS (postural orthostatic tachycardia syndrome) had to a greater degree disabled her. As physical doors have shut the mental ones have opened. She swears the characters in her head are trying to run away with her remaining sanity. Kristina has so many ideas it is anybody's guess where this will now lead

Connect with Kristina Online:
Facebook: https://www.facebook.com/home.php#!/wyndwitch
Twitter: http:// twitter.com/kj_author
Blog: http://kristina-jackson.blogspot.com